The Midas Death

An Inspector Kajiwara Mystery

A Novel

By

Diana M. DeLuca

Other titles by Diana M. DeLuca

Extraordinary Things

A Dream of Shadows: A Novel of Reincarnation
Winner Reviewers Choice Award, 2015

For

Hiroshi Kato and Albert J Simone
Gentlemen and Scholars

Preface

ANYONE READING THIS book should understand that there is no Hawaii State University, and that the campus is not meant to represent any one institution. HSU is an amalgamation of many institutions spread across the world. Frankly, no one university can get into this amount of mischief, even given the talent collected on campus. HSU is meant to represent any major research campus trying to remain competitive and prestigious while fishing in international waters.

The reader is asked also to recognize that the Hawaii Police Department described in this book shares only a location with the real Honolulu Police Department. There is no intention here to comment on police procedures or personalities. Inspector Kajiwara is unique to this story. I hope that his bemused take on higher education, while dealing with campus egos and trying to solve a murder, will provide a new and amusing viewpoint into life on campus.

Similarly, there is no kingdom of Kuthan, although after writing about it, I could happily believe that it exists.

And while it may be tempting to try to identify characters with real people, readers should remember this is a work of fiction. Any resemblance to people living or dead is accidental and unintentional.

In the interests of the story, I have located the events in Hawaii during the late 1990s. This decision reflects not only the time I was active in higher education, but also a time when universities grappled with their identities, caused by increasing demands for them to become self-sufficient. Tuition increases became common during this time, sparking student protests. Departments, particularly in the sciences, sought corporate support, causing an inevitable clash between the ideal of open sharing of new knowledge and business interests in patents, rights, and trademarks.

The attempts to merge science and profit created rather fascinating conflicts that endure to this day. One science institute, for example, has openly admitted that any research using their facilities must be supported by outside funding. In other words, the research requires a contract and its topic is driven by the needs of the funder. As the dean of my story says, the modern research university found it had struck a Faustian bargain in trying to attract financial support while having to face the inevitable interference that the money brought.

Mark Twain once called Hawaii, "The loveliest fleet of islands moored in any ocean." Only the most discerning visitors may take the time to learn the Islands' history and about the overthrow of the Monarchy (for which the US Government issued an apology in 1993, one hundred years later). But many more will recognize that today's Hawaii faces the same urban problems and economic challenges as any other modern American city, except in a unique blend of Pacific, Asian, and European cultures.

The Midas Death is the first of four planned novels. Taken together, they present my personal perceptions both of higher education and of the State of Hawaii, based on my forty years of living and working in these rather wonderful, complex islands.

Many thanks are due to the people who read this book in draft forms and guided its development. I want particularly to thank my reading group: artist and biographer, Rosalyn Roembke Hurley and Tyler Tichelaar, Michigan author and historian, for their years of support and wisdom. Thanks also to Larry Alexander who took on the graphic and typographic challenges of getting the manuscript into print. And last, but not least, I need to acknowledge the work of my editor, Jonathan Glasscock (mr.johnnie@hotmail.com) who, as the Kuthanis might say, was almost able to read my mind.

However, despite their good advice and assistance and that of many others who kindly read and critiqued the book, particularly those dealing with crime investigation, forensics, and autopsy, any and all blunders herein are my own.

1

Honolulu, December, 1997

THE NIGHTMARE JERKED him awake. Dirt exploded into craters, bullets splattered across tattered palm fronds, and the screams of the wounded were muffled by the sound of automatic fire and mortars. Blinking and disoriented, he lay tangled in sweat-soaked sheets, trapped in the mist between dream and waking, desperately wanting to change the past but knowing that he couldn't. The clock beside him on the nightstand clicked 4:30 a.m. The sound ricocheted in the quiet.

Inspector "Kaj" Kajiwara sat up and ran his fingers through his hair, feeling the dampness and humidity of the Hawaii winter. The December sun rose late in the Tropics and then dropped into the sea at night without twilight. It was a time of overcast, rain, and nighttime lows that made families pull their heavy futons out from storage.

He knew he couldn't sleep again, not after one of those nightmares. He knew the only way back from them was to distract himself, which couldn't happen lying restlessly in damp sheets, staring at the clock until the light turned pale grey outside the bedroom louvers.

But he also knew he had to be careful. He didn't want his wife, Linda, stumbling bleary-eyed into the kitchen, her dressing gown wrapped around her pajamas, offering to make him coffee. She'd want to know what was wrong, and he wouldn't have an answer.

He looked down at the familiar shape lying beside him, a jumble of arms and legs only half under the covers, hoping he had not disturbed her. But she was breathing deeply and regularly, as happily untidy in sleep as she was in life.

He climbed out of bed, pulled the covers up over her shoulders, and gently touched her hair. She smiled in her sleep and nestled deeper into the pillows. Then he put on his old, police-athletic-team t-shirt, sweatpants, and rubber slippers. He shut the bedroom door behind him quietly as he left.

He didn't understand why the dreams were returning. Vietnam should have become only memory by now. These new nightmares were telling him that it wasn't.

They were making him relive that day. He experienced again the moans of the other casualties, the sting when the corpsman put in the IV and told him that a Dust Off chopper was on its way, the weary cynicism of the pilot who smelled of cigarettes and cursed the monsoon season, and the glimpse of the Evacuation Hospital's calendar that showed the date of February 11, 1968. They performed surgery and then sent him to Tripler Army General Hospital for more surgery and rehab.

During those painful and frustrating months after his return, his parents tried their different forms of encouragement. "You forget the war," his father, Goro, said. "They tell us forget when we get back from Europe." As a dutiful son, Kaj nodded and tried to listen. "You only 21, you go back to school," his mother, Ai, told him firmly. "You go get an education." He listened to her too. Those memories unpacked now like a newsreel of someone else's life. Another place, another time.

But why now? Was it because his major life distractions were gone? His career was well established, the house nearly paid for, and his daughter, Annie, was about to graduate from Hawaii State University. Those had been his main goals once. Now that they were done, or nearly so, were they leaving a void in his life? One large enough for dreams to haunt him like an old uncle, creepy and probably declining mentally, who couldn't keep his hands to himself?

Knowing that he had to get his mind off the night, Kaj began his morning routine: Aikido workout in the garage, followed by the morning newspaper retrieved from the money tree outside the front door where the newsboy threw it, then eating breakfast—Kona coffee, black no sugar, and his favorite Kings Bakery lilikoi or guava Danish—and reading every front page story, twice. No need to worry Linda. As usual, he would say nothing.

The sun was starting to rise by the time he came back into the house. He could hear the old guy's rooster crowing down below. Half the hillside wanted that bird gone, but the man's house was outside the subdivision boundary, so the home-owners' association couldn't fine him for his nuisance rooster.

Kaj wasn't upset by the bird though. It was a link to the past, like the Sumida watercress farm down in Aiea. He'd heard that farm was fed by artesian wells. Maybe that's why the cress fields were always dark green. It was good to have something of life endure, better than seeing just another row of high-rise apartments blocking out the view.

Anyway, Linda bought eggs from the rooster man. The yolks were the brightest yellow he'd seen since his childhood visits to his grandfather on the Big Island. Everyone, including his grandfather, raised chickens up country. Kaj remembered his house. It had wooden sloping floors and a corrugated tin roof that sounded like a drum during heavy rains. The chickens were everywhere. You had to know where the birds roosted to find the eggs.

The wall mirror caught his eye in the hallway outside the kitchen. He found himself looking at a middle-aged Japanese-American man, slightly grey at the temples, not quite fifty but close, not in bad shape, but looking skeptical and perhaps even dour.

He stepped back, startled. When did that happen? He smiled crookedly at his own foolishness, letting the laughter creases around his eyes transform his face into a younger version of himself. For a moment, he wondered if he should smile more. His left eyebrow rose in embarrassment at the thought. He went into the kitchen, and took down the Lion Coffee cannister.

While he sat at the table drinking his first coffee of the day, he watched the Arizona Memorial emerge white from the grey sea of mid-December. It was as close to a spiritual experience as you could get in Pearl City. He let his mind wander back to that Sunday when children in Navy housing waved at aircraft with round suns on their sides.

Pearl Harbor changed everyone's lives, not the least his father's. A Big Island boy, Goro told him that he hadn't seen a *haole* face up close until he joined the army. Goro enlisted once the US government said Japanese-Americans could. At first it was a big adventure. He trained at Fort Shelby and became part of the 442nd Regiment. Once they shipped out to Europe, he learned quickly what that adventure meant.

Goro was one of the lucky ones. He made it home. But his survival came with a price. Over fifty years later, when he'd drunk too much, he'd sit on the garage floor, his arm curved around Fluffy, their wild-haired poi dog, and retreat into an unreachable silence.

The telephone's sudden ring made the air buzz and the mood dissipate. He snatched up the receiver before it could waken Linda. Given a call this early, it had to be another fatality at the gun and bottle club, the name that the Criminal Investigation Division gave to the ER at Queen's Hospital. But there had been something different about this one. It raised the hair on the back of his neck. It felt like trouble.

The voice on the line belonged to Bob Wilson, his boss, the head of CID.

"Got one for you." Bob's voice boomed so loudly that Kaj held the receiver away from his ear. "Hawaii State University professor Harrison Whitworth DOA on the driveway of his Manoa home. You know who he is, don't you? Only the Governor's best hope for economic development. I want you there, taking the lead."

Kaj listened sourly. Past experience had taught him that HSU did not like having police on campus. He guessed it was the bad publicity. Last time, the powers-that-be mired him in campus politics and grudging or non-existent cooperation. He might be an HSU grad himself, but he made a point of not following the university's sports' teams and still threw the alumni association's glossy brochures into the trash. He never felt he'd graduated from the campus, more that he'd divorced it. The feeling, he was sure, was mutual.

"Isn't anyone else available?" he asked, knowing full well what the answer would be.

Bob cut him off. "I know how you feel about HSU. I don't disagree. But I need my best detective on this one. The press is going to be on our tails. They may cut you some slack because you're a local-boy war hero . . .."

Kaj clenched his teeth. "I don't . . ."

"I know, I know," Bob interrupted again, "you don't trade on your service, and you won't talk about it. But this time, you need to take one for the team. The Governor's been briefed and has ordered full cooperation among executive branches. The Chief's called it: Priority One for all HPD departments. You know what that means. All hand on deck. No vacations. No days off. You're the lead. So, consider it done. Now, who do you want? Your partner, Jill Nakamura, she's still new. Do you need someone more experienced?"

Kaj didn't hesitate. Bob would interpret silence as indecision and an invitation to decide matters himself. "She's fine. Give me Kaipo Kahana and Cliff Lee."

"Your old team, eh? Okay, you got 'em. Meet them on site."

The phone clicked dead without Bob saying thank you or goodbye or even telling him where the crime scene was. Kaj would have to phone in to ask, but he wasn't surprised. Bob was always abrupt, particularly when avoiding political hot potatoes. He came from a long-time *kama'aina* family but never felt totally comfortable around local politics. Maybe it was the local *haole* thing about trying to find a place to fit in.

Yet why, Kaj wondered, did Bob think that Kaj, whose father grew up on the Pa'auhau sugar plantation on the Big Island and whose grandfather maintained the irrigation system there, would handle the politics any better?

Moodily, Kaj threw the last of his pastry into the trash. He'd lost his appetite anyway. He took one final glance down at the Arizona Memorial and watched a passing cloud turn its white walls grey. It was not a good omen.

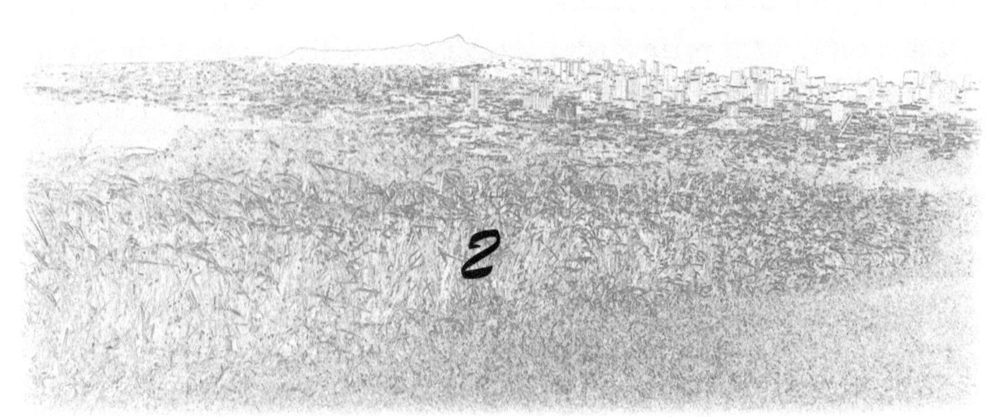

2

KAJ HAD TIME to think as he sat stuck in H-1 traffic on his way into Honolulu. Bob had to be joking. How could anyone not know the name Harrison Whitworth? Who could escape knowing? Surprisingly, KHVH didn't have the story when he tuned his car radio to Radio 830 AM. That wasn't going to last. Whitworth was too big and too prominent for his death not to be headline news.

The frenzy had begun last October, when the Nobel Prize committee announced that Harrison Whitworth would share that year's prize for Medicine. The *Honolulu Advertiser* ran a banner lead: "Hawaii's first Nobel laureate." They reported the award as if Whitworth had won gold in the medical Olympics.

Others rapidly jumped on board. The Governor claimed credit for the State funds already appropriated to support Whitworth's research. He foresaw a bright future for State economic development, not to mention his reelection campaign. The legislature rushed to appropriate ear-marked money to support the Sciences, hoping for even more prestigious research on campus. The university's administration sent out bulletins inviting various colleges to see if the prize could be leveraged into further federal research dollars. Hawaii residents took note because the prize was validation coming from outside the state.

With that kind of political attention, Whitworth's death was going to mean unleashed media lined up at the starting gate. With Whitworth dead, the Governor also faced a major political problem, and no one, let alone CID, would be able to solve the case fast enough or well enough to avoid being second guessed. High profile needed to be written in bold and underlined twice.

Jill Nakamura, Kaj's partner, was waiting for him next to the crime scene tape. As usual she managed to look calm and professional. It was a wonder to Kaj how she did it, particularly in the Kona weather season when the trade winds stopped.

"What have we got?" he asked briskly. He prided himself on being first on scene and didn't like to ask, particularly when he was tutoring a younger and less experienced investigator. But, this time, even with blue lights on, he couldn't manufacture road space that didn't exist. Hawaii's newspapers and politicians agreed there were too many cars for Honolulu's congested roads. Yet each year Matson barges delivered more and more cars to the Islands, and God help anyone working in town when there was an accident during the morning commute.

"The vic is Harrison Whitworth, 53. The body is under the portico. Local patrol officers found him at 6:30 a.m." Jill pointed to a blue and white police cruiser parked on the road in front of the house. "No witnesses yet. TOD around midnight. Forensics is on site. Cliff and Kaipo are canvassing the neighbors. The murder weapon is some sort of arrow."

"Arrow? What kind?" Kaj's eloquent left eyebrow rose in a quizzical arch.

"That's all they've shared so far."

Jill shrugged, making an attempt to appear professionally nonchalant. She was California Japanese-American, first woman and first minority to serve in a detective unit near the Mexican border, a pioneer of sorts, although she didn't talk about it. Kaj understood not talking about things. Everyone had something not to share.

"Any report from Forensics?" he asked.

"I'll see if there's an update." Jill pursed her lips, held her jacket closed, and ducked under the tape.

Kaj watched as she went down the driveway toward the house. Bob had insisted that Kaj partner her when she joined CID. Kaj's former partner had retired, so it made sense. His only concern was that she might be a distraction to the HPD unattached.

"We need the diversity," Bob told him firmly. "We want her to succeed." Translated, that meant it was Kaj's job to fend off anyone making her feel uncomfortable. As it turned out, Kaj didn't have to worry. Jill did a remarkably good job of sending people on their way all on her own. She shut Kaipo down quite definitely when he tried to ask her out for coffee.

Kaj looked up the road at the patrol car. The officers would be expecting to present their report personally to him as the lead detective. The morning sun's glare prevented him from seeing them through the windshield, but for the second time that day, the hair prickled on the back of his neck. Warning, red flag, it said. He approached the cruiser warily.

"Good morning, Kaj," a cheery voice called out to him from the interior. "Long time, no see."

Kaj knew the voice and stopped short. There was no mistaking who it was. He watched as the senior officer unfolded himself from the passenger seat. Instantly, Kaj's war-time memories, the ones he had worked hard to suppress that morning, came flooding back.

"Hello, Moses," Kaj said with a crooked half smile that had to pass as a welcome. It was the best he could do. "How long have you been on the Manoa beat? I thought you were Windward side."

"Transferred last spring. Needed to be closer to home." Moses' smile was genuine. So was Kaj's silence. Moses Mahi was Kaj's past. They trained together, served together, were wounded together, and came home together.

But where Kaj listened to his mother and used his GI education benefit at HSU, Moses joined the police force once he was physically recovered. That gave him three years of seniority over Kaj. They maintained their connection even when Kaj made detective, that is, until Kaj's nightmares came back. For two years now, Kaj had been avoiding him.

At a loss of what to say beyond hello, Kaj looked for something to cover his confusion. He settled on the junior officer leaning over the cruiser's driver's side door, staring intently down onto the crime scene. The young officer's shock of red hair was cut to bristles above his collar, and his chest and shoulders bulged, stretching the creases out of his blue uniform shirt. The younger man was so absorbed that he hadn't looked up when Kaj approached.

"New?" Kaj asked Moses, inclining his head.

Moses grinned. "Yep. Jason Rogers. First murder, first crime scene. Can't you tell? I remember yours. Drug deal gone bad in Waikiki. You were assigned to drive with me. Remember?"

Kaj remembered. It's not often one saw a corpse hissing with escaping bacterial gases on a Waikiki sidewalk. That's when he learned that decomposition didn't take long in the Tropics.

"You were first on scene?"

Kaj fell back on routine to maintain his composure. Inside, he churned with embarrassment. He knew he should have talked with Moses and admitted that the nightmares were back. He should not have just walked away from their friendship without explanation. He wondered what Moses must think of him.

Moses seemed not to be bothered by the same sort of regret. He took out his notebook and read from it. "We drove our usual route up East Manoa Road. At 6:30 a.m., we passed this house and observed the garage door was open and the light on. That was unusual. When we pulled over, we spotted the body on the driveway. I called dispatch at 6:35 a.m. We secured the scene and closed off the street. There were no other individuals observed on the property and no movement in the house."

"I received the call just after 7:15 a.m.," Kaj said. "The Governor had already been briefed, along with the Brass and CID. That's fast even for this town."

"Not often a big shot like Whitworth gets killed."

"What's the deal with the house?"

Kaj looked down at the New England style, two-story white clapboard with a wrap-around, open lanai, gray window shutters, and a formal portico where horse-drawn carriages must have unloaded their occupants. It was a typical old-Hawaii period piece with remaining vestiges of charm, although it looked run down and must once have had a lot more land around it. Each sale of the original property must have broken someone's heart, because the site provided an unobstructed view down the valley, over the wall of high-rises marking the start of the Makiki condo zone, and then *makai*, out to sea.

"It's what's left of the old Isaiah McKenzie estate," Moses replied. "The vic bought it a few months back. The house needs work. But it's only fifteen-minutes from campus. Ideal for university types."

Kaj took a moment to take in the setting. A slight breeze made a gentle, rustling sound as it blew through ferns and grasses, filling the air with a damp, woody smell. The doves gave their piping calls, interrupted now and then by the mynahs' rusty-hinge squarks. A dog barked somewhere down below. Across the valley, the houses, built in tiers along the walls, looked as if they were drowsing in the morning sun.

For a moment, he was mesmerized. He could understand why someone would want to buy this property, even if it did need work. The house had the feel of the Missionary Houses downtown and Queen Emma's Summer Palace in Nu'uanu. It was an ancestral home, a place of silence and repose, a house that a kama'aina family such as Bob Wilson's ought to have somewhere.

"Emelie McKenzie was the last of them." Moses gave a nostalgic smile. "She said she'd lived in the house since the '60s. Wouldn't tell me how old she was, but she was covered with age spots. A remarkable lady. Every time I saw her, she had on a muumuu and pearls. She did her hair up in a bun with a tortoise-shell comb. When she died, the heirs sold on the spot."

Emelie McKenzie was a safe subject. Kaj warmed to it. "I remember her. She was the grand dame of the Ladies Garden Club. She had a beach house in Kailua that she dismissively called a cabana, but I remember it was large and had a bank of windows all across the sea side of the house. Every couple of years, she'd host a garden show as a fundraiser. Dad never missed it. He wanted ideas for the landscaping business. I was more interested in the body surfers. I remember there were good waves and the beach went on for miles. I wanted to be in the water, not looking at plants."

"Smart kid." Moses smiled. "I'd have wanted the same thing if the surf was up. Neighborhood gossip says it was a private sale to Whitworth. The house never listed."

"Who belongs to that second driveway?" Kaj pointed to an access road that ran parallel to the main driveway before disappearing behind the house.

"House below. Places up here barely meet the minimum setbacks, and sometimes have side-by-side driveways like these two. Even then these places cost plenty. Better hope you like your neighbor. I can tell you this one didn't."

"Who's down there?"

"HSU art prof named Arthur Stone who likes loud parties. We were called there twice last month. The complaints came from this house. One night, I issued Stone a warning, and he agreed to tone it down. Then an hour later we're called back. This time I wrote him up for a noise violation. He was abusive until I told him we could take him in for disturbing the peace. I could have done without both of them."

"Enough bad blood to kill?"

Kaj wondered if Moses remembered the angry knife dancer who threatened his wife with a machete. They had to wrestle him to the ground to get the cuffs on him. But why would Moses remember? They'd answered many domestic calls where people squabbled over what seemed minor things and ended up in the hospital before heading to jail. His past with Moses was memory mingled with regret. The regret was all his.

Moses shrugged. "Like Waikiki. People crammed in together. Some places up here, you can almost shake hands out of your bathroom windows. You can hear a toilet flush two houses down. Easy enough to get on people's nerves."

The conversation lulled, and Kaj surreptitiously studied his former partner. Moses' face was fuller, but the two years since Kaj had last seen him had not made him look skeptical or discouraged. The scars on his face and neck, the visible reminders of their time in Vietnam, were still there, but his hair was uniformly dark and his skin was still unlined. In fact, the years had only made him look kinder. Kaj shifted uncomfortably. How could he have abandoned his friendship with Moses? What made him think that if he didn't see Moses, the nightmares would go away? Now he felt ashamed as well as guilty.

Something had to be said about the lapse in their friendship, but where to start? Certainly not with the dreams. What could he say about them, anyway? That, two years ago, they started coming back and Moses was in every one of them. Would Moses understand that he had cut off their friendship rather than admit he couldn't deal with them? He hesitated as he struggled to find the words to begin.

When he saw Jill coming back up the driveway, he took the reprieve with a shamefaced surge of relief.

"Forensics is processing multiple sets of fresh footprints. They're working three different areas: one up on the ridge behind the houses across the road, the second in the trees to the side of this house, and the third going down a ravine to the street below. They say that between the rain and the large number of foot prints, they need time to map the area and then work out sequences back at the lab."

Kaj looked apologetically at Moses. "Looks like it's getting time to go down. You staying on scene?"

When Moses replied that he was, Kaj gave him a quick nod, an acknowledgment that there was unfinished business between them. They would talk, he was implying, just later. That was Kaj's intention. When later happened, Kaj might even know what to say.

3

THE FORENSICS DIRECTOR was a bluff, generous man in his late fifties who retained some of his youthful athleticism. He stood a head taller than anyone else and used his arms to direct his team as if they were on fourth down and three to the goal. Kaj respected him enough not to call him by name. He thought his real name, Richard Eagle-Bott, and his nickname, Dickiebott, both sounded slightly insulting. Usually, he avoided using any name at all. Not that the FD cared. He said his name had been good enough for his football jersey when he played for the Gators in the Orange Bowl.

The FD was supervising the pouring of plaster at the site near the trees beside the house. "Okay coming down?" Kaj called to him.

The FD waved them on with large hands that looked as if they could still catch a pass. He came over to meet them.

"The victim fell on the pathway fronting the house. The reporting officers found the front door of the house open. A briefcase was on the first step of the interior staircase. Car keys were on a hall table beside the front door. The silent alarm was disarmed. The luggage was where you see it, next to the body with airline tags attached. His car is in the garage with shopping bags and receipt from Manoa Safeway. The garage door was open with interior lights on, but the front porch and interior house lights were off."

"House lights off?" Jill interrupted. "Does that make sense?"

"I'm getting to that." The FD paused and turned his head slightly to one side. Kaj suspected it might be for effect since his profile was really quite noble and might justify his claim that Eagle-Bott was an aristocratic surname. "More than the rest of you can say," he once told them.

"We processed the house on the assumption the killer was inside at some point and was responsible for turning off the lights. No signs of forced entry and no signs of struggle. Last night's rain potentially washed away exterior evidence. That's it, except that the ME told his staff to wait for you before moving the body. We're still working the perimeters and house exterior."

"And the murder weapon is confirmed to be an arrow, as in shot from a bow?" Jill called this to the FD's back.

The man looked back at them over his shoulder. "See for yourself. Haven't seen anything like it since that fellow in Waianae got killed by a spear gun."

Kaj and Jill walked under the portico to look at the body. The man was slender, elegant, and recognizable from his newspaper coverage. His suit was mellowed silk but creased from travel. His luggage, now encased in a large plastic evidence bag, was soft, monogrammed leather with airline tags showing international first class. His left arm was bent up revealing a heavy gold watch. His right arm was bent across his hips. He might have seemed asleep except that a fledged projectile pinned his jacket and shirt to his chest. There was surprisingly little blood. Only his mouth was ringed with blood-stained froth.

"Either the killer was close or skilled," Kaj said as he kneeled down beside the victim.

"Or just plain lucky," Jill said. "Sight lines can't have been easy in the dark, even with the victim silhouetted against the house lights." She looked up at the trees and dense plantings down the side of the property. "It's hard to see where someone could stand to get this shot."

"If he fell backwards, the shooter may have been in that upper clump of trees." Kaj pointed up towards Moses' police cruiser where Officer Rogers was still staring at forensics team members who were taking pictures. "Forensics seems to have the same idea," he added.

"Is there anything that might suggest a burglary?" Jill asked. "He's wearing a watch. Is it a Rolex?"

Kaj leaned in to look. "It's still running. It says Vulcain stem-winder on the face. Never heard of the make, but it's probably valuable."

He stood up and looked back down at the body. The man's face was frozen into an expression somewhere between surprise and confusion. Kaj agreed with him. Who would have thought a man like this would die on his own driveway? But then how many truly safe places are there in the world?

"Let's go in," he said. He followed Jill up the front stairs and into the house.

In front of them, a formal hallway extended the length of the house. Large rooms opened from it on both sides. Towards the back, a carved wooden staircase with pineapple finials led to the upstairs rooms. Behind the staircase was what looked like a butler's pantry that must lead into the kitchen. Only one of the downstairs rooms had any furniture—an armchair and side table that seemed dwarfed by the space and far too modern for the stained-glass pattern of entwined plumeria and orchid set into the upper half of the windows.

They walked through the pantry and into the kitchen, a large room with wood cabinets thick with layers of cream paint. The refrigerator and stove were avocado green, with matching green and white floor tiles laid out in a checkerboard pattern. The room looked as if it had been featured in *House Beautiful* thirty years ago and was afraid of renovations.

Jill walked down the bank of cupboards, opening each one and letting it spring back to close with a bang, filling the kitchen with the musty smell of old wood cabinets that haven't been opened for a long time. "Nada. Bare. Clean. Not even dead roaches. No ants on the windowsills either."

Kaj opened the refrigerator door. "Here's why. He's put everything into the fridge: evaporated milk, coffee, and cereal. The bread's in the freezer, along with some TV dinners and butter. The dishes and cutlery are in the vegetable drawers. Makes sense. Not a bad idea if he didn't want unpleasant surprises when he came home."

"It feels very lonely, very solitary."

Jill rubbed her arms as if she felt a chill. Old houses depressed her, particularly if they gave her the sense that they were trying to stay alive on rapidly fading memories

Kaj looked out of the window over the sink and watched as forensics team members went through ferns and elephant ears in the back garden. He could just make out a rooftop through the gap between two Norfolk pines. He assumed the roof belonged to the noisy, bad neighbor down below.

"Maybe there's more upstairs," he said.

Jill walked first into the largest bedroom directly over the entrance hall. On one side, it had a view over the portico and up to the deeply incised hills that formed the Manoa Valley walls. On the other, it had what hopeful real estate flyers might describe as a million-dollar view down the valley, over the masses of houses flowing like lava down to the variegated blue and turquoise sea.

She took a quick inventory of what was in the room. "Sparse. Bed, dresser, night stand, and a louvered closet. Was he moving in or moving out?"

'In," Kaj replied. He opened a drawer in the night stand.

"Just a couple of books: Winston Churchill's speeches and something called *The Spiritual and Transformational Creativity of Science*." Kaj's eloquent eyebrow raised in its quizzical arch again. Academic intellectuality did that to him.

Jill opened each of the drawers of the high-boy dresser, the carved eagle resplendent over the curved drawers beneath it. "Underwear, socks, and shirts. Nothing unusual. But the dresser itself is interesting." She stepped back to appraise it. "Looks period and in good condition. Expensive."

She glanced at Kaj by way of explanation. "My family owned a small hotel. I grew up around antiques."

Kaj went into the bathroom. "A few towels. Shaving cream. The medicine cabinet has over-the-counter meds, no prescriptions."

"They may be in his suitcase. But he was living simply." Jill shook her head. "Almost camping out."

Kaj looked around the room with some understanding.

"He was furnishing the house from the top down. You have to start with somewhere to sleep. Hope he understood what he was taking on with a house this old in a wet valley."

"Money solves everything, and I suspect he had some. In San Diego, it was becoming popular to spend big money restoring haciendas and pueblos. This place would be worth a fortune once he fixed it. Maybe he saw it as an investment. The land alone . . .."Jill let her voice trail off.

Jill's comment made Kaj ruefully remember what he and Linda had paid for their small house on fee simple land in Pearl City. The land cost as much as the house. The only alternative was to lease land from one of the big estates, but that meant a possible huge reckoning when the lease was up.

The next room was the man's office. It contained a desk, an IBM computer and printer, a pile of discs, several file cabinets, an elaborate record player with large Bose speakers, and a set of matched koa wood floor-to-ceiling bookcases round the walls.

The chair in front of the computer was soft polished leather. Kaj was tempted to sit in it just to see how it felt. Next to the printer, a heavy, crystal tray held a half-full bottle of Talisker single-malt Scotch and a glass with an etched design that sparkled in the light. Everything was clean and looked freshly dusted.

"Waterford crystal glasses," Jill said. "Hand blown. Irish."

"The man had good taste." Kaj eyed the bottle of whiskey respectfully.

"And could indulge it," Jill agreed. "Like his luggage and clothes. Must have had plenty to afford this house. Does the university pay its faculty enough for a place like this?"

"The university is probably paying a lot to keep him in Hawaii, but you're right. You'd think he'd be at one of the big-name colleges on the Mainland."

Jill looked quizzically at Kaj. "You think there's some special reason he's stayed in Hawaii? Something that augments his salary?"

"Something to look into," Kaj replied.

Kaj studied the man's computer. Forensics would gather it later, so he didn't touch it, but taped on the frame, where most people would put their passwords, was a sticker with a phone number and a name.

"Look at this" he called to Jill. The note had the phone number of a Mrs. Sam. "Maybe the house keeper?"

"Or a girl friend or what passes for one?"

Jill primly recorded the information while Kaj resumed his own inspection. He looked through the man's impressive collection of LPs, noting that Whitworth seemed to have had particular interest in Mahler.

Kaj approved of Whitworth's taste. The HSU course he took in classical music to fulfill a humanities requirement had turned out to be one of the few things he was prepared to thank the campus for. Whitworth was becoming someone Kaj might have enjoyed sharing a Talisker with, particularly if they raised a Waterford glass to Mahler's fourth symphony, played on Whitworth's top-flight, play-back equipment.

Kaj stopped next in front of one of the few things on the wall, an oil painting of a yacht in full sail with pine-covered hills and a lighthouse behind. He could make out the name of the boat, 'The Traveler.' The boat seemed pinned against a New England sky.

"A memory of home?" he wondered out loud.

Jill stopped opening desk drawers and walked over to take a look. "It might be. He was from the East Coast. There's a diploma from Harvard back on the wall over there."

Kaj glanced to where she was pointing but didn't go over to look. Certificates told him nothing. Books, on the other hand, were a way into a man's mind.

He started browsing the titles on the bookshelves. Many dealt with scientific topics and with philosophy and history, the type of reading he expected of a scientist, but there were also books of American literature and European poetry, suggesting a broad, eclectic mind. What's more, the books had creased spines suggesting that the man had read each book at least once. Some were well used enough to show that their owner had returned to them often. The extensive library was clearly for enjoyment and not just for show.

"He was old school," Kaj told Jill as he closed a book of Robert Frost's poetry that had dog-eared pages. "He wanted real books. I get that."

"They take up a lot of room. Most people are switching to computer storage these days. Books weigh a lot if you have to ship them."

"Yes," Kaj agreed almost wistfully, "They're heavy, but computers will never replace them."

"You do know that you can store an entire encyclopedia on a set of discs, don't you? It spares whole bookshelves of storage."

"Not the same," Kaj said definitively and moved on. He'd long had a hunch about libraries and what they showed about their owners. There was always a telling obscurity. In the end, he found Whitworth's in four paperbacks in the sea of hard copies. The books were all written by the same female author, a Janice de Mello. The books were neither scientific nor philosophical. All had angry titles containing the words *woman* and *class*.

Kaj turned one over to look at the author's picture. An energetic woman with no-nonsense dark eyes, a grim smile, and slightly menacing shoulder-length hair stared back at him. She looked as if she could do a bicycle trek in the Pyrenees and do her own repairs, or jog the Pacific Crest trail carrying a thirty-pound pack.

"Take a look at these," he called to Jill.

She came over and took all four books off the shelf, turning them over in turn to read the summaries on their backs. "They don't seem like they belong in this library," she admitted. "I think he'd be more likely to read that book of Churchill speeches he had in the bedroom."

Kaj opened the de Mello books' front covers. "They're not signed. An angry student or colleague, perhaps?"

"Something else to rule out. If she's an offended colleague, it's interesting that he would have kept them."

Jill took out her notebook and added the book titles. She noted not only the books but also the fact that de Mello was a faculty member in the Women's Studies Department at UC-Berkeley.

When they were through with the room, Kaj stood in the doorway and looked back at the desk and expensive furnishings.

"Is this what university club rooms look like back East? Do they have dark wood paneling, bookcases, and Savonarola chairs carved with the university crest? If that's the case, we were cheated at HSU. All we got were folding tables and plastic, stacking chairs."

Jill looked at him with sardonic merriment. "My school had a mural of a Mexican farm and donkeys on the wall. Does that count?"

"You win," Kaj grinned. They went down the stairs together.

4

CLIFF WAS WAITING for them when they emerged from the house. Kaj had requested Cliff and his partner, Kaipo, for good reason. They had worked the last HSU case with him, so they had an idea about the university. But they also complemented one another.

Cliff was meticulous and detail oriented, particularly adept at seeing connections and sorting inferences. Kaipo, on the other hand, had a particular ability in getting witnesses to trust him. His charm was still intact even though he was recovering from a divorce. He'd come home from work one day to find that his Mainland *haole* wife had left him, claiming that CID intruded too much into their lives and that she'd felt claustrophobic living on an island.

Cliff stood under the portico, pulling his collar away from his neck and shrugging his shoulders. Like many Korean-Americans, he was well over six feet, only slightly taller than Kaipo but several inches taller than Kaj. He always looked groomed and well dressed, unlike Kaipo who seemed to have lost any sense of color coordination since becoming single.

Cliff had taken off his jacket because it was becoming warmer as the sun rose. When the trade winds failed, as they did every fall, the result was Kona weather, a time when humidity made the air feel sticky and close. Even the mynahs stayed in the shade.

I checked with the neighbor down the hill," Cliff told them. "He's a piece of work."

"HSU Art professor named Stone?"

"You know him?" Cliff looked at Kaj with surprise and then sympathy as if to say that the best view of Stone would be the back end of him heading out to sea, preferably headed to some Antarctic destination where the penguins might eat him.

"Just of him. What did he have to say?"

"All he heard was a noise around midnight. But he also said that he was delighted that Whitworth was dead, and he hoped the death was slow and painful. I told him you would want to talk with him."

Kaj's left eyebrow rose again. In his experience, outbursts like Stone's were often fueled by alcohol or local grown weed. It was always interesting to find out which, although people usually did everything they could to prevent him from finding out.

"All right," Kaj said drily, "let's not keep this gentleman waiting."

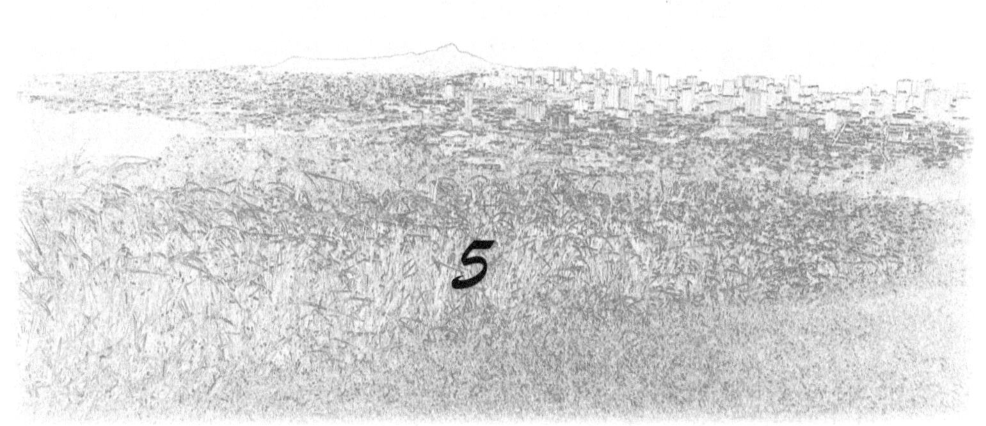

5

KAJ STUDIED STONE'S house as he and Cliff walked down the driveway. It was a wood frame one-story with crawl space, typical of houses built in early-fifties Hawaii. But this one had an almost insolent determination to stand out for the wrong reasons.

The house's turquoise roof clashed with the dingy pink of the siding. The big picture window and louvers on one side of the white front door didn't balance the small louvered windows on the other. A ramshackle shed half hidden behind the house appeared to function as a studio, while the unkempt yard was filled with large pottery pieces, many shaped like tamarind pods. Manoa rainstorms had reduced some of the pottery to jagged shards, making the path to the front door crunch under foot. It was impossible to imagine that this house might be worth a fortune, but that was land in Hawaii.

Kaj took a moment to study the puffy-eyed man who opened the door. His crumpled Aloha shirt gave the impression he had woken up on a park bench with an empty bottle of vodka he didn't remember drinking. His breath smelled like kerosene, and his skin looked pasty gray. He also made no secret of his feelings for his dead neighbor and

~ 29 ~

even seemed proud of them. What bothered him more was being disturbed.

"He was a would-be patrician, a pretentious asshole, sitting up there in what he fancied was a historic house and trying to tell me how to live. Mainland, East Coast, *pilau*, rotten stinking haole."

Kaj's eyebrows both raised. Stone's drawn vowels and clipped endings weren't anywhere close to sounding local. In fact, he mispronounced the Hawaiian word and made it sound like "plow." If he had to guess, Kaj would say Stone was a Texan trying too hard to be part of the local scene.

"He told me I wasn't living up to the neighborhood standards. Make that his standards. Acting like he's some god because he's won a prize. Whoever killed him did the world a favor. Everyone's got a life, but on some people it's wasted. I've already told your person over there all I know." Stone stabbed his finger in Cliff's direction.

"If you prefer, Mr. Stone. I can arrange for one of the officers to take you down to the station."

Kaj put on his blank, detective face, the one that made him seem to peer into someone's psyche and come away disappointed. His late mother, Ai, trained him to observe. She always knew when he was fibbing, although it turned out later that he had a giveaway, a "tell." He curled his fingers when he lied. His instructor at the Police Academy, not knowing the family history, told him the stare was a talent that could make even a drunk feel guilty.

"Right now? How long will that take? You know who I am, don't you? My paintings sell around the world."

Stone preened as much as his disheveled appearance permitted. He waved his pudgy hands in the air as if fending off the cops and the unpleasantness they brought with them. Kaj noticed how pink and soft his fingers were; they glistened like uncooked pork sausages.

"Most of the day, I imagine." Kaj allowed a slight raise of his left eyebrow to suggest interest but then lowered it in indifference. At that point, his indifference was real. He knew that threatening to take someone downtown was trite, but it usually worked because going downtown sounded time-consuming and tedious.

Kaj would not feel sorry for Stone if he did go. The man would be in air conditioning at CID headquarters, which was better than the Manoa humidity making Kaj's shirt stick to his back and sweat streaks form at his hairline.

Stone stepped back from the threshold reluctantly and waved them in. "All right, then. I don't have all day." He turned his back on them and pulled up the bamboo blinds, letting in a splash of light.

Kaj stepped into the house gingerly and elected not to remove his shoes. Underneath a thatch of dust, the faded wood floor had turned a shade of grey, and the threadbare carpet was felted and looked sticky. The walls, however, were covered with paintings of rocks of all sizes and shapes and seemed to be free of dust.

"Are these yours?" Kaj asked, modulating his voice to imply interest.

Stone took Kaj's words to mean admiration and evidence that the man might be smarter than the average cop.

"Look. We got off on the wrong foot. I'm not at my best in the morning. Let's sit down and start over."

Stone gestured him to a rattan sofa, kicking aside an empty pizza box and throwing magazines off a chair for himself. "I need to clean this place up," he admitted as he splayed his bare feet on the floor in front of him.

Kaj looked around at the disarray. The house smelled of cigarette smoke, stale beer, and incense. In the kitchen, the open oven door revealed blackened baking pans, presumably where the pizzas had been cooked, while on the floor, roaches of different sizes were eating a couple of abandoned pizza crusts. Cleaning up seemed an understatement. The place needed to be hosed down.

The only exception to the chaos seemed to be an object of some kind resting under a velvet cover on a side table. Kaj could not make out much, except it was about three feet long, ten inches high, and had some form of undulating shape. He wondered why it was covered.

The sofa's stained floral cushions weren't inviting, but there was nowhere else to sit. Kaj took his place and smelled the Manoa mildew clinging to the fabric.

Cliff wrinkled his nose. "I'll stay back by the door," he said.

"So, you paint rocks?" Kaj began.

"Monoliths," Stone bristled. "An asteroid landed in our backyard at the ranch. I took it to be a special, spiritual icon, at least until Dad sold it. The asteroid inspired me." He pointed to the painting hanging behind him. "I paint the Polynesian spirits who choose to live in the mineral world. Can't you tell?"

Kaj looked at the painting of a shaggy lava rock with a fern growing out of a crevice. The more that he looked at it, something seemed wrong. It took him a moment to figure it out. The fern looked as if its leaves were growing in the wrong direction. He turned his head sideways to look at it. "Is that hanging the right way?"

"Of course, it is," Stone thundered, "I don't hang material things upside down. The Hawaiians tell me that would trap the spirit occupant inside."

His chair creaked in protest as he shifted his body to stare at the painting. He too put his head on one side. "Oh, crap," he said after a few moments.

Kaj left him to reconsider the direction of the painting. "What did you hear last night?"

Stone turned away from the painting reluctantly. "I heard a noise somewhere around quarter to twelve. That's it." He gave a dismissive wave of his hand as if he expected Kaj to dissolve. He turned to look back at the painting.

"You told Detective Lee that it was closer to midnight."

"Did I? Then that's what I meant. Don't make me regret saying that I heard anything. I don't wear a watch."

Stone looked as if he had just found a dead roach in his dinner and was planning to sue.

"Can't you see I'm guessing? Someone else around the neighborhood had to have heard it. Go ask them for chrissakes. Someone heard it. You can't fart in this valley at night without everyone hearing."

"Tell us again what you heard." Kaj's voice was cold. Stone's bluster had to be cover for something.

"How many times do I have to tell you people? Don't you keep notes or something? It was a dull pop like returning a fast tennis serve. At first, I thought was a backfire and didn't take much notice. How many backfires do you remember?"

"Was it like a gunshot?" Kaj persisted.

"Not that. Someone around here drags lanai furniture under cover at sundown. It sounds like banshees screaming. A gunshot would echo, and all your sleeping princesses in the valley would be out in their pajamas demanding protection from home invasions."

Kaj moved on. "What was your relationship with your neighbor?"

"Relationship!" Stone lunged forward and gesticulated in the air with his pink, sausage fingers.

The sudden movement made Kaj tense and prepare to take the man down if he had to. Cliff took a step further into the room, his hand hovering over his holster. Kaj gave a small shake of the head to him, and Cliff stepped back. Stone seemed not to have noticed.

"Relationship?" Stone spat the word again as he settled back. "There wasn't one. Look here. Do you really think I'd do anything to him?" Stone's passion spewed out of him.

"I wouldn't waste my time on one of the most self-righteous bastards I've ever known. He was the patron saint of snitches, calling the cops and trying to control everyone's lives. It's not my fault that my house is near his. I bought this place twenty-five years ago when property was affordable. Now I can hardly afford the property taxes. That was long before he showed up. He even reported me to my dean. Claimed I had sex parties over here. Said he saw me with a dark-haired woman giving me fellatio—you know, head, blow job, oral sex."

"I get it. Go on."

"You can't see in my house unless you come down the driveway and trespass. When I called him a Peeping Tom and the morality police, he looked offended and backed off. But, and it's a huge but, there is no way I did anything to him."

"We hear you had a party last night. How many people were here?"

"Five plus me. But no one from here was involved." Stone did not meet Kaj's eyes.

"We need their names and contact information."

Stone hesitated for so long that Kaj thought the trip downtown might be necessary after all, but he finally whispered the names: Amanda Byce, Cheryl Aki, Brian Souza, Antonio Mendoza, and Cheterinda Singh. To Stone's discomfort, Kaj repeated them loudly and had Stone spell out the names so Cliff could record them.

"Did you have a personal relationship with any of them?" Kaj had to work to contain his distaste for the man.

"Sex? God, no. They're students. Whitworth reported me because he was trying to make my life difficult. University policy says you don't date current students. I always wait a semester, and they're the ones who initiate it. I don't have to beg for sex."

"Then what were you doing here last night?" Kaj leaned forward. The rattan couch creaked under his weight.

"How is any of this relevant?" Stone squirmed in his seat while Kaj sat silently waiting. Stone finally caved. "I was thanking the students for helping me find South East Asian Buddhist meditation art. I've been building a collection. The final piece just arrived."

"That one over there?" Kaj pointed to the covered form.

"It shouldn't be here. I'm donating the collection to the university. I brought it back from my office so everyone could see it up close. It goes back today. It's far too valuable to leave here. Not that the university is any safer, but if it gets stolen on campus, their insurance has to cover it."

How did you get it?" Kaj's judgment of art was personal. When Linda gave him an Ukiyo-e print a few Christmases back, he thought it was a subtle invitation. She corrected him. The lady looking at herself in a mirror, her hair falling down her back, her kimono loose, and one shoulder bare was the artist's lament for passing of the floating world and with it a particular concept of beauty. Kaj preferred his own theory.

"I'm told that it came out of Tibet with a family fleeing the Chinese. The family had owned it for generations and didn't want to part with it. It was one of their last possessions." Stone seemed to enjoy the idea that one family's loss was going to be the gain of his academic and artistic reputation.

"When did these students leave?"

"Before dawn this morning. Before you people woke me up trying to kick my door in."

"Why didn't you or they report seeing the body?"

"Never saw it. We didn't use my driveway. I know better. The great man was due home, wasn't he? They went down the ravine alongside this house. It comes out on the street below. I went down with them. They drove off, and I came back up to bed where I was when you people arrived."

Kaj sat back on the sofa, hoping that his clothes would not smell of mildew when he stood up. "So how did you know Whitworth was gone and when he would return?"

Spittle foamed at the edge of Stone's mouth.

"It was in all the papers, wasn't it? Stories about the super star supposed to end the State's economic problems. That figures. Win a prize and people lose their minds. Ever try reading the books they give the international literary prizes to? They're unreadable. People put them on their shelves for show and never get beyond page two. I heard they planned some sort of greeting at the airport for Whitworth. I hope no one showed up." Stone's mouth turned down sulkily.

Kaj ignored Stone's outburst. "Now, these students. Who was driving? What type of car was it?"

"Oh, come on! I'm not good on cars. Why would I pay attention to that sort of thing? All a car has to do is run. Chet was driving. It's his car. I suppose it's whatever you expect students to drive. Blue, I think. I never asked about its make."

"And what do you drive?" Kaj had not seen a car on Stone's driveway. He assumed Stone must park it on the lower road to avoid driving past Whitworth's driveway. He was right.

"A Volvo. An old one. Still runs well but drops oil now and then. Now here's another example of what I had to put up with. Whitworth had the gall to tell me not to park on my driveway, because he didn't like the oil stains. My own driveway. My property, not his. I told him what he could do with himself, freaking Mainland asshole."

"This Chet is a current student?"

"He was a graduate student last semester. He was one of my paid assistants on the project, hired to find and catalog the collection. I let him stay here when he was working with me on the inventory."

"Do you provide lodging for all your students?" Kaj could not imagine any of his instructors having made that offer to him.

"No. I help out my friends. You got a problem with that?"

"How do we get hold of him?"

"I don't know. He didn't say. You could ask the art department. They may have a current address for him. Unlike Whitworth, I don't intrude on someone's personal life."

Kaj stood up at that point and stared back down at Stone. It wasn't one of his penetrating, soul-searching stares, but one that, in its own way, was equally impressive.

"Professor Stone. Do you plan all your parties when you know your neighbor will be out of town?"

Stone sneered. "That's a stupid question. If you were in your right mind, wouldn't you?"

As Kaj stepped over the party debris on his way out, he passed the covered object that was Stone's presumed capstone to his collection and wondered again why it was covered. Stone had given him a lot to think about. For one, he wondered if Cliff had also noticed that Stone's fat little fingers had curled several times.

"What do you make of him?" Kaj asked as they walked back up to the crime scene.

Cliff shrugged. "He's a technician. He must have had one creative flash about painting rocks and now paints to a formula. It might almost be paint by number. His challenge is in not repeating himself."

Kaj looked at him sideways. "I meant—do you like him for the crime?"

Cliff laughed apologetically. "That's what happens when you get around academics. You mean, is he bad tempered, crude, with low impulse control and maybe had one fight too many with the victim? I'd say possibly. With his attitude, I'd also say he could open his mouth and easily clear a room of offended people."

"I wonder," Kaj said, "what it says when someone paints only one thing over and over. It sounds obsessive."

Cliff shrugged. "Well, to be perfectly fair, he may be interested only in solving a series of technical challenges with each painting. In that case, it doesn't really matter what he paints if all he wants to do is experiment with light and texture and perspective. I suppose someone could say that we're obsessive in solving crimes. The crimes are really just variations on a theme. Our challenge is not to become too cynical."

"I look on solving crimes as helping people," Kaj objected mildly.

"Agreed," Cliff said, "but I doubt that Stone is thinking in terms of the students that he's helping. He reminds me of one of my more disreputable former profs who was more into using students. Don't be the last one to leave one of his parties, I was warned, because he'll come out wearing a speedo and gray pubic hairs. Very enticing."

Kaj winced and looked sympathetically at Cliff.

"Forgive me if I try not to picture that," he said.

6

J ILL WAS WAITING for them at the top of the driveway. She had her notebook out, which prepared them for a lengthy report.

"The crime scene is complex and dispersed," she said. "Forensics has called for backup and another photographer."

Kaj was not surprised. Stone's party alone accounted for six people tramping through the crime scene.

"Kaipo and I split up the different active sites. I took the ridge above the road. There are two tracks up there, one size ten, possibly male 140-160 pounds, and another, male size eight about 130 pounds. The ridge is accessed by a trail starting across the road three houses down. From the ridge, you get a good view of this house. That's why Forensics hiked up to check the area. They also found human waste up there."

"Fresh?" Kaj asked.

"Hard to tell after last night's rain. They sampled it anyway." Jill looked glad she didn't work in forensics.

"Two sets of prints in the trees next to the road," Kaipo reported. "One male, size ten, the other size nine with pronounced ridges, as from boots. The tracks overlaid one another. Then in the ravine down behind this house there's a fresh trail of what looks like half a dozen individuals leaving from the house below. The ravine appears to be used as a regular pathway."

"Size ten shoes. Maybe 140-160 pounds." Kaj's eyebrows knitted in frustration. "That certainly narrows it."

Jill looked grim. "It gets better. They say they need casts and photographs to work it all out. One of the techs said it was like Grand Central Station. Prints on top of prints."

Kaj turned to Kaipo. "What did they say again about the ones in the trees next to the road?"

"Two people, one maybe size nine in boots and one size ten. The ground was boggy, and there was a lot of tracking as if one of them was pacing. They'll let us know more once they've worked with the casts."

"And the ones down below?"

"Probably a group from the lower house. Plus, the boots left the scene the same way. There are a lot of overlapping tracks and the area looks like it's heavily used as a shortcut."

"So, we've got a disturbed crime scene and three separate groups of individuals," Kaj said. "Two up on the ridge, one long enough to relieve himself. Two in the trees by the road. Six coming and going down to the road below. That's ten by my count so far. And that's without any neighbors who might have seen something."

"Where do you want us to start?" Cliff asked pragmatically.

"You and Kaipo follow up with Stone's guests. You have their names. Also, check the neighbors. Plus, we need to know Whitworth's movements yesterday. What flights he was on. How he got home. Where he went. Jill and I will follow up with the ME's office and Forensics. Then we can meet back at headquarters."

Officer Rogers interrupted the moment. "Need to move your car, Sir," he told Kaj. "The ME is ready to move the body. Also, Officer Mahi says to tell you there's a television truck and camera crew arrived on scene. The reporter's asking to talk with you. What do you want done?"

Kaj looked up at the road. He could just make out the front of the KHVH news truck. "Tell them no comment at this time," he growled, "and keep them away from me."

Kaj edged his Ford Bronco forward into a bush, missing a telephone pole by inches but giving enough clearance for the ME's van to get out behind him. He could hear the bushes scratching his door as he backed up to repark. The road was so filled with police cars and technical vans that if he looked for another space, he knew he'd have to go outside the crime scene tape. That's where the KHVH news team was lurking. It was an older car. He preferred the scratches.

As he got out of the car, he glanced up at the jumble of A-frames with protruding decks that formed the upper row of houses across the road from the crime scene. It would be dark up there. A single street light burned where the road turned up from the main valley, and any house lights would be blocked by the jumble of plants in people's gardens. In Manoa, put a stick in the ground and it jumped up ten feet. Most of the residents would be working now. Everyone worked in Honolulu. It was how they afforded a house, and they might not be joking about eating peanut butter sandwiches for dinner after making the down payment.

As Kaj turned to look back at Whitworth's house, he felt the prickle that told him he was being watched. He didn't need to be told who was doing it, and he also knew that he couldn't put things off any longer.

Reluctantly, he walked over to the parked patrol car, this time resolved to start the delayed conversation. But the intervening time hadn't helped. He still didn't know what to say.

"You're looking good, Moses. How are things?" Kaj spoke awkwardly. He kept his voice low.

Moses rubbed the hair at the back of his broad neck. "Can't complain. But how do you do it, Kaj? You don't look any older than you did in 'Nam."

"We were just kids then," Kaj replied and rapidly changed the subject. "How's Malia?" he asked.

"She's fine, except there's trouble brewing. Believe it or not, we're about to add number two. Right around New Year's. One out of college and now one in the crib. Auwe. Don't know what we were thinking. Talk about a ratoon crop."

"They say they're the sweetest."

"Pineapples, maybe, but how old will I be at the first-year luau? I'll be retiring before this kid's in college."

"How's your boy?"

Moses gave a proud smile. "He's great. Alan's working for the fire department. Wasn't interested in police work, but that's okay as long as he's happy."

"Say hello to him for me." Kaj felt too uncomfortable to say any more. "And hello to Malia." He nodded awkwardly and started to walk away.

"Take care of yourself," Moses called out to Kaj's departing back. "We miss you and Linda."

Kaj raised his hand in acknowledgement, but his heart sank. The walk back to his car felt like a march to the gallows.

7

THE CHIEF MEDICAL Examiner pulled on rubber gloves, walked to the lockers where he opened a drawer, slid out what was left of the elegant victim, and threw off the cover. He then looked quizzically at Kaj and Jill as if expecting them to ask some question or display some reaction.

Dr. Robert Howes, now in his young sixties, had been a general surgeon who retired because of a slight hand tremor he knew the surgical nurses would report. He took a forensic pathology residency and found new professional life cutting up the already dead. Unless he was in the field or doing an autopsy, he wore a suit and tie even in the warmest weather, kept his gray hair clipped short, and projected an air of permanent discouragement. Behind his back he was called Mainland Howes because of the tie.

Dr. Howes was the one who broke the silence.

"I hope your Chief and the Governor appreciate how many cases my staff set aside to rush this autopsy. Customarily, we need 24 hours to report and even then that's rushed. And don't expect results from the tox screen for several weeks." Howes looked disgruntled and unimpressed.

"We're all under the gun on this," Kaj said blandly. He wasn't about to get caught in interdepartmental politics. "The Brass is expecting national and international pressure."

"Politics and pressure," Howes snorted, "the bane of my life. Everyone wants something yesterday. Well, here you are. Take a look."

Howes pointed to the surprisingly neat stellate hole where the arrow had forced its way into Whitworth's body. "Cause of death is acute cardiac tamponade. Blood accumulated in the pericardial space resulting in hemodynamic compromise that stopped the heart."

He looked over his glasses at Kaj. "You getting this? The fatal wound was caused by a projectile equipped with a tripartite tip. It entered the body 2 centimeters to the right of the left nipple, proceeded into the left pericardium, and entered the left ventricle where blood accumulation stopped the heart. The projectile lodged between the T4-T5 thoracic vertebrae. Rigor mortis was well established, particularly in the upper torso. Internal temperature read on site, allowing for the effect of the rain, indicates he had been dead approximately seven hours. That makes probable TOD midnight. No evident bruising or defensive wounds. No evidence the body was moved. Death was rapid if not instant."

The ME picked up a photograph and handed it to Kaj. Jill stopped taking notes to look. "This is the projectile."

What he showed them was an arrow fledged in red and black with a tip swelled with an outcropping that came to a three-sided, razor-sharp point.

"The original has been forwarded to your Forensics section. In my estimation, unless the bow used to kill this victim was specifically equipped for low-light situations, you're looking for a highly skilled bowman who selected the entry point with almost surgical precision. The victim was certainly not expected to walk away from it."

Jill still stared at the photograph as if she was mesmerized. "Not your usual murder weapon?" she asked.

"Not so strange." Howes puffed his chest slightly and looked quite professorial. "Archery has a long history in Europe and Asia. The Otezi man was killed by an arrow, and he lived around six thousand years ago. Certain Buddhist teachings promote archery as a form of meditation."

Jill mustered enough tact to look suitably impressed.

"What was the entry angle of the arrow?" Kaj asked. Since he'd never used a bow and arrow except in pretend games of cowboys and Indians, he had to talk about the arrow as if it were a bullet.

Howes picked up a pointer and inserted it part way into the hole in the victim's chest. "Based on the crime scene layout, my estimate would be that this projectile was launched from a position geographically higher than the victim and somewhat to the left."

Jill tried to picture the hillside and the road. "How much higher?"

"One plausible scenario would be that your victim was walking along the path from the garage to the house, heard a sound in the trees up by the road, and turned his body to the left to look. You'll need your FD to confirm that. That's as much as I can tell you at this point."

Abruptly, the ME pulled the sheet back over the body, pushed the shelf back into place, and clicked the locker door shut. When he deposited his gloves into the waste bin, it was with an air of finality. Kaj and Jill both understood he was letting them know he had other bodies waiting.

Kaj felt his usual autopsy depression as he and Jill left. He wondered how it felt to cut people apart. It didn't seem to bother Dr. Howes. In fact, he once said he preferred dealing with the dead, because they did what they were told.

Kaj remembered an autopsy he attended during his training. It was a decomposed woman in her twenties killed by a stab to the neck. He watched the ME confirm cause of death by an instrument with a serrated cutting edge (it turned out to be a fish-gutting knife). The experience convinced Kaj to avoid them as much as possible. Until then he had no idea of how bad the human body could smell. "Not a bad idea to carry air spray," that ME had smirked.

8

JILL DROVE THEM from the ME's office back to headquarters while Kaj checked his phone messages. There were multiple calls from the media for comments that Kaj wasn't prepared to give, and one from Bob wanting to know where they were. He and Jill went down to the Scientific Investigation section in the HPD basement together.

"Here's your murder weapon." FD Eagle-Bott held the bagged arrow up for their inspection. "No prints, and the blood and body traces on it were all from the victim. It's a field arrow, with a screw-on hunting tip. We'll continue to check if the fletching is unique, but I've seen those colors in sporting-goods shops. The upside to this choice of weapon is its relative silence; you hear a sharp twang and then a slap when the arrow hits. The downside is the skill and power needed to be accurate. This arrow was launched by a powerful bow in the hands of someone who knew how to use it."

Kaj nodded. "That was the ME's opinion too. The shooter knew what he was doing."

Jill studied the arrow thoughtfully. "If we brought you a bow, would you be able to identify whether it fired this arrow?"

"No chance of that." Eagle-Bott laid the arrow back down on the table. "Bows don't have unique characteristics like guns. We'll have a better chance with the footprints. You just need to find us the feet."

The FD guided them over to a metal examination table laden with Whitworth's possessions. "Here's what your vic had with him," he said.

"On the body, one antique mechanical gold watch, a Vulcain. In case you didn't know, these watches were preferred by a number of US presidents. Quite sought after, these days. One gold, oval signet ring with crest and the word *Harvard*. One wallet containing various credit cards, driver's license, Hawaii State University identification card, and medical insurance cards. A parking receipt from the overseas terminal parking at Honolulu Airport, date stamped 10:15 p.m. Cash grocery receipt from Manoa Safeway for $24.64, time stamped 11:30 p.m.; $431.00 US dollars; and £56 Stirling in coins and paper.

"In the briefcase: a notebook and small pair of opera glasses in leather case marked *Concorde*, a travel wallet with itinerary and tickets, one gold Nobel Prize medal in box, one passport, one envelope with check made out to Harrison Whitworth in the amount of . . .." Eagle-Bott stopped for a moment. "How much is the Krona worth in real money?"

"About ten to the dollar," Jill replied.

The FD indulged his sense of irony and whistled. "Nice chunk of change. Also, hotel receipt from the Hotel Langham in Regent Street, London, for a suite for three nights. My God," he threw up his hands in horror, "is this bill correct for only three nights? It must be a ten-star hotel catering to royalty."

The FD was enjoying himself.

"Various receipts for lunch and dinner—Harrods, the Cheshire Cheese pub, all for one person but there was one lunch for two at the Hotel Langham dining room. There's an admission ticket to Chartwell issued by the Winston Churchill Trust. Plus, there are a couple of taxi receipts."

"Any indication who the other diner was at lunch?" Jill asked.

The FD nodded. "Note on the back of the receipt: 'Lunch with Sutter Wind-Trenton.' Otherwise, one leather file folder with three pages typed, handwritten corrections, with the words "Acceptance Speech" at the top. There are six business cards, including one for Sutter Wind-Trenton, who it turns out is a rector at Cambridge University. The other five cards are from Swedish government people and foreign academics."

Kaj looked at the pile of possessions. The box containing the Nobel Medal was open and looked out of place. The gold gleamed in the light, showing the raised figure of a woman with an open book in her lap, holding a basin to collect water pouring from a rock. It all seemed too academic for the police forensics lab. It was like seeing an orchid growing in a Maui onion field.

"And the suitcase?"

"Getting to that: suit and shirts in a plastic bag. Various underwear, scarves, socks, two pairs black shoes, and one tuxedo with shirt and bow tie. The tuxedo had a stain on the pant leg, so we ran it. Turned out to be champagne. Other than that, all fingerprints on the briefcase and wallet are his.

"There are scuffed prints on the handle of the suitcase—not usable. In the house, all prints on the door frame, light switches, alarm control panel, and hallway table were his. Any foreign substances on the body are mud from the sidewalk, typical Manoa clay, and sleeping-grass thorns. Nothing in the car to indicate there was anyone with him."

The FD stopped briefly for questions. Hearing none, he resumed.

"Now, we managed to isolate the footprints from the three locations. It wasn't easy. On the upper ridge across the road from the crime scene there were two sets of footprints. One was ten-C men's smooth sole, a loafer given the stitch pattern. The other was an athletic shoe size eight. The size tens were the most recent.

"Down beside the house, there were another two sets of tracks in the trees. One was size nine rubber boots except the impression from the front of the boot is fainter than at the rear, suggesting the foot inside was smaller: The size nines came up the ravine from the road below, paced around, and then went back down the ravine. The second set overlaid a portion of earlier ones. This second track was size ten made by a man's dress shoe, quite fancy with a pointed toe. We lost track of pointed toe when he walked down to the house.

"Further down behind the house, we've identified six sets of distinct individuals coming and going from the house below to the lower street. The exiting tracks covered the size nine exit tracks, so they were made after the size nines left the scene." He stopped to look at the two detectives quizzically. "Keeping all this straight?"

"What's your take on this?" Kaj asked.

"Working theory: the shooter, or maybe we should say the archer, was in those trees up beside the road. The slope flattens out there, and that's where the size nine boots were pacing. This means that either the size nine boots or the size ten pointed toes may be your perp. The tracks from the house down below were made by rubber slippers or athletic shoes. I wouldn't rule out involvement by unidentified others on site that night, but there's where I'd start."

"Now," the FD said with an emphatic flourish that only he could manage, "there is something else. The stool sample we took from the upper hillside. We found occult blood and sepsis in the sample. The blood is type B-Positive, quite common in Asia. Even given the rain, it was not more than 12 hours old. There were traces of undigested cumin and sesame seeds, both of which are used in Southeast Asian cooking, so, putting this together and making an assumption, you may be looking for an Asian male weighing approximately140 pounds. What is not conjecture is that he is seriously ill. He needs immediate medical attention if he doesn't want to lose part of his colon. It's advanced enough that if he does nothing about it, he'll develop septicemia and die."

The FD pointed significantly at Kaj.

"Word to the wise," he said. "Don't waste any time finding him if you want him to be able to tell you what he was doing up there."

9

BACK AT CID, the crime board awaited the start of the entries. Without being asked, Jill sighed grimly, picked up the marker, and walked to the front. At her previous CID, she was used to having the office work delegated to her. Her boss said it was because she was good at it. She thought it had more to do with his uncertainty about how to work with a woman detective.

"Kaipo can do that," Kaj said immediately.

"No one can read my hand writing," Kaipo objected. "At least, that's what you all tell me. I'm not being lazy." Kaipo looked genuinely concerned.

"No one said you were," Kaj replied irritably. He was feeling the length of the day and the burden of discomfort he carried from seeing Moses.

"I'll do it," Cliff said quickly. He strode to the board and took the marker from Jill's hands. "We need you free to use your analytic eye," he told her with a smile.

"TOD midnight," Jill said as she sat down next to Kaj.

Cliff wrote it and circled it. "Let's have the flight details, Kaipo."

"According to his travel itinerary, it was overnight United to New York, then British Airways Concorde to London Heathrow. He checked into a suite at the Langham Hotel in Regent Street for three nights. Then he flew Scandinavian Air Lines to Stockholm for another three nights, where he was the guest of the US Embassy. The Nobel Prize ceremony was held on his second day there. Coming home, it was Air Canada to Vancouver, Canada, and then Vancouver to Honolulu."

Kaipo handed the list to Cliff, who copied the flight details down at the top of the board.

Jill looked at her notes. "We know what he did for those three days in London. He visited Winston Churchill's house, Chartwell, and had lunch with a Cambridge University rector named Sutter Wind-Trenton. He had his business card."

"He was scheduled to arrive in Honolulu, at 7:30 p.m. last night," Kaipo continued, "but the plane was an hour late arriving. Some delay in Vancouver. The guy must have been done in even flying first class. He may have been in a hurry to get home, because he didn't arrange for a layover coming back. Nothing unusual coming through immigration. Customs remembers him, because they gathered around to look at the Nobel medal and made everyone else wait. Airport Security tapes show him exiting international arrivals at 9:30 p.m."

"He had a parking receipt that showed him leaving the overseas parking garage at 10:15 p.m." Jill looked at the time sequence starting to snake its way across the board. "Kaipo's right. That's a brutal schedule coming back. Going over, the Concorde flight and the three days' rest in London would have helped with the jet lag. I wonder he was able to drive himself home from the airport."

Kaipo squinted to look at the board. He knew he should get glasses but didn't want to admit it.

"I checked with the parking attendant working the overseas terminal that night. He didn't remember Whitworth's car. But he did remember a university group leaving about 10:30 p.m. One of the vehicles was a truck with a rickshaw in the back. Someone tipped the newspaper about that rickshaw because there's a story in this afternoon's paper showing Whitworth at the airport next to it. Airport Security remembered Whitworth being interviewed on camera, so I called the TV station and asked for the raw footage. They sent it over a couple of hours ago."

Kaj looked at the newspaper Kaipo pushed across the table. It showed Whitworth and the rickshaw behind him. There was no sign of the group. "Okay. What else?"

"He had a grocery receipt that indicates he completed his shopping at 11:30 p.m. I checked with Manoa Safeway. He's a regular there, and the checker remembered him. She didn't notice anything different or see anyone with him."

Cliff started a new line at the top of the board. "Let's get a timeline for his arrival. He leaves customs at 9:30 p.m. He left the airport at 10:15. The rickshaw group left around 10:30. With no traffic he gets to the grocery store at maybe 11:15. It's a quick run to pick up a few things. The grocery receipt says he left the store at11:30 p.m. He'd be tired, maybe hungry. He'd go straight home."

"Has anyone checked the time from the supermarket to the house?" Kaj asked impatiently.

"I did," said Kaipo. "Ten minutes. I caught a light."

"All right," Jill said. "He's at the house at around 11:40. Give him time to open the house, turn on the lights, put his briefcase in the hallway, and go back to the car to get his luggage. He's hit on the return trip. Midnight fits. Did any of the neighbors see or hear anything?" She looked over at Kaipo.

"An aunty in the house up above says there was party noise from the house below his," Kaipo said. "She says something kept disturbing the birds in the trees next to the victim's house last night. They're mynahs, so they're noisy."

"Did she say when?" Jill was catching a little of Kaj's impatience. It seemed to be in the air.

"She thought the last time was just before midnight. She was watching television, saw car lights, and went out to see if her grandson and his wife had come home. They'd been at a concert and didn't get back until after one a.m. Turned out they'd stopped at Likelike Drive In for hamburgers. The kids both work at Pearl Harbor, so they left for work this morning at 5:30 a.m. Youth. You've got to admire its ability to function without sleep. "

Kaj frowned. "Come on. Did the other neighbors see or hear anything?"

Kaipo and Cliff exchanged glances. "Only the aunty," Kaipo said. "The other neighbors went to bed early. Cliff and I covered Whitworth's street and the ones above and below. Anyone further away couldn't have heard anything."

Kaj tapped his fingers on the table top. "There was an anomaly with this picture. Forensics noted it as well. Why were the front door and house lights off?"

Jill nodded in agreement. "If I'm bringing luggage into the house, I want the lights on so I can see what I'm doing."

Kaj tried to imagine himself in the situation. "Let's assume that the vic turned them on when he first entered the house. He would need them on to unlock the door and turn off the alarm. Is there any reason he would have for turning the lights off?"

"You might do it to discourage termites, but they only swarm in May and June. That's the main thing I remember from Entomology 107. Rest of the year they're eating your house." Kaipo looked pleased that he'd got something out of the four years he'd spent on the HSU campus.

Kaj ignored Kaipo's joke, but Cliff suppressed a small smile. "Then if the victim wasn't battling insects," Cliff said, "the perp must have turned the lights off as he or she left. It might have been impossible to get in before because of the alarm system."

Jill looked up from her notes. "That would mean the killer knew about the alarm but not the code."

"What kind of alarm is it?" Kaj asked.

"Koa Kane Alert," Cliff said. "State of the art. An intruder trips an infrared beam, the alarm sounds, the video recorder turns on, and a call goes out to the monitoring company. If the killer broke in before Whitworth was out of town, the alarm would trip and security would be there in minutes."

"Check with the security system for a record of entries on that day. In the meantime, let's go with the theory that there was something in the house that the killer wanted. Nothing seemed out of place when Jill and I went through it, but that doesn't mean something wasn't taken. Since the money and valuables were untouched, we'll assume that it was something beyond what Whitworth had in his possession. Did anyone say anything about a cleaning service? He must have had one. Everything was dusted and clean, and there was no sign of roaches."

Kaipo nodded. "The aunty in the house on the hill also told me she saw a Suite Leilani Home Maintenance car sometime in the afternoon."

"Okay, get on that. They'll have records of time of arrival and the security system should confirm it. Now what about Stone's guests?"

Cliff read from a clipboard. "We've set up interviews with four of the art students for tomorrow on campus. We're missing Cheterinda Singh. The art department said they didn't have current information on him, but they did say he was an international student. That's something Stone left out. We can check with the foreign student office tomorrow when we're on campus. If they won't give us anything, we can check on his student visa, assuming he has one."

"What about the victim's next of kin?" Kaj asked.

"His mother," Jill said. "The State personnel office gave HPD her name. The Boston police department was asked to inform her. I'll contact her myself first thing tomorrow. I'll see if she needs anything."

Kaj nodded. "Okay, everyone, that's a start. Let's have the TV coverage now."

They watched as the screen filled with random images of the crowds outside Honolulu Airport international arrivals on the lower level. People came through the double doors pulling luggage and blinking at the camera, their startled eyes wide in the glare of the lights. The film panned the groups waiting for arrivals and then found the rickshaw. It was festooned with ribbons and had a cardboard replica of the Nobel Prize medallion attached to the back of the passenger seat. The camera zoomed in and out on the medal and then took a wide view to show the group standing beside it.

There were five of them. One was an older man with grizzled hair pulled back in a ponytail, the others were wearing t-shirts and shorts and appeared to be in their late twenties. One stood out, because the camera focused on his t-shirt which said "Save the Seals." He was taller than the others and sported a dark, bushy beard. Then the camera turned back to the door where Whitworth appeared. The camera followed a woman, whom Kaj recognized as the KHVH science reporter, as she thrust a microphone into Whitworth's face and asked how he had felt when he was given the award. Whitworth looked exhausted but concentrated on replying.

After a few minutes, the man with the ponytail took him by the elbow, picked up his luggage, and escorted him to the rickshaw. Whitworth looked at the rickshaw and hesitated. The last of the film was Whitworth in the rickshaw being pulled off camera by the five people who had brought it.

"He didn't look pleased," Kaipo said. "Not as if he was expecting it."

"Get names for the five," Kaj said.

"Already have them." Cliff flipped open his notepad. "The TV crew had asked them for their names: Paul Nguyen, Eddie Gow, Brendan Hope, and David Marks, plus Curtis Dawes, who told them he was faculty on the Whitworth project. We're set to interview them tomorrow."

"Leave Dawes to Jill and me. We'll interview him after we're done with Whitworth's dean," Kaj stood up abruptly. "It's a good start. Now let's get it done."

Kaj stomped back to his desk without explanation. He knew they were staring at him, unaccustomed to his abruptness, but there was nothing he could or wanted to explain.

Every man's demons are his own. Their whispers curve like smoke around the barriers that even the strongest and wisest try to build against them. Sometimes, they even speak the truth.

Right now, Kaj's were telling him that he didn't like the feeling of not being in control of his life, he didn't like not living up to his own code of personal behavior, and, most of all, he didn't like the fact that the past wasn't staying where he thought he'd put it.

10

K AJ ARRIVED HOME too late for the ten o'clock news, but he imagined that the Whitworth murder had been the lead story. It was being picked up world-wide, and soon the international press would descend on Hawaii. It would be nice if by that time they had solved the case.

From the driveway, he could see the television flickering behind the curtains, as well as the glow from the Christmas tree. Although Linda liked real Christmas trees, they used the fake one they bought when the cargo container ship arrived late one year and unloaded shriveled tree skeletons.

"Might as well use the old one again and get our money's worth," Linda said each year, but they both knew they didn't have time to shop for a fresh one.

Seeing the tree lights reminded him that he still needed to shop for Linda's gift. If he were lucky and settled the Whitworth case, he'd be among the men crowding the stores in Ala Moana or Pearl City on Christmas Eve. If he wasn't, and it wouldn't be the first time, he'd have to ask her forgiveness and make it up to her later.

Linda had fallen asleep watching the television and woke when he opened the door from the garage.

"You look tired." She stretched as she stood up and gathered herself from sleep.

"It's been a long day," Kaj admitted. He locked his gun and badge away in a drawer and tried to navigate the drop back into family life. It usually took a few minutes. With a major case, it could take longer.

"Hungry?" Linda tried to make his transition as easy as possible. Food was a good bridge.

"I'll eat anything you've got."

"Portuguese bean soup, rice, bread, and salad. All you can eat," Linda laughed as she took food from the fridge and put it into the microwave.

"Your sister sent us a card. It's up on the fridge if you want to read it."

Kaj looked sideways at Linda. "What did Aileen say?"

Christmas cards were all anyone heard from her. The family learned about her wedding when she sent them a picture.

"She says they're okay. Said we should go over to visit, that the weather's nice in Orange County this time of year."

"Anything about Dad or coming back to visit Hawaii?"

"Nope," Linda said. "By the way, your dad was over here this afternoon. He was surprised to find me, but I told him I was on school break for Christmas. He'd forgotten."

"What did he do to the yard?"

Kaj's voice was anguished. Goro would *monku,* complain, because they didn't care for it the way he thought they should. He was appalled when they spray-painted a dead pine in their front yard rather than afford its replacement. "What will the neighbors say? My son with a dead, green-painted pine in his front yard. And me owning a landscape business. They'll ask how come I raise you so bad," he complained.

Goro had absolute standards. "The Kajiwaras were samurai," he said proudly, as if that meant their modern descendants should be also. The code was so revered that there were times when Kaj felt he was growing up in a Toshiro Mifune movie. Who knew? Maybe his desire to set things right by solving crime started while he was watching *Yojimbo*. Goro was the one who insisted on calling Kaj by his traditional Japanese middle name, Kenji, and enrolling him in Kendo. His mother, Ai, shortened Kenji to the affectionate, Kenbo. In the end, Kaj decided the matter of names himself by refusing to answer to anything but Kaj.

"He did some pruning is all," Linda said. "No big deal."

"Should he be driving in heavy traffic all the way from Palolo?" Kaj asked.

Linda shrugged sympathetically. "I know, Hon. I wish he would sell his house and move in with us. But when I told him we could make a nice studio apartment for him downstairs, he just said 'memories.' I hate to think of him in a buffet restaurant during senior discount hour eating his dinner alone with all the other solitary seniors. Not when he has family who care for him. I know he misses your mother."

"I'd like to see him and my sister make up before it's too late. He's not getting any younger."

"Any chance of that?" Linda glanced over at the Christmas card that she had taped to the refrigerator door.

"I doubt it. My sister is as hard headed as he is."

"Honey," Linda said, changing the subject as she always did when she could see a topic becoming painful. "Don't forget that Annie and I start our temp jobs at Ala Moana Liberty House tomorrow."

Kaj had forgotten. "That's a long way to go. Last year you worked here in Pearl Ridge."

"We told you we wanted something different this year." Linda tried to look winsome and appealing. "You'll have to humor us. We want to be independent and not become boring and predictable."

"Do you know what you will be doing?"

"Annie and I are going to be gift wrapping."

Both Kaj's eyebrows rose unasked. Linda had tried many things to gain this elusive independence. Despite his good intentions, he could not suppress a chuckle.

"Why are you laughing?" Linda looked at him indignantly.

"I'm sorry. I can't imagine you wrapping presents." He knew he was falling into a crevice. His deadpan expression had never worked with his wife and had even less chance with his daughter.

"Why not?" Linda said with a mutinous tip of her head.

"All the presents you wrap are loaded with scotch tape. Last Christmas, ants got into them." He knew he was going to pay for this. The only thing uncertain was how much and when.

"You can't blame us for ants. Ants can get into anything."

Linda gave a dismissive sniff: a sharp intake of air through her nose and a quick expulsion through her lips. Kaj remembered her doing it when they first met on the HSU campus. He called it her cheerleader's honk, although she wasn't a cheerleader. When she did it, she sounded like a bull getting ready to throw off a rodeo rider.

"I know Annie has a degree in history and insight into people," he said, trying to backtrack, "but let's face it—she lost her job at Kuni Dry Goods, because she couldn't cut fabric straight. How's that different from cutting paper?"

"Are you saying we aren't capable of doing it?" Linda's indignance had now become a deep, rebellious frown.

"No, Hon. I'm all for you feeling independent. I'm always supportive. You know that. You have no idea how many huli-huli chickens, Portuguese sausage, Zippy's chili, and Leonard's sweet-bread fund-raising tickets I buy every year."

"Because of us?" Linda gave a small, surprised grin. "What do you mean?"

"You remember when you sold Tupperware and Avon? Well, ever since, whenever one of your former customers sells fundraiser tickets, they come straight to me. I'll bet I've bought more than you ever earned in your ventures into finance. I don't even ask anymore. Just as long as I don't have to do the selling, I just ask how much?"

"No kidding?"

"Trust me. No kidding."

"But you don't bring much home."

"The Portuguese sausage I do, because you use it. The other things I'll eat for lunch or leave by the coffee machine at work. They don't take long to disappear."

"It's for a good cause. It's for us," Linda giggled. "By the way, the HSU story was all over the TV news tonight. It ran as the lead story, and they kept showing the rickshaw greeting at the airport. He looked uncomfortable."

Kaj sighed at Linda's rapid change of subject and gave in to the inevitable. "I imagine he was. The newspapers have the story. They'll run with it tomorrow."

"Guess we won't see you for a while." Linda tried to sound more resigned than she felt. Big cases meant no days off until they were solved. It was part of his job and part of her life.

"You know how it goes. Besides, you'll be so busy wrapping presents that you won't even miss me." Kaj tried to joke because he knew she was right. There were times he had worked right through Christmas. It all depended on what pain Hawaii's citizens decided to inflict upon one another.

"We always miss you. You're our rock."

"By the way, Moses Mahi was the reporting officer." Kaj stumbled over the words.

"How was he?" Linda stared at Kaj intently.

"He looked fine. He says Malia is pregnant and getting impatient. I didn't know. I felt bad about it. I should have made time to stay in touch."

"Malia and I talk," Linda said. "We keep up."

"You never told me about that." Now it was Kaj's turn to be indignant.

"Kaj, I have to have some friends. We never see anyone but your dad anymore. We haven't had a real holiday in years, just days we take here and there. But it's okay. That's what CID does—your life belongs to the job. We all understand."

Linda put another bowl in front of Kaj without his having to ask.

"I feel bad about Moses and Malia." Kaj stared at the soup but made no effort to eat.

"Christmas is a good time to renew old friendships."

"Not now. Not with this case just starting."

"I saw you on TV," Linda said. "They caught you driving away from the Whitworth house in Manoa. You waved them off and looked quite stern. Cutely stern, of course. TV news interviewed people who knew Whitworth. Sounds as if he was a tough nut."

"Depends on who you ask. I'd hate to hear what people say about me."

"Only good things if I'm asked."

Linda smiled and reached across the table to stroke his hand. It was her knowing smile, the one that made the years fell away. She was once again the exuberant, talkative college student always protesting something. He was again the reserved warrior she loved to tease. It was a sweet moment, one of the many they had shared over the years of their marriage.

Her smile had the power to make him regret having to get up the next day to go to work. He even wondered for a moment what it might be like to have a ratoon-crop baby.

11

"You're wanted in Director Wilson's office," the department clerk told Kaj as he walked in next morning, "and he said to tell you to step on it."

Kaj assumed it had to do with the Whitworth case and involved the need to keep everyone informed. He turned around without a word and walked down to his boss's office.

Rank did not have many privileges in CID. In fact, the only difference between offices amounted to their privacy. As CID head, Wilson had the single office equipped with blinds that could shut out the telephones, conversations, and the endless people who came and went.

Otherwise, detectives shared the same functional furniture, coffee-mud color scheme, and cubicles. Senior staff had more pictures and framed newspaper clippings on their walls, because they'd worked there longer, but that was it. The one bow to the season was a plastic holly lei draped around the office bulletin board and a chipped Santa figure by the coffee machine.

"Come in and shut the door," Bob snapped. "I need your help. The Governor has called a press conference for 2:00 p.m. today to discuss the Whitworth case. His office has asked us to report where we are with the investigation. The Chief and I will be there, but I'll need you at the Capitol as back-up. What do you have on tap this morning?"

"Nakamura and I have an 11:00 a.m. with Andrew Goodyear, Whitworth's dean. We should be back in plenty of time."

"Be there—please—or it will be messy. We've got to get out in front of the media."

"Why is the Governor holding a press conference this soon?" Kaj asked. "He must understand this is only day two."

Bob shrugged. "I'm sure he does, but he wants more than a press release expressing outrage. He wants to show leadership and involvement."

"Understood." Kaj resigned himself to possible follow-up calls from the Governor and the Brass as well as those from the media. He could ignore the media, more or less, but not the others.

"This case is top priority. Whatever you need, you get." Bob sounded very definite.

"So far, the ME and FD made us a priority, which was our immediate need," Kaj assured him. "Whitworth worked with dozens of people, some at the top echelons of State leadership. We may need help with contacting them. We don't know yet if Whitworth's work has national security implications. We'll have a better idea once we talk with the dean today."

"Watch the time," Bob said decisively. "Meet me at the State Capitol before the briefing. All departments are on ready alert and heads are going to roll if this case falls apart."

12

Things hadn't changed on the HSU campus since Kaj's time there. He was a student for three years plus summers, feeling unwelcome because of his military service and with no desire to linger longer than he needed to in order to graduate.

The campus was still a jumble of buildings planted wherever space allowed, hemmed in from planned expansion by surrounding, expensive residential property. Where there was no room for a major structure, temporary buildings clustered like toadstools under banyan trees that State Historic Preservation wouldn't let the university cut down.

The students joked back then that nothing was more permanent than a temporary building. They were right. The walkways around the temporaries, euphemistically called annexes, still splayed out at odd angles and disappeared during heavy rains. In winter, when torrential downpours turned Diamond Head from dusty brown to green, students walked barefoot to class, carrying rubber slippers. Kaj remembered sitting in class soaking wet and writing his class notes down on damp paper.

The one good thing about his years on campus was meeting Linda Correa. She taught him that mayonnaise tastes good on strawberry Jell-O and the best cracked seed was worth the drive downtown. But more seriously she challenged him to look for beauty in the world and not just see crime and war. She also taught him how to laugh at life's absurdity. When he once said she'd look good in a kimono, she'd burst out laughing. "You're such a romantic," she teased him "You gotta have boy's hips to wear a kimono. Imagine me on my knees doing that cute little rocking stuff to get up. I'd eat the carpet. That's Cherry Blossom Queen stuff."

To prove her wrong, he gave her an antique pink and gold kimono one Christmas. Instead of wearing it, she hung it on a stick hanger in their dining room, with a plastic dust cover over it. It looked pretty, but it wasn't the outcome he'd imagined when he bought it. Still, it was a happy memory and, ever after, they called any attractive Japanese girl a CBQ.

Rather than think about campus life, Kaj glanced instead at Jill. Linda would probably call her a CBQ. Kaipo must have thought so when he tried to flirt with her. Kaj knew that she had been raised in San Diego. He also knew she had studied pre-law with a minor in psychology in college. He didn't know what made her join the police force, only that she graduated in the top ten percentile of her class at the academy. San Diego CID at least pretended they were sorry to see her leave when she transferred to Hawaii.

As soon as they reached the campus north entrance, the familiar parking dance began. The attendant, a student employee, claimed he was authorized to admit only vehicles with university permits or police cars painted blue and white. If they wanted to use the pay lot, they should turn around and go to the *makai*, sea direction, gate on the other side of the campus. Offering to put the portable blue light on the car roof didn't shake him. Getting nowhere, Kaj told the attendant to call the dean's office at the Kamaboko Institute.

Just when Kaj was about to get out of the car to find his own solutions, the attendant came out of his kiosk and told them that the institute had failed to arrange for a temporary parking pass, but that it had now been corrected. He handed Jill an official looking piece of cardboard that authorized parking in a numbered lot. He then pointed them in the general direction of the institute.

Jill drove around the parking lots several times until she found their designated lot, but having the pass didn't provide an actual space. When they returned to the parking attendant to report their failure to find one, they were told to park in the institute's delivery zone. If they were issued a ticket, they should give it to the dean's office. The delay, of course, made them late.

Dean Goodyear's office was located in a building officially named the Kamaboko Institute of Marine Biology. It was named for U.S. Senator Kamaboko, who, behind his back, was called the Pork Master for his ability to lay hands on federal money. The grateful university waived the policy reserving building names for the dead, perhaps hoping the grateful politician would divert even more taxpayer money the university's way.

The institute was a large square stone building with windows only on the second level, set back behind tall grass and ferns. Behind it were adjacent smaller buildings for storage, pumps, and power units. For most people the building was a mystery, and after the last protest march over research animals, the university preferred it that way.

When they finally found the delivery dock and parked, yellow-gray rain clouds had begun creeping down the valley walls, promising the December downpours that thundered onto rooftops and cars. The showers never lasted long, ending as abruptly as they began, but they left steaming rivulets and muddy puddles glinting in the sunlight. Kaj didn't want to be drenched any more than he wanted to remove his shoes and paddle, so they ran around the building to get to the entrance.

Once inside, they found a large, airy atrium filled with ferns and a few unseasonal hibiscuses, a welcome relief from the outside austerity. But not even the greenery could lessen Kaj's irritation. It intensified after they took the elevator up to the dean's office on the first floor.

When he introduced himself and Jill to the woman behind the reception desk, she looked at the clock. Her manner reminded Kaj of his first-grade teacher who had curled gray hair and stared at him through her bifocals. He hadn't liked her very much. While the woman ignored them, Kaj read the nameplate on her desk. It said she was Mrs. Gladys Hoffstra.

When Mrs. Hoffstra finally acknowledged them, Kaj told her where they had parked and attempted a pointed comment about the parking pass being a hunting license rather than a reservation. She didn't smile. Instead, she muttered something he couldn't quite hear. This was invitation enough for Kaj to unleash his mischievous side.

"The dean is expecting us," he said, emphasizing the verb as if she might have forgotten. "If it's more convenient, we can arrange for a squad car to bring him downtown."

The woman was not impressed. "That won't be necessary. He'll be with you in a minute." She did not invite them to sit while they waited.

"And where would we find Professor Whitworth's secretary?"

"His assistant," Mrs. Hoffstra corrected him, "is on the second floor. Her office is next to his."

"And her name?" Kaj could as well have waited to ask the dean, but he didn't like being disrespected. He'd had enough of that during his student days when his instructors automatically assigned him to present the pro-position in the Vietnam war debates. I may have fought in it, he wanted to protest, but that doesn't mean I supported it. Saying he was drafted made no difference. The classroom intellectuals, the ones who managed not to get drafted, thought he should have gone to Canada.

Mrs. Hoffstra spoke the name of Whitworth's assistant with delicate distaste. "Harriet Noguchi."

"Do you and Mrs. Noguchi work together?"

"The dean's office is quite separate from Professor Whitworth's. We work with the administration, not the faculty or students." Mrs. Hoffstra's tone was icy. Kaj assumed there must be history there.

Then, as if admitting some defeat, she stood up and motioned them towards an inner door where she knocked twice on the heavy wood panel and stood back to let them in.

13

DEAN ANDREW GOODYEAR was an energetic, hearty man with white hair swiped across his forehead. His eyes were observant, and his hands moved in constant motion when he was animated, which was often. He wore a blue and white shirt printed with a pattern showing Hawaiian flags and Hawaiian geese, *nene*, the kind worn by bank managers when they want to honor Aloha Fridays without looking like waiters.

Kaj noted that the office windows looked out onto a well-manicured Japanese roof garden invisible to anyone outside the building. But it was the office furnishings that most impressed him. Three walls had floor to ceiling koa-wood shelves much like those in Whitworth's home office. Unlike Whitworth's shelves, however, these were overflowing with small carvings, stone images, pottery, coins in velvet boxes, fans, scrolls and paintings.

"Protocol gifts," the dean explained in a strong British voice as he saw the amazement in Kaj's face. "Visitors and students bring little presents. It's a lovely custom, but it takes up room."

He motioned them to sit on soft chairs while he occupied an opposite sofa.

"We must apologize for being late," Kaj began. "We had difficulty finding parking."

"I understand," Goodyear said. "Over the years, this campus has built impressive new buildings without long-range planning for where to put the cars. Now there isn't any land left to accommodate the demand."

"We have to apologize that our lateness upset Mrs. Hoffstra." Jill's voice contained more than a hint of irony.

"Gladys does like things ordered," the dean smiled knowingly, "but I'm sure you didn't come here to discuss our problems. How can we help you with the investigation?"

Kaj started out with the traditional first question. "Do you know of anyone who would want to harm Professor Whitworth?" He knew that most people would have rehearsed their answers to that one.

"Absolutely not," the dean replied, his mustache bristling as he rose to the bait. "He was a highly respected faculty member. We will struggle to find someone of his stature to replace him."

"Then, can you tell us who he was?" This was the unexpected follow-up question. As Kaj hoped, it caught the dean by surprise.

Goodyear looked momentarily unsure. "As a person or a scientist?"

"I'm most interested in him as a person right now. What was he like to work with? Did he have friends or any enemies?"

"He was a private person, if that's what you mean." The dean's shoulders had stopped their little dance. Kaj noted that the dean's energy muted when he was uncertain.

"Did he have any close friends?" Kaj persisted.

Goodyear frowned again and hesitated. "I don't recall anyone," he was forced to admit. "He had many professional colleagues, and as I said, he was well respected."

Kaj assumed his professional deadpan expression, the one he had used on Stone the previous day. Ai also told him if you want to know a man, look at his friends. He wondered what his mother would say about a man who had none.

"I understand he wasn't married. Did he have personal friends?"

"I believe he was seeing someone in the history department. He'd bring her to receptions, and I saw them once at the theater. But I don't know anything more than that."

"What's her name?"

The dean struggled with the idea that if he identified her, he might be implying she ought to be a suspect. In the end, the need to cooperate overcame his desire to be discreet.

"Helen Malcolm," he admitted. "Her office is in Pendleton Hall."

"No wife, no ex-wife, no ex-girlfriend, no ex-companion, no children, no students close to him?" Kaj remembered the four books in Whitworth's library. The man might be a loner, but there had to have been someone once.

"None that I knew about. But my relationship with him was professional. We occasionally had lunch so he could keep me informed, but otherwise, we didn't socialize except at university receptions and the like."

"How about his co-workers?"

A cloud of what Kaj took to be doubt passed over the dean's face. His answer was careful. "Harrison was responsible for administering over five million dollars in State and federal funds, the latter mainly from the National Institutes of Health. In addition, there were proprietary contracts for joint research with pharmaceutical corporations as well as direct Congressional appropriations. His project touched everyone in this institute and in several other colleges."

"Who was working most closely with him?"

"Curtis Dawes. He's the Co-Principal Investigator of the anemone project. He manages the main lab and coordinates with sub-contracted projects in other colleges."

"We're going to need the names of people who worked with him, his students, and anyone else who had contact with him outside this department."

The dean nodded. "Gladys can give you the project directory as you leave. It's quite a list. But as I told you, what I know about Harrison's life outside the department is limited, beyond the obvious fact he worked well with the university's administration and regents as well as the legislature and Governor's office."

Jill, who had been taking notes, spoke up for the first time. "You mentioned that you had lunch with him so he could keep you informed. Does that mean you weren't directly involved with his project?"

Goodyear nodded. "That's right. To the extent Harrison reported to anyone, it was to President Halstead and the Governor."

"Then the Kamaboko Institute did not provide funds for Whitworth's project?"

The dean's shoulders jerked into life at Jill's question. His mustache twitched with what Kaj sensed was repressed indignation.

"That is absolutely not the case. Buildings need to be operated, salaries paid, and electricity and water turned on. That all comes out of the Institute budget. The university charges grantors an overhead fee to cover these services, but it's never enough. It's even worse when the grant administrator persuades the administration to reimburse part of the overhead back to the project, as Harrison did. I couldn't take that lying down on my back. We have fifteen other funded projects, smaller, but still needing things like travel funds. After I raised my objections, Harrison was given his own line budget item, and Vice President Napa picked up the slack for my operations in this institute."

"Were you all right with this?" Kaj asked.

"It was presented to me as a done deal. The project was to be based in the institute for convenience and for academic credibility. We're ranked among the top ten nationally for our marine programs and research, in case you're interested. We're not a glossy brochure." The dean scowled, making his mustache rise high on one side.

Jill looked thoughtful. "So, you were responsible for providing space and support for a program you did not control. That seems a convoluted management structure."

The dean looked at Jill with new respect. "You see the challenges. Once a university accepts public money, accountability measures come with it. Sometimes interference comes along as well. Harrison worked with the Governor directly, so it was left to me to fend off legislators and potential investors who would have liked to benefit from his work. I had to defend his autonomy while fighting to get enough funding to keep his lights on."

Kaj's eyebrow rose. "Did Whitworth know this was happening?"

"I'm not sure what Harrison knew. I think he believed he could be a scientist and run a major grant without outside oversight. He asked me once how I negotiated the university's politics. I told him I accepted that when I became an administrator, I became a whore. Harrison looked quite appalled at my language, but it was true. You see,

Inspector, Harrison wasn't the only one with ideals. Like the others, I wanted to do science for the love of it. But I had to become a realist. Science today needs money to operate, and money attracts wasps."

Here it was, the university politics that Kaj hated.

"Was there any particular legislator or regent who wanted to intervene?" he asked.

"All when it suited their purposes. There was one senator who wanted to move the entire college to the Big Island. The regents are another matter. I never read them correctly and leave them to the president. I recall that Regent Takai seemed especially interested in the project, but the president's office is in a better position to know."

"How is Whitworth's death going to affect the college?" Jill asked.

"It's going to be terrible." Goodyear's shoulders slumped. "Vice President Napa asked me if we had anyone competent enough to take on Whitworth's work because the university doesn't want to return the grant funds. It was insulting, but he was right. We need someone with an international reputation who can work with Hawaii's government. Harrison could do it, because he looked the part and overawed everyone, but there aren't many people with that type of clout. We may have to go with a series of visiting directors instead of a permanent position."

"What was Whitworth working on? And can you please explain it so I can understand." Kaj smiled as he made the request.

"His project was designed to analyze the genetic structure and the mechanism of action of a poisonous Micronesian sea anemone. After it was discovered by the University's submersible, Harrison believed that it had pharmaceutical applications. If that worked out, there would have been potential for licensing as there had been for his previous work. The Oceanography Department is working to propagate the anemone. Harrison's anemone lab is performing chemical and genetic analysis. The medical school is working on its applications. The initial results seem promising enough that NIH—the National Institutes for Health—recently renewed the grant for another three years."

"Was this what he won the Nobel Prize for?"

Goodyear shook his head. "No. That was for his previous work developing a break-through pharmaceutical to contain the onset of malaria. He shared the prize with colleague researchers, one from South Africa and another from Thailand."

Kaj nodded. So far, he understood, or thought he did. "How long had Whitworth been with the university?"

"He came here from Harvard twenty years ago. They could do accelerated tenure in those days, and he became full professor almost immediately. Since coming here, I've fended off other universities trying to lure him away. I think he liked his life here, and we were always able to match or at least counter the offers."

The dean's mustache twitched. "By the way, I believe that your investigations start with asking for alibis. Just in case you should be interested in mine, I was attending the Christmas Concert at the Blaisdell Center last night. My wife and I reached home after midnight. I don't know when Harrison was killed, but we live up the Old Pali Road in Nu'uanu, so we weren't anywhere near Manoa."

"Is there some reason you might be suspected?" Kaj's eyebrows showed his bemusement.

"Of course not. I'm trying to be helpful. I'm an amateur criminologist. I've written a couple of detective stories with a Hawaii setting. If you'd like to read one, I'd enjoy your opinion."

Kaj changed the subject. "What about Curtis Dawes and the other assistants?"

"As I said, Curtis manages the day-to-day operation of the project. The assistants report to him and he in turn works—or did work—with Harrison. Curtis is a good scientist in his own right, so the project was in good hands whenever external fund-raising or collaboration was needed and Harrison had to be in Washington."

"What's his background?"

"Curtis is an associate professor. He joined the department about the same time as Harrison and was tenured ten years ago. He published a peer-reviewed book on Dendrobatidae, which was the basis for his receiving tenure."

Jill and Kaj both stared at the dean.

"Poisonous tree frogs. He was studying the pharmaceutical application of the venom. He moved over to the anemone project once it was funded."

"Then he gave up his own research to work for Whitworth? How did he feel about that?" Kaj asked.

"It was a matter of timing. His NIH project officer told him that since his proposal for grant renewal was similar to that of the anemone project, both of them seeking pharmaceutical application for components in venom, NIH was more interested in receiving an umbrella proposal that might include both projects. The university was more interested in the anemone component since it gained political backing from the State."

"And possibly because Senator Kamaboko had particular interest in that project?"

"I think the senator's interest was mainly in working with Harrison rather than any particular research. Pork barrel projects rely on a handshake and trust. Harrison's background and work gave him immediate credibility on Capitol Hill."

"Is there any reason this investigation needs to be sensitive to federal restrictions?" Jill asked.

"You mean was Harrison doing classified work? No. We're not Los Alamos or JPL in Pasadena. I can't rule out the State Department, given Harrison's international significance. But I'm sure the State Department won't be shy about letting you know."

"What about the research assistants?"

"They're a combination of post-docs and graduate students working on dissertations. Some also teach part-time for the university while they are paid by the anemone project. This means a living wage, so there is heavy competition for the available slots. They report to Curtis, and he can do a better job of introducing you to them. I recognize them but don't know that much about them otherwise."

"Was there any trouble with these assistants? Someone fired perhaps? Someone with a grievance?"

"This is a university, Inspector. What happens in these programs can affect the entire course of a student's future career. Where there is competition, there can be failure. Sometimes students become upset with negative assessments."

"Was there such a case?"

"Harrison taught a graduate seminar each year. Recently, a student was upset to receive a C. In graduate school that is the equivalent of failing. He filed a complaint with my office and demanded that his grade be reviewed."

"Was it?"

"We never had to convene a committee to investigate. He withdrew from the university. As I understand it, the student in question returned to the Mainland. I don't know what happened after that, and if I did, FERPA, the federal privacy laws, would prevent me from discussing it."

"It may be important for us to know that information."

"When that times comes, Inspector," Goodyear said with a dismissive finality, "you will need to bring a subpoena and work through the university's legal department."

14

The rain started as they left the dean's office. At first, there were isolated drops like someone's tentative tap on a door, then the sound became insistent, heralding the cloudburst Kaj had dreaded. They could hear the drumming through the elevator shaft as the doors opened at the second floor onto the entrance of the anemone lab.

The lab was a large room with banks of cupboards down the walls. It was furnished with long tables divided into individual work spaces. Down the center of the room, mechanical aerators bubbled air into a series of large glass tanks. The atmosphere in the lab was humid and smelled of salt water.

A small cluster of people were holding a meeting at one end of the room. Kaj immediately recognized two of the rickshaw haulers among them as well as Curtis Dawes. The only one who noticed the detectives was a woman in a dark suit and sensible shoes. Kaj assumed she was Harriet Nogawa, Whitworth's assistant. He looked around for Cliff and Kaipo until he finally spotted them through a window at the back of the room. They were interviewing another student who had been at the airport.

Mrs. Noguchi stared at Kaj and Jill with a cool appraisal that made Kaj remember his early days on the Waikiki beat when he and Moses were patrolling for pickpockets. Ordinary citizens looked at the ground, anywhere but at one another. Those bent on mischief stared intently, looking for victims or for the police. For the moment, the woman did not alert the others.

Dawes was wearing the same slacks with heavy leather sandals as he had at the airport, except this time his clothes were covered by a lab coat. His gray-streaked hair was again pulled back into a pony tail that hung down below his collar. The others were in various shorts, undistinguished t-shirts, and rubber boots. Kaj assumed they were dressed for comfort.

'You have your assignments. There's no need to change those." Dawes' voice was raised as he had to compete with the rain splatter on the lab windows. "The funding is secure, so carry on as usual. If you have questions about reading times or protocols, Mrs. Nogawa will have the master list."

At the mention of her name, Mrs. Nogawa took the moment to speak up. "The university plans a memorial service for Professor Whitworth next week. That's after final exams. We should plan to attend."

"Sounds like a good idea," Dawes agreed. "Put that on your calendars. Now let's get back to work. If you're needed again, the detectives will find you."

As the small group broke up, Curtis noticed Kaj and Jill. "Can I help you?"

"Inspector Kajiwara and Detective Nakamura. We'd like to ask you a few questions."

Kaj might have imagined it, but Dawes looked momentarily embarrassed.

"Let's do this in my office," he said and guided them back out through the lab's main door.

15

DAWES' OFFICE TURNED out to be a small, dark room that looked like a converted broom closet. The only natural light came from a small window set high in the wall; otherwise, the overhead fluorescent lighting gave a pasty tint to everything beneath it. Even faces seemed to settle into an all-consuming veil of gray.

The occupant lifted papers off one chair and a backpack off another and invited them to sit. Then he went behind his desk and plopped down on a creaking office chair.

Dawes gave the impression that he was a direct man, so Kaj came right to the point. "Tell us about what happened at the airport last night."

Dawes didn't look surprised, but he spoke almost defiantly. "I want to make clear that nobody here had anything to do with the TV cameras being at the airport. We didn't know they were coming. We were not trying to get our pictures in the newspaper. We were simply trying to show Harrison a special welcome home."

Kaj leaned back, slightly dazed by Dawes' unexpected vehemence. Judging from the man's reaction, the rickshaw episode at the airport must have attracted a lot of pushback, none of it positive or comfortable.

"Why don't you start at the beginning," Kaj said evenly. "Take us through what happened."

Curtis looked at them with sad eyes. He looked as if he were a penitent pleading for absolution.

"We met at Simeon's house in Kaimuki after dinner to decorate the rickshaw with Nobel medallions. We planned to put Harrison in the rickshaw, maybe crown him a wreath of bay leaves, and transport him up to his car in the parking structure. Looking back, it was crazy. I don't know what we were thinking."

Dawes seemed to be only now realizing the extent of their folly, and how it looked that a faculty member had been involved.

"We arrived at the airport around 8:00 p.m. and tried to park outside the overseas terminal. Right away we ran into problems. With the rickshaw on the truck bed, it was too high to get under the parking gate. We had to unload it outside the parking area and drive the truck in by itself. The attendant then wanted to charge us for parking three vehicles including my van. We got that solved and then drove over to overseas parking. There it got worse. We hadn't considered how many dark blue cars look alike. We had to walk every level looking at license plates. Harrison has a custom plate: HRVD 1."

Curtis rubbed his shoulder and stretched his arm. His chair creaked with the movement.

"When we hauled the rickshaw over to the door outside overseas arrivals, the security people were the problem. They didn't want the rickshaw in the road blocking traffic or on the sidewalk blocking pedestrians. That was one thing good about the television crew. Once they turned on the camera, the security guards didn't want to be seen harassing us. They allowed us to put it in the taxi zone as long as we removed it once he arrived.

"Today we're paying for the escapade. Paul's pulled a muscle in his back, David's limping because one of the rickshaw wheels ran over his foot, and I think I've damaged my rotator cuff. It was harder to pull the thing with five when there was meant to be six."

"Is your welcome to Hawaii always so physical?" Jill looked somewhere between perplexed and amused.

"No. Usually just leis. This was meant to be special. I thought he'd expect it. But he wasn't into it at all."

Curtis looked at Jill as if he were looking for assurance that the high drama at the airport was not complete lunacy.

"What did he say about it?" Jill wasn't able to give Curtis absolution. The word *bizarre* was too firmly fixed in her mind.

Curtis shook his head sadly. "He thanked us. I think he used the word *unusual*. That was it."

Jill imagined that the word *unusual* resonated with several layers of meaning. "Where did you go next?"

"We loaded the rickshaw back onto Eddie's truck and I followed them back to Kaimuki. After we returned the rickshaw, I dropped Brendan at his apartment on University Avenue before I took Paul and David back to their dorm on the campus. Eddie lives in Aina Haina, so he took off in the opposite direction."

"Who's we?" Jill asked.

"The five of us, including me. We should have been six, but one didn't show. Your detectives have interviewed Paul Nguyen and David

Marks. Eddie Gow is still with them in the lab. The four of us are the only ones who showed up for work today."

"Who's missing?"

"Mark Gottschalk and Brendan Hope. Mark's not showing up last night or this morning doesn't surprise me, because he relies on buses to get here. But I'm worried about Brendan. He was with us at the airport last night."

"The kid with bushy beard and the Save-the-Seals t-shirt?" Kaj asked.

"Yes. He's the reliable one, so I'm not sure what happened. He should have contacted us by now if he's not coming in. We have to take timed readings."

"What time did you get to the dorms?" Kaj pictured the route: Waialae Avenue to King Street to University Avenue to drop off Brendan and then a short run up the hill to the dorms. Traffic would be light.

"Around 11:30pm. Brendan lives with roommates who may have seen him come in. I'm not sure anyone saw me drop the others off. The dorms may have a check-in system. I'm guessing at this point."

"It's important to know exactly" Jill said. "The five of you were among the last to see him alive. Where did you go after you dropped them off?"

"I went home. I thought about getting a chili-rice bowl at Zippy's on King Street, but I realized they'd be closed. I cooked a box of instant chicken ramen soup at home instead and went to bed."

"Where do you live?" Kaj asked.

"Two-bedroom on Liholiho Street."

"Let's talk about the project itself," Kaj said. "Has there been any trouble with people connected to the grant?"

Curtis frowned slightly. "If you mean personnel, there's always turnover. Someone doesn't work out for some reason. It could be anything. But I wouldn't say any more than usual."

"What was the last one?"

"We had a kid who couldn't show reproducible results. We were lucky it was a side experiment, or things could have been serious. We let him go."

"Was anyone angry enough to want to harm Whitworth? Someone who didn't graduate. Someone who might have a grudge. Someone who was fired. Someone who might have become an enemy?"

Curtis thought about his answer for a few moments. "One graduate student was upset with Harrison over a grade, but he withdrew from school, and federal policy says I can't discuss that. Otherwise, I'd say there might have been people with professional differences who could hold grudges. But I wouldn't use the word *enemy.*"

Have to remember that one, Kaj thought to himself. "What kind of differences?" he asked aloud.

"You'll think they're minor, but they're quite usual. Harrison and Dean Goodyear went a few rounds about overhead funds until Vice President Napa negotiated a settlement. But I never heard of anything that would be enough for someone to get violent. Faculty kill one another in writing. Conflict with the administration is par for the course."

"How did you get on with him?" Kaj asked.

"Once I learned to work with him, everything was fine. He supported my tenure, and I didn't mind asking him questions in a certain way and not breaking in on him when he was focused on something. But I also had to learn to work with the dean, who is quite an enthusiast about things, so I consider adjusting to personalities part of the job."

"What about your own projects?" Jill broke in. "You worked with tree frogs, didn't you?"

"I did." Curtis glanced sadly at a poster on his wall showing what would have been, under better light, a vivid-red frog on a dark green leaf spattered by rain drops. "Until the money dried up."

"The dean says the university decided to continue with the anemone project and let yours go to the wall. That couldn't have been pleasant." Jill felt some sympathy for Dawes but also remembered that they were hearing his version of events.

"There wasn't much I could do about it. I was newly tenured, which was a major factor for me. If I hadn't been, it meant packing up and leaving the islands. It was hard to accept my project being terminated, but there's a big difference between Big Science and little science. Harrison represented Big Science; although, he preferred Pure Science."

"Pure science?" Jill frowned.

Curtis smiled. "Science done for new knowledge alone. In other words, absolute creativity detached from commercial application or political advantage. Tough to find except in little science where only a handful of scientists in the world may be interested in your work. Harrison crossed the threshold to Big Science once he developed anti-toxins with patent and licensing that made a lot of money."

Kaj studied Curtis skeptically. "You and Whitworth arrived in Hawaii at the same time. He got tenure and promotion immediately, but you had to wait for years."

"Still waiting for promotion to full professor. Don't get me wrong. There are times I've been resentful. But it's been of science. I'm glad to have a job. I started my career at the same time as his. But there's a cachet to Harvard and winning a national Young Science Researcher of the Year award for your master's thesis. He fit in with the university's ambitions. But let me emphasize that I had no reason to harm Harrison. I'd be hurting myself and the students."

"Professor Dawes," Jill said, as she and Kaj rose to leave the cramped office. "Earlier, I noticed in the lab that the students were wearing rubber boots. Are they all the same?"

"Yes, they're community boots for general use." Dawes looked at Jill curiously. "Why do you ask?"

Jill ignored his question. "Do you mind if we take a sample pair with us? We'll see they're returned."

"Help yourself," Dawes said with a shrug. "They're kept in the changing room next to the lab's front door."

When Kaj and Jill left the lab a short time later, Jill had a plastic bag under her arm. It contained what looked a lot like a pair of muddy boots, size 9.

16

Tʜᴇʏ ɴᴇᴠᴇʀ ᴍᴀᴅᴇ it to the elevator. Mrs. Nogawa darted out and stood blocking their way, giving every indication that she expected to be heard. Kaj was in no mood to deny her. Here was yet another powerful middle-aged woman with glasses. He consoled himself by remembering that these ladies knew where the bodies were.

She introduced herself with authority. "I'm Harriet Nogawa. I am Professor Whitworth's executive assistant. Follow me."

She led the way into yet another koa-wood paneled room. Kaj stared in awe at the wood both for its beauty and its cost.

"Would you like something to drink?" she asked without much enthusiasm. Jill and Kaj knew she expected they would refuse.

Kaj shook his head. "We're fine. Thank you anyway."

She nodded and settled business-like into what she wanted them to know. "This is Professor Whitworth's office. I heard you introduce yourself to Professor Dawes. I didn't think he would be candid with you, so I wanted to correct any misconceptions he might have created."

Kaj relaxed into what looked like a wild ride: "I am sure you can be helpful."

"Professor Whitworth was a great man." She dabbed her eyes with a handkerchief produced from some pocket in her coat. "Little people envy what they can't achieve." She glanced at Jill as if she would understand more.

"Would anyone be envious enough to kill him?" Jill tried to sound reassuring and invite confidence.

"I don't know that." The woman recoiled and sat upright in her chair. "I'm not accusing anyone."

"We understand. You just want to help," Jill said soothingly.

"I can only tell you what I know. There are people who will benefit from his death." She clenched her hands until her knuckles turned white.

Kaj leaned forward with interest. Benefit meant money or power, always good motives for murder—right up there with revenge and jealousy. "Who are they?" he asked.

"Take a look at them," Mrs. Nogawa scowled, throwing her earlier caution to the winds. "The president who feared a successor, because Harrison got on so well with the Governor. The jealous associate who couldn't compete. The student who couldn't accept honest appraisal and threatened Harrison."

"A student threatened him?" Kaj echoed her words. "Was this reported to the police?"

"Reported?" She sneered. "Universities don't report things. They handle things." She sniffed into her handkerchief.

"Who was this student? When was it? What happened?"

Mrs. Nogawa looked startled by Kaj's demanding tone. "It was a project assistant several months ago. He made threats and everyone was in a hurry to make it go away. No one worried about Harrison's safety." She dabbed her eyes again. "The university decided to have the student drop out of school. So that's what happened. It was covered up."

"What threat did he make?"

"He tried to attack Harrison. His name was Douglas Williams. He went back to the Mainland."

"What part of the Mainland?" Jill asked.

"Somewhere in Oklahoma. Curtis would know, if he's willing to tell you. Curtis supposes himself the graduate students' best friend. I'm not supposed to be talking about this, but with Harrison gone, what does anything matter?" Tears were forming again in Mrs. Nogawa's eyes.

"Did anyone else make threats?"

Mrs. Nogawa shook her head and looked blankly at Jill. "I didn't hear about any others." She took out a tissue from a desk drawer to augment her damp handkerchief.

"What about Andrew Stone?" Kaj said.

Mrs. Nogawa's hand froze in midair. The tears were immediately gone, replaced by contorted rage "That man!" she spluttered.

"I understand there was trouble between him and Professor Whitworth." Kaj didn't tell her they had already talked with Stone. He wanted to hear her version.

Mrs. Nogawa prickled with resentment. "Stone lacks morals and ethics. Harrison thought he was not a credit to the university."

"Do you know what caused him to say that?" Jill could see the direction that Kaj wanted to go in.

"He was jealous. Harrison's project needed space, and there was even a design competition for this building." Mrs. Nogawa's voice swelled with emotion and pride. "It was about to be sent out to bid when Stone protested that the building would block light from the art gallery. He organized sit-ins and wrote to Congress. It was terrible. He was a faculty union organizer and said the administration wasn't listening to faculty and threatened a vote of no confidence."

"What happened?" Kaj sat back with yet another bemused stare.

"President Halstead called a meeting of the dean, Stone, and Harrison. He told them that the Kamaboko building was going to be built, period. To make Stone agree to stop making trouble, he found money to renovate the art gallery and put in new lighting. The Asian Art Gallery it was supposed to be called. It's been sitting empty ever since except for occasional student art shows."

"And that was acceptable to everyone?" Kaj asked.

"Acceptable? All it did was show everyone how self-serving Stone was. He'd protested this institute building just to get the gallery renovated. He didn't care what he was doing to the university or to Harrison. Now they say he wants to make some donation and have his name plastered on the building. Can you imagine? The Arthur Stone Art Gallery? It's shameful."

Kaj looked around the office while she dabbed her eyes again. The pictures on the wall showed Whitworth with people Kaj didn't recognize except for the most famous politicians. He waited until she seemed to be recovered.

"Do you keep Professor Whitworth's correspondence files and records?"

"I log every phone call and every letter. All electronic mail comes to my computer."

"Did he have his own personal computer in the office?"

"No. He always dictated his correspondence. He'd write notes for his telephone calls, and I'd type them up for him. He didn't like working with computers."

Kaj remembered Whitworth's computer in his Manoa home. Its presence in the house said something else. Forensics had taken it to the lab for downloading. If Whitworth ran all his business through his assistant's system, what was he using the home computer for?

Mrs. Nogawa gave a proud, victory smile. "He didn't do anything without it crossing my desk."

"We'll want to review the correspondence and calls with you," Kaj said. "But was there anything unusual over the past two months or so."

Harriet shook her head. "He was working on a grant proposal, so that took up his time. Otherwise, it was quite usual."

"Was there anything unusual about the grant proposal?"

Harriet glanced at Kaj as if she was remembering something. "Well, there was one thing. A graduate student complained that he thought his name should be included on the project's research reports. He was quite adamant about it."

"Was it resolved?"

"It must have been, but I don't know how. The dean and Professor Whitworth met with the student, and I didn't hear anything more about it."

"What was the student's name?"

"Mark Gottschalk."

"And for the record, Mrs. Nogawa, where were you last night?"

"I was at home alone." Mrs. Nogawa looked defiant and stared hard at Kaj. He felt the start of a prickle at the back of his neck but it would have to wait.

They were running late when they left the institute. Kaj imagined that Bob Wilson was getting agitated not seeing them at the State Capitol. If they used the portable blue light and siren and were lucky, they could still make it, but there couldn't be any more delays. They ran to the car.

When they got there, Kaj snorted with disgust. A university ticket had been pinned under the wiper demanding that they send $50 to the parking office. If they didn't pay up, they were told that the car would be towed if it ever appeared again on campus.

17

Jill dropped Kaj at the State Capitol fifteen minutes before the briefing began. He ran across the rotunda and took the elevator up to the office floor. Bob Wilson was waiting for him outside the press-briefing room. He was near panic.

"What have you got?" he demanded.

"TOD midnight, COD cardiac trauma, travel itinerary, televised arrival at the airport, possible witnesses, interviews with project staff on campus and last people to see him alive, several persons of interest. We're following up with international contacts."

"Did you get their accounts?"

"We've interviewed the vic's project manager, dean, and staff. Kahana and Kim are on campus right now interviewing the students who met him at the airport as well as a neighbor's party guests, plus we're looking for two research assistants who failed to show this morning. Autopsy is done. Forensic evidence has identified at least two persons of interest."

Wilson frowned as he focused on weaving a coherent narrative out of preliminary disconnected details. "Anything we're holding back?"

"Yes. We're not releasing the fact he was killed by an arrow."

"You stay here. I may need you for questions. Think hard about what you're going to say if I do." Bob took off grimly and disappeared down the hallway.

Kaj nodded at Bob's fleeing back. He wasn't going anywhere. He wondered why the Governor felt such a rush to talk to the media, but the political process was one of life's mysteries.

Since he wasn't on display at the podium, Kaj found a place along the back wall of the briefing room. From there, he had a good view of the lectern. It was on a dais under a huge State seal suspended from the ceiling.

By now, the room was jammed and getting hot. Regular beat reporters filled the rows of chairs toward the front. Assistants and hangers-on carrying clipboards and binders lined the walls. At the back, where Kaj was, television cameras lit up sporadically to set focus, the sudden glare creating the impression that the sun had suddenly come out from behind a bank of clouds. The room's buzz of indistinguishable conversation created a gotcha anticipation. Kaj imagined that commentators who had questioned the governor's economic strategy were out for blood.

The occupant of the chair on the end of the last row of seats closest to Kaj lounged sideways, his legs thrust insolently out into the passage between the chairs and the wall, meaning that if Kaj wanted to move forward, he would have to step over him. The culprit was young and looked as if he were trying on a nonchalance several sizes too large for him. Kaj leaned forward to read the press pass hanging round his neck. It said he represented the HSU student newspaper. Kaj smiled slightly and wondered if the larger dogs arrayed in the front seats, deadlines looming, would allow the puppy in the back to have even a nanosecond of the Governor's time. The kid would have to be lucky.

The Governor entered briskly and more or less on time. He brought an entourage with him that included the university president, whom Kaj recognized from his numerous appearances in the local newspapers. The latest was an athletics scandal set on fire by a passionate TV sports reporter whose tirades about the university's suspension of a star player had caused the president to be booed at an HSU basketball game. The president had waved back at the hecklers, producing great footage for the evening broadcast. It was said that his name recognition was as great as the Governor's.

The Governor stepped up onto the dais and took up position behind the podium. He looked appropriately grave as he beckoned the police chief and university president to join him. He was young for the office, with a mixed heritage of Hawaiian, Portuguese, Chinese, and Caucasian. He had dark eyes, honey skin, and strong personal charm. It was difficult to take an unflattering picture, a great advantage to his campaign. A hush fell as the television cameras flooded the room with light.

"Let me thank you for coming on such short notice. I have a prepared statement. Then Hawaii State University President Halstead, Police Chief Akana, and I will take your questions."

Kaj studied the room as the Governor began. He recognized television political commentators, the more publicly visible of the chairpersons and members of the house and senate economic development and higher education committees, and assorted members of the less powerful who might hope to provide a sound bite if asked. The university president had come with staff who stood in the doorway. Kaj noticed that Dean Andrew Goodyear wasn't among them.

In his remarks, the Governor expressed his condolences to the Whitworth family and promised that Harrison's work would continue uninterrupted despite this terrible crime. In addition, he pledged that no effort would be spared until whoever was responsible had been brought to justice.

He then invited questions and the sky fell in.

Hands waved in the air and anxious shouts of "Governor, Governor," filled the room. Kaj noticed that the student newspaperman had his hand up along with the rest of them. He didn't get called on.

The first questioner recognized was a long-time television reporter and commentator known for an intriguing antagonism to the powerful. Kaj recognized the Governor's strategy: get the ring leader out of the way right off.

"Governor," the man said almost triumphantly, "there were a number of legislators who warned you that it was dangerous to rely on the work and reputation of one man for something as important as state economic development. Would you say now that they were right?"

"I'm going to invite President Halstead to help answer that question in a minute," the Governor replied.

I bet you are, Kaj thought.

"But first, I want to be clear that I never viewed the economic package relying on the work of one man, no matter how eminent. I thought of us as a State relying on the work of our university system as a whole, working in tandem with our business and investment communities. Harrison Whitworth may have been the face of research for the campus, but many others were involved in moving us forward."

The Governor then stepped away and made room for President Halstead. But before the president had the chance to speak, a reporter from the largest local newspaper, a string-haired, flaxen man who seemed never to have seen a beach, forced his way out of the pack. "Do you really have personnel on campus qualified to replace a Nobel Prize winning scientist?" he shouted. A murmur of assent circled the room. It was the question of the day.

The president glanced at the Governor, gave a half-smile, and coiled himself to deliver the powerful response that was called for.

"Of course, we do. Professor Whitworth has a co-Investigator responsible for day to day operations of the project, so the work is on-going and there will be no gap in the research. I spoke with Senator Kamaboko this morning to reassure him that the project's integrity is the university's number one priority. He's fully supportive.

"We have begun to assemble a blue-ribbon search committee of local and national leaders charged to identify the best qualified candidates anywhere on the globe. We plan to appoint a highly distinguished interim leader while the search for the permanent replacement continues."

"Who's going to be on this search committee?" This time the Governor had time to select his questioner, a woman reporter from a business journal.

"We will be issuing a press release once we receive confirmation from the people we're inviting. I can tell you that members of the Hawaii legislature, Hawaii's delegation to Congress, the local and national business community, and the campus will be involved."

Kaj lost interest as the conference droned on, at least until there was a question about the police procedures in handling of the case. As to be expected, everything rolled downhill. The Governor handed off to Chief Akana who handed off to Bob Wilson. Bob at least, didn't hand off to Kaj. Instead, he managed to answer with a confident air that implied he was providing important breaking news. That was Bob's special talent with the media: making do with little and creating a masterpiece, even though he hated doing it. Kaj was pointed out as lead detective for the investigation.

The questions and answers lasted an hour until the Governor's press secretary called a halt. Then the Governor and his entourage departed, and reporters converged on whoever was left. Kaj was trying to slip away when he was cornered by the student reporter.

"I'm Frederick Lee from the HSU student newspaper. I heard them say you were the lead on the investigation. I'd like to ask you some questions since I couldn't get the Governor to acknowledge me." Fred tried to sound professional but only managed to sound officious. "If that's all right," he added lamely.

"All we know was covered in the presentations," Kaj replied kindly. "There's nothing more to add."

"I know that," Lee replied. "But there's another dimension here that may not be so obvious. The students have a right to know what's going to happen to them when a professor dies like this. It can affect the entire climate on the campus, and we're all concerned about our education. I wanted to ask what special means anyone might be considering to keep the students informed."

Before Kaj could answer, a voice intervened. "Well, now, Fred, I see you're on the job." HSU President Halstead edged the student aside as he extended his hand to Kaj with a charming smile. He was somewhat shorter than Kaj had expected from seeing him on television, and boyish looking with large horn-rimmed glasses. "I'm Charles Halstead," he said, "but just call me Chuck."

"I was conducting an interview, President Halstead," Fred protested.

"I'm sure you were," the president replied, "but you can do that after the detectives have met the people critical to the investigation. I'm sure you wouldn't want to interfere with that." He took Kaj's arm and guided him away, leaving the student newspaper stranded.

Chuck, as he had invited Kaj to call him, took him to the front of the room and called over the vice president for research whom he introduced as David Napa. Kaj recognized the name from his talk with Dean Goodyear. He was already on Kaj's list, but there was little chance to ask questions as the president wanted to extol Napa's distinguished career as a scientist in his own right. Kaj glanced over to where the student reporter was still standing and gave him a slight smile. The kid brightened.

"I'm sure you want to interview us both—at length," President Halstead was saying, "so I have asked my assistant to set aside an hour at eleven o'clock tomorrow at my official residence. We can discuss Harrison's project and explain how it fits into the university's mission and Hawaii's future. Will that be satisfactory? Is there anything else you need?"

"Any help with the campus parking situation would be good," Kaj said.

Chuck turned to Napa. "Can you take care of this for them." It wasn't a request.

Kaj nodded and half-listened to the ensuing promises of full cooperation. At length, the president released him. By then, Bob Wilson, and with him Kaj's most likely ride back to headquarters, was nowhere to be seen. He would have to call Jill and ask her for a ride.

Kaj went down the elevator and walked across to the hunched statue of Father Damien where it would be easy for Jill to see him as she drove down Beretania Street. It was also easy for the student newspaper to spot him as well. He was looking at his watch when a voice materialized beside him.

"Can we still have those few minutes?"

Kaj turned to see Fred. He thought the kid had left.

"President Halstead takes the floor wherever he is, so I've learned to work around him so to speak. And by the way, you can call me Fred." Fred grinned at having his moment with Kaj. All was not lost.

"You work with the president a lot?"

"He'd say I work around him more than with him. I like to look into things at the university to see if the administration is telling the truth. Sometimes they're not. They tell us that they are training us to think and ask questions, but not of them it seems. I ask questions anyway."

"Like what?" Kaj was slightly interested. His own frustrations with HSU had been refreshed by the parking ticket

"How the university budget works for one thing. The university justifies increased budget requests by claiming it's to serve the students, yet classes are the first thing cut when funds get tight. The latest thing is a crazy plan to build a marine research park on Kahoʻolawe. You've heard of that, right? Kahoʻolawe, for God's sake. Why there? The island has no water. It's been used by the military as a bombing range, so it's littered with unexploded ammo. The Hawaiian students are up in arms, because it was supposed to be a refuge. No one can figure why the university would be even interested."

"Did you ask?" Building on Kahoʻolawe didn't sound right. It had only recently been returned to the State by the feds, and the general consensus was that it was uninhabitable.

"Of course, I asked. I was told it has to do with the university's research, but if so, it's tangential. I'm betting that there are private interests tied to this. As usual, everyone will benefit except the students. Come to think of it, your interests and ours might overlap."

Kaj doubted it but was willing to listen. He had nothing else to do until Jill arrived.

"Professor Whitworth was the fat cat in this Kahoʻolawe stuff. I heard they were building it for him. Perhaps that's why he was killed. I don't know, but I'd love to find out, and I bet that people will be willing to talk now he's dead."

"You need to leave the investigating to us," Kaj said sternly. He didn't need students muddying things up. "If you know something other than speculation, now would be a good time to share it."

"I heard the president set a time for his audience with you. You can bet he's going to give you the official version of it. We'll be in the student newspaper office putting out the new edition in the morning if you want another take. You can find me there before you make the pilgrimage—if you're interested."

Kaj saw Jill coming and started moving toward the road. "What was it you wanted to ask me?"

"I've already asked you. I'm going to assume the answer is yes." Fred then walked off with a smile and a salute.

18

K AJ WENT TO the crime board and picked up the marker himself. Bob Wilson was attending their afternoon debrief to see how far they were in the investigation, and Kaj didn't intend his boss to have a front-row seat to arguments over whose turn it was to play recorder. Kaj was also determined that Jill not feel pressured into becoming a de facto clerk. She was too good for that.

He was all business as he rapidly drew a series of radiating lines and boxes to collect the information into usable silos for further investigation.

He wrote the label "Witnesses on site" in the first box next to the names of Stone's party guests. He looked expectantly at Kaipo and Cliff for updates.

"We interviewed all but one of them," Kaipo reported. "They corroborate what Stone said. They left his house and went down the ravine around dawn, but they don't recall hearing the sound Stone described. They did admit that they might have slept from time to time. That leaves Stone without a solid alibi. No one else heard the noise he described."

"We couldn't locate Cheterinda Gowda," Cliff added. "Since Gowda is a foreign student, we've asked the State Department to see what they have on his visa. Otherwise, the university keeps throwing this FERPA privacy act at us. It made things difficult. People are reluctant to talk with us. They don't seem to know what they're allowed to discuss."

Kaj wrote the names Stone and Cheterinda Gowda and circled them. He wrote the words *visa* next to them and *alibi* with question marks next to Stone.

Kaj wrote the word *university* on the next box and entered the names Goodyear and Harriet Noguchi next to the names of Dawes and the student rickshaw pullers. "Goodyear said he was at Blaisdell attending a show. Noguchi says she was home. What do we know about the others?"

"The research assistants confirmed the events and timing at the airport and how they got back and forth to the airport, but they couldn't confirm if Dawes went straight home as he claims," Cliff said "We still need to corroborate the times that Dawes claims he dropped the students off. Then we can judge if there was enough time left for him to drive back up to Manoa."

Kaj nodded. "If there was, we'll need to know if Dawes has experience with archery. He had possible motive. The university ended his project in favor of Whitworth's."

"Right now, though," Cliff continued, "Our primary focus is finding Brendan Hope and Mark Gottschalk. We also heard about a student who tried to commit suicide over a bad grade and was removed from school three months ago."

"That sounds like Douglas Williams," Jill said. "Whitworth's assistant told us about him. She says he made threats but that it was swept under the rug."

Cliff shook his head. "He did more than make threats. The students told us that they caught him trying to set fire to the lab. They heard that campus shrinks diagnosed a psychotic break and said he needed to be hospitalized. A family member flew over from the Mainland and took him home."

Kaj circled the names of the two missing graduate students on the board. Beneath them, he added the name of Douglas Williams. "Noguchi said Williams was angry about a course grade Whitworth gave him. We need to find out if he could have come back to finish the job.

He labeled the next box, *Crime Scene.* "Where are we on the cleaning service and security system?"

"Whitworth's cleaning service, Suite Leilani, confirms they serviced the house Thursday afternoon. Their usual time is morning, but since they knew Whitworth was out of town, they changed the schedule and came late. They claimed everything seemed normal in the house."

Kaipo flipped open his notebook. "Koa Kane Security confirms a code assigned to the cleaning service deactivated the alarm at 2:00 p.m. and reactivated at 3:25 p.m. The alarm was not deactivated again until 11:45 p.m. by the primary code holder which, as far as they know, is Harrison Whitworth. The alarm has not been reactivated since."

Kaj paused with the marker in his hand. "Then the only anomaly is that the cleaning service changed their schedule." He noted that on the board. Then he turned to at Jill. "Did you hear back on the boots you collected from the lab?"

She nodded. "The report came in an hour ago. The pattern on the lab boots matches the crime scene casts, and the soles had sleeping-grass leaves and mud consistent with the soil samples from

Whitworth's front yard. That doesn't prove much because that type of soil is endemic to Hawaii and the boots are common, but it makes it possible that someone from the lab was in the trees by Whitworth's house. Forensics already told us that the foot inside was smaller than the boot size. It could be either male or female."

Kaj then created another box out toward the edge of the board. That he labeled *HSU administration.*

"Has anyone heard about a possible research building on Kahoʻolawe? A reporter from the student newspaper said the building was supposedly linked to Whitworth's project."

Kaipo snorted loudly. "Kahoʻolawe? Somebody's pulling someone's leg. No one goes there. Besides being dangerous, it's not even legal. An activist was killed trying to land. The place is full of unexploded ordnance. The military used it as a bombing range."

Bob Wilson, who had been silent up to that point, suddenly turned in his chair to shoot a quick, reproving glance at Kaipo.

"I wouldn't be too quick to dismiss it just yet. I heard staff members from Ways and Means asking about it down at the legislature. They've been getting irate calls from the Hawaiian community. No one seemed to know where it got started."

Kaj wrote *Kahoʻolawe* on the board with three questions marks. "Doesn't sound credible," he said, "but we'll need to check it out if involves Whitworth."

He hesitated over the next box. In the end, he just labeled it with a question mark. Into that area, he put the names of Mrs. Sam, Helen Malcolm, Janice DeMello, and Trenton Wind-Sutton, the unverified unknowns of the case.

"Mrs. Sam's name and contact information was on Whitworth's computer," he explained. "According to the dean, Helen Malcolm was one of Whitworth's very few friends, plus Whitworth had four books by the DeMello woman that didn't seem to belong. Wind-Sutton is from Cambridge University. He had lunch with the victim in London and might be in a position to know if there were threats made over there."

"Anything else?" Kaj looked round the room. "Okay," he said when the meeting seemed to be complete. "Priority one is these missing people. Let's get them tracked down. Jill and I are meeting with the HSU president tomorrow. We'll ask him about Kahoʻolawe then."

Bob Wilson lingered as the detectives left the briefing. His mood had mellowed since the press conference. Perhaps it was relief that the investigation so far seemed to be under control. But it may also have been the further confirmation of his respect for his lead detective. He'd noticed the way Kaj kept his team together and the tact and inclusion with which he treated Jill.

"Keep me informed," he told Kaj. "Let me know what you need." It wasn't Bob's style to express overt appreciation. But Kaj knew his offer of support was real.

"There is one thing," Kaj said, "if you hear anything more about Kahoʻolawe, let us know right away. It may be just a rumor, but something doesn't feel right. When the island was returned to the State, it was clearly to become a preserve for Hawaiian culture. It would take someone very powerful to change that. I'm not seeing anyone stepping forward to take responsibility. I don't like it. It feels wrong."

"Don't worry," Bob assured him, "if I hear anything, you'll be the first to know. That sixth sense of yours is well known around here."

19

T HE SUN HAD long made its sudden drop into the sea by the time Kaj made his way home. Sometimes it didn't make sense to go home any earlier because it meant sitting in traffic.

They bought the house in Pearl City weighing the commute. But there weren't many options. Living in a condo was not where they wanted to raise Annie. Hawaii Kai was too expensive; Nuʻuanu, Niu, and Manoa were completely out of reach; Waialae Kahala was for millionaires only; and the Windward side was developing so fast that the Pali Highway would soon rival Nimitz for congestion. They bought what they could afford because they needed to get out of Goro and Ai's small Palolo home.

Like its owner, the Palolo house was becoming an additional worry for Kaj. The fifty years of its life lay heavily on it. Goro had tented the house several times in his on-going battle with the termites, the plumbing needed regular routing because of tree roots, and the outside electric wires needed periodic adjusting as the house shifted. Sooner or later, Goro would not be up to caring for the place.

Kaj drove up to his garage, expecting that Linda and Annie would be exhausted from their first day at work and gone to sleep. But the lights were all on, and Linda and Annie were drinking hot chocolate, watching the late show, and looking quite pleased with themselves.

"How was your first day?" he asked.

"Nothing like we expected," Annie chirped, "it was exciting. They called today 'familiarization.' We'll be working there only two weeks but they still gave us the full introduction."

"Tomorrow they're going to train us on the cash registers," Linda chimed in.

"Sounds challenging," Kaj said. "Glad you're enjoying it."

"We get some neat benefits," Linda said. But then she stopped. "You look tired, Kaj. I stopped at Shirokiya and bought teri-chicken bentos. It was that or Patti's for Chinese, but there were long lines at the food court. Would you like hot chocolate?"

The promised food and drink appeared right away, and he ate without bothering to remove the food from the plastic box it came in.

As his wife and daughter happily bantered over who would learn the cash registers fastest, he felt himself start to relax. He couldn't imagine living alone as Whitworth appeared to. He sympathized with Kaipo. A divorce is the ending of a dream, coming as it does with an inevitable sense of failure and rejection, and that's before the loneliness sets in.

Linda had accepted all the challenges that came with him, and they'd worked hard together to make their lives combine. It wasn't easy. His job was demanding but so was hers, teaching high-school English. The more Kaj saw of the failed marriages at CID, the more he knew how profoundly lucky he had been. He shuddered to think what he might have lost had he not literally bumped into Linda that day in the campus cafeteria.

That night, snuggled against Linda's back, he was too tired to dream. But just being with her somehow righted the world, if only for a few hours.

20

EARLY NEXT MORNING, Kaj sat at his desk and read the newspaper. The *Advertiser* had spent much of the front page quoting the international coverage of the Whitworth murder.

The Nobel Prize committee had issued a statement regarding the professor's death, calling it an American tragedy. *The Times of London* claimed Whitworth was the victim of America's preoccupation with guns and violence. *Corriere della Sera* wondered when the US would outgrow playing cowboys and Indians. *Der Spiegel* wondered about a streak of American anti-intellectualism that spilled over into the sciences. The *Asahi Shimbum* hoped that Professor Whitworth's death was not the start of a move away from Asia-Pacific scientific cooperation. The coverage was a kaleidoscope of the world's opinions about America.

Locally, it seemed that reporters had interviewed everyone even remotely connected with Whitworth and encouraged them to speculate. Unimportant people now had their chance to provide sound bites, most of them gloomy judgements about whether the police department knew what it was doing.

"No Suspects Yet," ran the column header across the top of the second page. The story rehashed the crime and included pictures of the Manoa house. The editorial page was occupied second-guessing everyone's political and economic futures. The Governor's press conference was covered but had done little to quell the speculation about his chances of re-election.

Kaj put the newspaper aside and took out Trenton Wind-Sutton's card. The man wouldn't be at work given the time difference. That meant that Kaj would call his residence number. He sat there for a moment, looking at a long row of digits constituting a telephone number that looked more like an appliance serial number.

"Anyone know how to call Europe?" he asked.

"I know how to call Japan," Cliff said. "It can't be that different." He came over to look at the string of numbers on the card. "The long-distance code is 011. It's not on his card, but that's what you start with. Then dial the 44 for the UK. It looks like it's 1223 for the town. The number should be the seven digits. But there are eight. Okay, there's an extra zero in there. I don't know what that's for."

"I'll try dialing it with the zero," Kaj said. A whine told him it was wrong. Then he tried without. A phone went brinng-brinng three times and a brusque voice barked "Wind-Sutton" using plummy clipped vowels and a tone that implied the call had better be important enough to be calling and disturbing his evening.

Kaj turned on the speaker so that Cliff could hear. Kaj introduced himself and when he asked the first question, a mild one inquiring as to how Whitworth and Wind-Trenton knew one another, the conversation veered out of his control. Cliff watched as Kaj's jaw became increasingly set.

Wind-Sutton began by making clear that anything not accomplished by the premier UK universities, of which there were two, was inferior. Whitworth's Nobel Prize, he implied, was earned because of the dead scientist's research association with collaborators at Cambridge University, which made his being singled out for the honor rather disappointing. When it came to whether he knew anyone with a motive to kill him, Wind-Trenton had no idea but assumed it was a drive-by shooting, since that's what people do in America.

When Kaj was able to get a word in and asked the reason for the lunch with Harrison Whitworth, for which the latter had paid a handsome bill, Wind-Trenton managed to finish up in grand style.

"He suggested a possible exchange program in tropical medicine," Wind-Trenton sniffed.

"Were you interested in seeing this happen?" Kaj could anticipate the answer and marveled at how much offense the man had managed in a very short time. He seemed a British version of Arthur Stone, except with a more polished and condescending tone. The man was not likely to improve Kaj's opinion of academic types.

"We're always interested in providing exchanges as long as expenses are covered and there is something to be gained from the experience. We investigate to be assured the receiving institution meets our standards. We don't intend to lower our expectations."

"Did you and Whitworth make any agreements?" Kaj stifled his desire to punch the man's nose through the telephone. A nerve twitched in his forehead.

"We didn't. There would be no question with research and medical programs such as Harvard's and Johns Hopkins'. Frankly, I was concerned about the academic rigor of a university located in the remote South Pacific Ocean. Whitworth's Nobel prize, no doubt, raised the bar for Hawaii, but we have the same or better qualifications among our own faculty. After all, one Nobel Prize doesn't characterize an entire faculty. What would our students and faculty gain from going to Hawaii beyond a nice suntan? The focus on tropical diseases made sense, but we felt we could accomplish the same through exchange programs with top institutions in Australia, Singapore or Thailand."

"What reason did Professor Whitworth give you for wanting to establish this research exchange?" Kaj's tone was now becoming controlled sarcasm as he was starting to think Wind-Sutton was putting on a performance for a hick Hawaii police detective.

"He said the university president—I forget his name—wanted to establish Hawaii State University as a center of excellence in select Asian and Pacific science and cultures. Whitworth thought they might better be achieved through faculty initiatives rather than by the administration. He was concerned about political interference in science. If I were you, I told him, I'd be more worried about religious interference. Those Puritans we sent over have gone off the deep end judging by what we read in the UK papers."

Kaj changed the subject in preparation for ending the call semi-politely. "Did Professor Whitworth ever indicate he had concerns about his safety?"

"None that I could point to. I told him he should consider moving to a European research university and coming in from the cold, or should I say in from the warmth."

Kaj gritted his teeth, managed to thank Wind-Trenton for his time, and barely avoided slamming down the phone.

"Who does he think he is?" Kaj snorted and threw his pen down on the desktop.

It was a rhetorical question because it was overwhelmingly clear that Wind-Trenton had a very clear idea of his position in the world.

Activity stopped for a moment as people digested their surprise at Kaj's outburst. Kaj gave them a wave designed to say, don't worry, I'm fine.

Cliff was the only one who chuckled. "Got to you, didn't he? It happens. I was in San Francisco a couple of years ago on a conference. Just as I was about to enter my hotel, a homeless man came up to me and said 'Gook.' I dropped my suitcase and turned on him. 'You like beef, Bra?" I was back in the halls of McKinley High; except I was a grown man who towered over him. When he sidled away, I yelled after him again, 'You like beef, Bra?' How's that for eloquence? I could see the headlines: 'Honolulu Detective Arrested in San Francisco Brawl.' I suppose I should have realized he was a homeless Vet and that, looking Korean, I brought back bad memories. But it gets you in the moment."

"Wind-Sutton isn't homeless. He doesn't know where Hawaii is located, and he behaves as if we're living in grass shacks. Pay me enough, he says, and I'll consider slumming and show you how a real university operates. People like him and Stone are why I don't like academics. That's all I can say. He'd better hope he never crosses my path. "

21

THE STUDENT NEWSPAPER office was buried in an annex not far from the administration building but largely out of sight. Kaj and Jill walked the short road access several times looking for it, and finally had to ask a bicyclist where it was. It turned out to be in a small, dark, wooden building linked to a larger one by a covered walkway.

The building functioned mainly as storage for one of the departments, and only hand-drawn arrows indicated that the newspaper was there at all. Inside the office, however, skylights streamed light into a large work room. Framed newspaper pages hung on the walls, and sheets of paper were tacked to cork boards above a handful of time-pocked desks. In the back of the room, two doors led to what passed as the editor's office and a room for the faculty advisor.

The clutter and purposeful confusion reminded Kaj of the CID office, but he entered this one with a cynical feeling that he might be wasting his and Jill's time.

Three students were hunched around a paste-up table and didn't see them when they entered the workroom. After a few moments, one looked up, a nervous-looking kid who didn't look old enough to be in college. When Kaj showed his badge and introduced himself and Jill, the kid grew wide eyed and almost started to tremble.

"It's all right," Kaj assured him. "Your editor is expecting us."

The student scuttled across the room and called something through a door in the back. The other two students, both girls, ignored them and seemed annoyed at the disturbance.

Fred then came out and invited them in. His office was hardly worthy of the name. It was cramped and seemed to be serving double duty as a storage room. After Kaj introduced Jill, she sat on the one chair available while Kaj sat carefully on a pile of boxes of paper.

"You'll have to forgive the clutter," Fred said as he settled into the dilapidated office chair behind the desk. "We're late getting out tomorrow's edition. I was on the phone negotiating a reprieve from the printer. We should be fine."

"You said you had information for us," Kaj said impatiently. He hoped that it wasn't just a waste of time.

"I do. But hang on a minute and let me check on what's going on out there." He went out to the main workroom, and they could hear him organizing how the paste-up pages were to be delivered to the printer. After a few moments, things seemed to have settled down.

"Done," he said when he came back into his office. "We publish twice a week, and it's always a rush no matter how well we plan. Events don't respect deadlines. This time we got backed up waiting for our faculty advisor to go through the copy."

"Have you had trouble?" Jill asked. "Your worker out there seemed nervous."

"Don't worry about him. That's Ronnie. He's a scared little rabbit. All newspapers get threats. It's part of the job."

"What kind of threats?" Kaj asked automatically.

"We got some letters two days ago. Nothing clever or even original. We were warned off a story we've been researching. In fact, it was about Whitworth's Kahoʻolawe project."

"Do you have them?" Kaj's interest level rose with the mention of Whitworth's name.

"The originals were turned over to campus police. I can show you copies." Fred opened a drawer, pulled out a folder, and pushed the contents over to Kaj. There were two. One said 'Don't run the story on Kahoʻolawe.' It was unsigned. The other said, 'You haven't stopped asking questions. This a warning'."

Jill looked quizzical. "You're right. Not very original. What did the campus police say about them?"

"They said there wasn't much they could do beyond increase their patrols in this area. The threat is not specific, and there wasn't much to go on. If you look at the angry letters we received when we investigated spending by Student Association leaders, these are not even worth the time . . .."

"Let's start with the pressing questions," Kaj interrupted. "What do you know about this Kahoʻolawe project and Whitworth's involvement?"

"I'll tell you what I know, and you take it from there. It's my understanding that Senator Kamaboko contacted the university and offered a set aside in the form of additional pork-barrel money for a new institute. He had one condition. Whitworth needed to head it and choose its focus. He made it clear, though, that it was that it be good for the state and defensible to Congress."

"Okay, where did you hear this?"

Fred leaned on his desk and cradled his fingers. His dramatic gesture reminded Kaj of how Fred had tried to assert his press credentials and ask questions at the Governor's press conference. But no matter what he might do, he was still a puppy amidst big dogs.

"Sources are confidential," Fred said pompously. "But I'll tell you off the record because it's a homicide investigation. Isn't that what they usually say on TV? We heard about Kahoʻolawe from an anonymous source. Somebody sent us an e-mail demanding that we look into it. The rest is conjecture, admittedly."

"Is that all you have?" Kaj stood up and gave every indication of leaving.

"Wait," Fred said and quickly stood up himself. "I'm not through. There's more. We heard there was some sort of rancor in the lab itself. A graduate student overheard Whitworth and Dawes shouting at each other."

"What about?" Kaj sat down but gave every indication of wanting to leave.

"My source wasn't sure, but he thought it might be because Dawes wanted the new institute to include his work on tree frogs. Whatever it was, Whitworth blew him off. Whitworth said he had the last word and it wouldn't be frogs. Then he told Dawes he'd brought it on himself. Dawes told Whitworth to go to hell, and a door slammed."

"And you're assuming that they were discussing Kahoʻolawe? Did you try to confirm this?"

Fred looked scornfully at Kaj. "Of course, I did. The administration clammed up. The regents said to talk with the administration. The dean said he knew nothing about it. The students, as usual, were told nothing and figured they were getting shafted again. We've got reason to be upset. We graduate in debt and no one cares. A degree is supposed to mean more earnings, but bunches of grads are working minimum-wage jobs. That's what happens when higher education sells out students for the money."

Kaj looked at his watch. Fred's indignation could have fueled discussion for hours over beers and Kaj might not have disagreed. But right now, he didn't have time for it. "Ok, Fred, this is all very interesting, but we need to get down to the matter at hand. Where were you on Thursday night?"

"You think I had anything to do with Whitworth's murder?" Fred looked aghast. "I was right here. Ronnie and I grabbed a burger in Moiliili and came back to the office to finish up. We didn't finish until past 11:00 p.m."

"Then where did you go?"

"Ronnie went home. He has a motor scooter. I crashed out in a sleeping bag on the floor. Sometimes I do that rather than drive home when it's late. I catch a shower in the morning at the gym. I keep a clean shirt and tooth brush here."

"Can anyone corroborate that?"

"Your friendly campus police. Our local gendarme stopped by and told me not to stay overnight again. Said it made his job more difficult. He's just pissed, because we wrote a story about Keystone campus cops."

"So far you haven't given us anything to go on except hearsay," Kaj said. "Do you have anything concrete about the Kahoʻolawe project. Does it exist anywhere except in rumor?"

"Well," Fred said, "you're about to meet with the president. Why don't you ask him? And I'd love to hear what he has to say."

22

The president's official residence was a fine old house built by a kama'aina family and donated to the university. It looked like Whitworth's house further back in the valley. But where Whitworth's house was austere and private, this one breathed life and light. It was situated on a hill and surrounded by tropical gardens and lawns. The house was so open that during receptions a velvet rope was hung across the stairwell to tell the guests that the upstairs rooms were reserved for the current occupants.

If Whitworth was private, old money well invested and never discussed, President Halstead's furnishings said he was the public man, who drew strength not from prior generations but from interactions with people. The yellow carpet near the front door was worn thin by the feet of guests invited to the almost continuous university receptions.

Kaj wondered why Mrs. Noguchi thought Whitworth wanted to become a university president. As Kaj was coming to know him, Whitworth, the man who wanted pure science, would not have tolerated the exposure required of public life. And yet, he was capable of dealing with the Governor and public officials when he had to.

President Halstead and Vice President Napa both rose as the housekeeper admitted Kaj and Jill.

The downstairs layout of the house reminded Kaj of Whitworth's: a large hallway with rooms on each side, a formal staircase to the upper level, with the kitchen to the back, But this house was furnished, and the sliding doors to the side rooms were thrown open, inviting shafts of sunlight to throw geometric patterns onto the floor. Paintings of Hawaii, some realistic but others color impressions of the Koʻolau Mountains, hung on the walls, and various side tables were covered with turquoise, blown-glass shapes. Labels identified the faculty artists responsible for them. There was even a semi-recognizable bust of President Halstead. Kaj noted that there were no paintings of rocks.

A pitcher of lemon water sat on the coffee table between two sofas. The windows were open, letting the scent of white ginger waft in with the breeze. Even more inviting was the printed temporary parking pass that Napa handed to Kaj as they shook hands. It was good for all zones and meant that Kaj could come and go, at least until the ten-day expiration date. Kaj wasn't disappointed. Any parking help was good.

"Just call me Chuck," the president reminded Kaj as he invited them to take their place at one sofa while he and Napa occupied the opposite one. He gestured to the water and offered to have coffee or tea brought to them, both offers declined with thanks.

Kaj studied both administrators as they settled. Before the Governor's press conference, Kaj had read about the president in the newspaper but never seen him in person. The president was dressed casually and sat with his left arm comfortably draped over the sofa arm. He seemed outwardly relaxed, but he also projected an almost contradictory, electric sense of possibility. Kaj could see why an ambitious young governor would be attracted by Halstead's expansive optimism and by the idea that State money pouring into higher education might be an investment rather than a subsidy. Kaj could also see that the president was diverted by the investigation and, under other circumstances, might have enjoyed jumping into the crime-solving process.

Napa, on the other hand, sat back and let the commotion stir around him. His face was creased like the cushions of a comfortable sofa. When he smiled, the lines became crevices into which his eyes almost disappeared. Unlike the president, he appeared reserved but approachable. He was taking notes on a pad resting on the coffee table in front of him. Kaj wondered if Napa was planning to write a book. That's what academics seemed to do.

Kaj already knew that Napa was a physicist by trade. President Halstead had told him at the press conference that Napa's research interest was studying the surface tension of bubbles, particularly in relation to decompression illness. Kaj's impression was that Napa was a man more comfortable with observation than conversation.

"How can we help?" the president asked. "What do you need from us?"

"Tell us about the Kaho'olawe project."

The president's eyebrows shot up. "I don't know what you've heard."

"Assume we know nothing," Kaj said, which in fact was true.

The president glanced at Napa then laced his fingers together on his lap. He didn't sound enthusiastic.

"The island of Kaho'olawe was suggested as a potential site for a new institute designed to support Harrison's anemone project. The entire project is only in the discussion stages. It would require federal support matched by State and possibly private funds. Kahoʻolawe was one site suggested. There are others."

"Did Whitworth suggest this site?"

"No-o-o," the president said with obvious reluctance. "I don't think he'd expressed an opinion. He'd requested new lab facilities and asked for additional space, but we hadn't sat down with him to outline what that might look like. Until Congress approves the federal budget, our lobbying firm can't move forward, which means we can't even start to think about feasibility studies and environmental impact statements. We could be talking years."

"Yet the Hawaiian community has protested the university's potential plans to use the Kahoʻolawe site," Jill pointed out.

"Someone alerted them. We don't know who." Napa glanced at the president. "Whoever released the information was very premature and extremely unhelpful. Two thirds of any project this large are upfront, mainly getting all the affected parties on board. That's the hard part. Once there's agreement, the project moves relatively smoothly. But we're nowhere near that."

"Hawaii has a biennial budget system," Jill said. "As I understand the process, you must be currently preparing yours. Is the Whitworth lab mentioned in either of the projected next two years? Are you making requests to the Legislature for planning funds?"

Kaj looked at Jill with interest. Her law studies in San Diego were suddenly very relevant.

"No. It's not included," the president said definitely. "Funding for the building, if it were to happen, would be an add-on, a special opportunity made possible by Senator Kamaboko's support in Washington. Obviously, a facility built primarily with federal funds saves State funds and is a win for everyone. But, while additional research space is an identified priority in the university's current Academic Development Plan, there is no specific mention of the Whitworth project in any planning documents."

Kaj adopted his deadpan face. "Then this new research facility is completely unplanned for. Is that what you're telling us?"

"It's a special opportunity," the president agreed. "The Governor is interested, although he cannot commit without bringing the legislature on board. The regents are supportive, but only in principle at this point. The university is interested but must follow university policies about consultation and review. Everyone agrees that Hawaii deserves first-class marine research facilities. But that doesn't mean that any agreements have been reached or any green lights issued."

"Am I to understand then," Kaj frowned, "that Professor Whitworth neither requested nor approved a facility on Kahoʻolawe?"

The president looked at Napa and went silent. The implication was clear. Napa was to take the question.

"The anemone project outgrew its space allocation very quickly. Professor Whitworth identified the need for more office and lab space and mentioned it to several regents and the Governor. Senator Kamaboko heard about the problem and thought he could help. All the university can say at this point is that there may be possible federal funding for a possible new research facility, delivery date and site unknown." Napa smiled his placid smile as he finished.

Kaj looked at the president and felt his prickling, warning feeling. The president knew more than he was saying, probably more than his vice president who had just earnestly presented what he believed to be the administration's position.

"Was there anyone who might have resented the recognition Whitworth was receiving from the senator?"

The president jumped into Kaj's question with enthusiasm. "University faculty are competitors, Inspector. They are expected to achieve pre-eminence in their fields, provide exemplary instruction, and serve their communities. This means they are held to the highest standards. On campus we have the most brilliant minds in the nation. Of course, they are going to use achievement as a motivator. They are competitors, but, in the end, they stand together and admire academic advancement."

"I assume that means you don't know of any?" Kaj found himself remembering Fred's earlier description of the president's passion. "But what about Curtis Dawes? I'm told the university preferred Whitworth's project over his."

Immediately, the mood changed. Since it was becoming obvious that the detectives had been informed about politics in the Whitworth lab, the conversation became more specific.

"We felt we had to choose," Napa said carefully. "Dawes' tree-frog project was credible and he had written a well-received, peer-reviewed book, but we felt we had to go with the project that had the greatest chance of being funded. That was the Whitworth project."

"Then why was Whitworth heard raising his voice and telling Dawes that he had brought some situation on himself? That sounds like conflict between them."

Silence reigned for several moments. The president glanced at Napa, who to his credit maintained his smile. Kaj wondered if the man had heard the question, but, apparently, he had.

"I believe you're talking about a personnel issue," Napa said finally. "It dates back several years to before the funding ended for Dawes' tree-frog project. It had nothing to do with Whitworth, but I assume he heard about it through loose talk in the college. I'm not sure how free I am to discuss it."

Kaj maintained his interview face. If he had to, he would ask for a subpoena for anything to do with the case as long as it was in the files. But was it in the files? Sometimes, the police department didn't record every detail of its internal affairs; perhaps the university didn't either.

"Is it in Dawes' personnel file?" Kaj asked.

Napa shook his head. "We handled the situation as best we could to save the university embarrassment and not jeopardize future funding."

"We'd better explain," the president cut in. "But we must ask you to keep this confidential."

"I can't promise," Kaj replied. "But if we feel it is relevant, we'll file a formal court request for the information." It was the best he could do.

Napa and the president conferred for a moment and seemed to reach agreement. Kaj looked away until they were through. Again, it was Napa who was designated to answer the question.

"Curtis's primary funding for his tree-frog project came from the National Institutes for Health, but he also worked with various corporations interested in isolating venoms for pharmaceutical application. One corporation provided him with personal funding.

"University policy requires such funding, checks made out directly to the individual principal investigator, to be processed through the grants office or handled by the university's foundation. That's how we ensure the money is properly spent and accounted for.

"Many faculty members are impatient with these restrictions, particularly because the university charges overhead for handling the money. In Dawes' case, he did not follow university policy; he cashed the check and placed the money in the ceiling tiles in his office. He took it down to pay for things that were not covered by his grant."

Napa looked inquiringly at Kaj. Kaj nodded that he understood. He doubted that the Brass would appreciate Bob Wilson hiding money in the CID ceiling tiles.

"An anonymous source brought it to our attention," Napa continued. "When we questioned him, Curtis freely admitted what he'd done. The university's attorneys informed us they saw no criminal fraud, because the corporate donation had no restrictions. Curtis had kept good records and did not personally benefit, but some of his expenditures were problematic. For example, he augmented research assistants' salaries when he considered the State had improperly classified their job descriptions, meaning he thought they were being underpaid. Rather than spend the time to try to have the State personnel office reclassify the positions to offer higher pay, he used the corporate donation.

"We could do retroactive paperwork on irregular acquisitions, but employee salaries required W-2 forms and possible public exposure. It could have been embarrassing since we were requesting greater financial autonomy from the State at the time. We were trying to make the case that the university was fiscally responsible."

Kaj noted the president's small, grim smile. Relations between the campus and the State's downtown accounting offices must sometimes be fraught.

"Dawes didn't understand the implications of what he had done," Napa continued. "He saw it as a pragmatic way to undo an injustice.

It took many staff hours to clean up the mess, and we made him open an account at the foundation for the remaining funds. After that, as you can imagine, we insisted on stringent oversight of his grant. When Whitworth's project was funded, we ended his but were still able to assure his employment by assigning him to be part of the anemone project. It seemed a good solution."

"Except Dawes wasn't thrilled," Jill observed.

Napa gave a shrewd grin. "When we told him that his position might be reassigned, he came around. That's why I can't believe he had anything to do with Whitworth's death. If anything, Whitworth was his protector."

"And how did Whitworth feel about him?" Jill asked curiously.

Napa thought for a moment. "I'd say he treated him as a competent assistant. Whitworth was a solitary man, and I'm not sure he considered anyone his equal. He sometimes behaved as if he were dropped from some other planet to be among mere mortals."

"He was that arrogant?" Kaj was immediately reminded of that morning's conversation with Sutter Wind-Trenton.

"You could like Whitworth, you could respect him, and you could admire him, but from a distance. That's a little different from the usual campus egotist who tends to be much noisier."

"What was Dean Goodyear's role in this?" Kaj asked.

"The dean knew about what Dawes had done," Napa said, "but he preferred my office to handle the fall out. We took on the paperwork and filing with the State and IRS. We would have been the public face if word had got out. We would also have had to deal with the media. But that type of situation is not unusual. When a college or institute doesn't feel prepared to deal with political fallout, the dean or director will bump the issue upstairs."

"And how did the dean get on with Whitworth?"

"Well, as far as we know," Napa said. "There was some argument from Dean Goodyear when Whitworth requested a reduction in the University's charge for overhead on the project. We rearranged the research budget to take care of the dean's concerns. Once he saw the broad political interest in Whitworth's work, he deferred project management to my office."

So that was why the dean was not at the Governor's press conference. Kaj wondered how many other university projects were restructured when they held political implication. But was it all so satisfactory? The dean had not sounded happy about it when he spoke with them in his office yesterday.

"We heard that there was a disgruntled student who caused problems for Whitworth. Was that also bumped upstairs?"

"This is a very confidential matter," Napa said. "I'm surprised that the institute is discussing it. Federal law prevents the university from discussing individual students. Let's just say that one student had personal difficulties and made some unwise statements. After he was counseled, it was decided that his best course was to withdraw from the university. We facilitated that decision."

"In the course of our investigation, we talked with Arthur Stone. I assume you know him," Kaj said.

"Yes," the president said in a tone that implied that Stone was a headache.

"He told us that he is donating Asian artwork to the university. Can you tell us what that is about?"

"Professor Stone wants to make a tax-deductible gift to the university," the president sighed. "We are proceeding cautiously because the university's attorneys have warned us about possible trouble with authentication and provenance. We haven't turned it down, but we are still working on the terms that would make it possible for us to accept it. I understand that he has some difficulty with taxes that he hopes to satisfy by making this donation. I'd hate to see the university lose something positive, and I'd like to help him out, but we can't accept something that is not legitimate."

"In other words," Napa grinned, "the gift is being looked into."

Kaj looked at his watch. "Gentleman," he said, "for the record, where you both were last night?"

The president's eyes gleamed with excitement, as Kaj had suspected that they might. He wondered if the president also wrote detective novels.

"I was at a dinner hosted by the attorney, Wilfred Fong. Many people can confirm that I didn't leave there until after midnight. I'm not a suspect, am I?" He sounded delighted at the thought he might be.

"My wife, Celia, and I were at the Blaisdell Center for the Christmas show," Napa said in his usual placid manner. "We saw Dean Goodyear there, the president's assistant Mara and her husband, Regent Rodrigues and his wife, plus Maui Senator Picoy and his wife."

"I can assure you, Inspector," the president said as he walked them to the door, "that this administration was not involved in Professor Whitworth's tragic death. There are at least twenty faculty on this campus who are more difficult, and not one can compare to the contributions he made to his field and would have continued to make. We celebrate excellence here, not snuff it out. The university has sustained a grievous loss."

Kaj's phone rang as he and Jill walked out from under the portico and over to where they had parked the car on the president's driveway. It was Kaipo.

"You're going to want to get back here fast, Boss. Looks like Officer Mahi may have matched a shoe to one of the footprints on the hill. And the good news is there's a foot it. They're bringing him in."

23

THROUGH THE CID conference room window, Kaj could see a disheveled Asian man sitting at the table and rubbing his wrists. He was around five foot six, slender build, with dark hair falling across his forehead and shading his glasses. His suit trousers were muddy, as was his light tan jacket.

Moses was standing guard outside the room with Rogers, both looking very pleased with themselves.

"Where did you find him?" Kaj asked

"We spotted him up on the upper ridge above the crime scene. We saw a car we didn't recognize down on the road. It had diplomatic plates registered to the Kuthani Consulate. We went looking for the driver. When Officer Rogers here started walking up the trail towards the ridge, he saw this gentleman trying to come down. It's muddy up there, and he slid down the hill right into our arms. We invited him to have a nice conversation, but he resisted, so Rogers cuffed him and put him in the patrol car. We brought him straight in. As you can tell, he's displeased. The words we can decipher have to do with immunity. Here's his wallet. It says his name is Liu, and he's on the staff of the Kuthani consulate."

Kaj nodded his appreciation but inwardly groaned. Consulates meant international implications. Just what the case needed. Still, he shared a cheery wave of appreciation as Moses and his junior partner left, despite what he suspected was trouble lying ahead. Jill and Kaj went into the muddy man and sat down with him.

"Sir, why were you on the hillside?" Jill asked. "You were in a crime scene area. What were you doing there?"

The man pointed to the wallet in Kaj's hand and repeated the word "immunity." Kaj opened the wallet again and looked at the State Department credential. It identified the bearer as a Kuthani citizen with diplomatic immunity.

"Diplomatic immunity," Kaj said slowly. The man nodded his head up and down vigorously. "We need to call the State Department," he said to Jill. "We can't hold him, but the State Department may."

"Not on your life," interrupted a loud voice from the office doorway. Kaj looked up as Wilfred Fong bounded into the room and slapped his briefcase onto the table. Kaj suppressed another small groan. Fong was attorney on call to an amazing number of important people. In the courtroom, he enjoyed high drama and played to the jury with a conspiratorial twinkle in his eyes. Most relevant, though, was the fact that he never forgot who was paying him.

"The Kuthani Consulate has retained me to represent Mr. Liu, and the first thing I can tell you is that you have no authority to detain a foreign national on the staff of a credentialed mission to the United States. You are going to release him immediately." Fong's face creased into an expression of disdain on behalf of his client.

"Mr. Liu is not being detained," Jill replied crisply. "We were about to ask him why he was present at a crime scene."

"You know better than that. He doesn't need to answer your questions." Fong looked like a cat sitting on top of a bird feeder, daring the birds to land.

"He may have witnessed a crime," Kaj said, already knowing what Fong was going to say. He was right.

"You lack authority. Mr. Liu, we are leaving. Now, return his wallet."

With a joyful abruptness, Wilfred Fong picked up his briefcase, made sure that Liu had his property, took his client by the arm, and swept them both out of the office. Jill and Kaj were left sitting in an empty conference room staring at one another.

Kaj had a good idea that there was going to be trouble, and it didn't take long. Half an hour later, Bob Wilson called them both into his office. His expression was indecipherable: confusion on top of incredulity on top of something approaching what the hell is going on?

"The Kuthani consulate just called to complain. So did the State Department. They say we harassed their diplomat. I assume this is you and it has to do with the Whitworth case. How the hell did you manage this?"

Kaj shrugged. "The Manoa patrol officers caught the guy at the Whitworth crime scene. They brought him in."

"They say his tranquility, whatever that is, was violated. What is that all about?"

Kaj shook his head. "No idea. Wilfred Fong showed up before we could question Liu. I don't know how tranquil investigating a murder is supposed to be."

"Well, look on this as the chance to learn. The State Department says there is to be NO further questioning until you and your team are briefed on how to conduct an investigation in a Kuthani-sensitive manner, whatever that is."

"Wonderful," Kaj groaned, but he wasn't surprised. You can't be raised Hawaii-Japanese and not know when you've stood on somebody's toes. "But does that mean they'll let us question him if we follow their protocols?"

"State's sending someone over later today to figure that out. In the meantime, don't either of you go anywhere. Get the rest of your team involved. You might as well all get briefed together. And while you're at it see that everyone gets their reports in. The two of you especially. No more nonsense. No more international incidents."

"Fong was enjoying himself," Jill said as they returned to their desks. "But how did Fong get here so fast? Who told him where Liu was?"

"Only one answer," Kaj said. "There was someone else up there at the crime scene."

24

THE UPCOMING MEETING with the State Department dashed Kaj's plans for finding Mrs. Sam. He looked sideways at the pile of unfinished reports on his desk. It looked far too high. Across the room, he saw Jill sit down at her desk, give a matching sigh, and pick up the top folder.

Two hours later, when Kaj was just finishing, he looked up to see an earnest looking man in his mid-thirties, clean shaven, well groomed, wearing the uniform of federal bureaucracy, a tan suit and tie. He crossed the room and presented his card to Kaj with a slight bow, suggesting a habit formed by spending much time in Asia. Kaj smiled slightly as he accepted the card.

"Greg Horne," the man said. "I'm told you are to be invited to the Kuthani embassy. I've been sent to brief you on Kuthan-US relations."

"Invited? I'd heard we wouldn't be welcome there."

"Things change," Horne said. "We have a lot to discuss."

"I'll take your word on that," Kaj said as he ushered the team into the conference room. "But can I ask how the State Department learned about our detaining a Kuthani citizen?"

Horne waited for everyone to take their seats.

"Mr. Fong called us on his way to returning Mr. Liu to the consulate."

"And he wanted you to brief us?" Jill asked curiously.

"No. The Kuthani Consul asked on behalf of his home government. The king personally directed that the consular staff be made available to you, but in a culturally appropriate way. That's why I'm here. The Kuthanis want to find whoever killed Professor Whitworth as much as you do. King Soöng considered Whitworth a personal friend."

"The king's friend?" Kaj leaned back in his chair. He wasn't sure how he felt about the increasingly bizarre twists and turns this case was taking. "How did that happen?"

"As I understand it, when the king was the crown prince and on a state visit to the Philippines, he contracted malaria. Professor Whitworth was giving a series of lectures there on his work with malaria and was asked to consult. He impressed the prince enough for Kuthan to make a formal request for him to be appointed special advisor the royal physician. The State Department was delighted. The personal connection between Whitworth and the royal family is the reason that their one consulate on US soil is located here in Honolulu."

"The king of Kuthan personally approved us interviewing them? Kaj's eyebrow rose.

"Yes. The local Consul is the king's brother-in-law. It's very high level. Maintaining good relations is important to both countries, but the reality is that we have to adjust to them, not the other way around. They find us brash and insensitive. We need you to provide an example of Americans who don't expect the rest of the world to speak English and have the same values."

Kaj threw up his hands in dismay. "And how are we going to do that? We're four detectives trying to solve a murder. Our job description doesn't include tact and charm. I don't think we're what you're looking for."

"Actually, we think you are. Your boss tells me that you have some sort of sixth sense."

Kaj gave a hand gesture that suggested he was pushing away a cloud of noxious gas. "I don't make any claims about that sort of thing," he said testily.

"It doesn't matter. You're our best shot at working with them. Liu is traumatized by his encounter with your officers. Getting him to talk will be difficult."

Kaj saw that resistance was useless.

"How much do you know about Kuthan?" Horne looked around the room. Kaipo and Cliff looked at one another and shrugged.

Jill had the only answer. "It's in the Himalayas, bordering on Bhutan, China, and India. It has some of the highest unclimbed mountains in Asia. Mount Sawanotsuro is almost as tall as Mount Everest and K2." She glanced at Kaj as if apologizing for her knowledge. "I knew someone once who wanted to climb there."

"That's a start," Horne said. "Kuthan is the Switzerland of hydroelectric power production, and its three neighbors want it to stay neutral. Kuthan's southern rivers feed a dam built by the British at the turn of the century. That dam generates enough power for the region. The only flat part of the country is around the capital city, Mongarthuā, where the palace and airport are located. US interest in the region stems from the stability the country provides. They have full employment, comparative wealth, and happy people unlikely to become terrorists."

"And you don't want blundering cops causing an international incident. Is that it?" Kaipo asked.

"Yes, but even more delicate." Horne allowed himself a small smile. "We do not want the Kuthani Consulate to close unless it transfers to Washington, which it won't. Kuthanis believe in building connections between individuals; it's their particular form of what they call Vedarinda, which is a form of Buddhism. It's symbolized by the image of the steady eye. They value art and sports that require perfect eye and hand coordination, which they say are prayers."

"Is this part of Mr. Liu's complaint about having his tranquility disturbed?" Cliff was starting to connect the dots.

Horne gave an approving nod. "But you also have to understand the connection between their present culture and their very bloody history.

"For centuries, the area was under the control of five war lord families who not only fought among themselves but also caused problems along the border with India. Their incursions were bad enough that the British army in India decided to pacify them once and for all. The British invaded, took over the country, and built roads, schools, and the dam. The people learned to enjoy their taste of peace and relative prosperity.

"When the British left, a power vacuum resulted. Now unchecked, the families and followers of the previous war lords started to reclaim their territory. They might still be fighting except for the Massacre of Kalyani, the stronghold of the Black Dragon clan. Their rivals conducted a surprise attack on them, killing everything alive—women, children, animals, crops—and destroying everything they couldn't steal. The country was so shocked that almost to a person, the people rose up and marched on their local monasteries demanding action.

The monasteries at that time had enough moral authority to impose peace."

Horne looked around the room at the four detectives. Jill and Cliff were listening intently. Kaj had a quizzical look as if wondering where this briefing was headed. Kaipo was the only one who didn't seem engaged.

"To make a long story short, the monasteries called the five families together and forced them to create a new governing structure. The families elected the grandfather of the present king to provide political leadership but under the direction and assent of a council of families and religious leaders. Then, to curb the violence once and for all, the monks preached a code they called The Five Ways of Virtue that was established as the state religion.

"The fourth and fifth "ways" pertinent to your case are the beliefs in tranquility and the spiritual connection between people. Those are what your officers ran up against in detaining Liu. The king had authorized the consulate to be established in Hawaii not for any other reason than because he felt a spiritual connection with Whitworth."

"You really have a major problem now, don't you?" Jill said sympathetically.

Horne looked grateful at her understanding and nodded. "That's an understatement. We're left hoping that someone can step into Whitworth's shoes to keep the consulate here in Hawaii, but as yet we don't see how."

"Has this government structure worked out?" Kaj had never heard of Kuthan before. He wondered where it had been hiding.

"It's worked for them so far. There have been no more civil wars. Their biggest problem now is protecting their southern border with

India. They have been experiencing a flood of refugees. In the interests of peace, Kuthan has made efforts to assimilate the immigrants. Unfortunately, they have encountered rising crime rates, particularly plundering of their archeological sites. Most recently, their most important monastery lost a national treasure, a carved teak dragon of immense antiquity. The Consulate staff may want to talk with you about this. They suspect it has been or will be shipped to the US for sale."

"Are the dams their only industry?" Jill asked.

"The dams are the largest because they sell power to their neighboring countries. They also have a very nascent tourism industry, as well as the usual agriculture and precious gem mining common to the Asian mountain nations. The country is also home to the hornless Kuthani goat. It develops a fleece so dense the un-sheared animal looks like a large hair ball. You have to see the animal move to know which direction it is headed."

Kaj contained his desire to chuckle because Horne was so serious. Kaipo was not so careful, he gave a guffaw as if his leg had been pulled.

Horne frowned. "A single fleece can sell for $10,000 US or more at auction if it can be exported. Most fleeces are not. Unmarried Kuthani women weave these into a strong and warm fabric, which they bring to their marriages as a dowry. Tradition is valued in Kuthan."

"What do you want us to do?' Kaj said before anyone else could blunder into sensitive topics.

"I'll be with you during the interview to help you observe protocol. Don't interrupt. You will be greeted by a small bow that you should return. The Consul is always addressed as "Your Serenity," but he will expect you to call him Sir. He's the king's brother-in-law, and if he were based in Washington, he would be called an ambassador. He studied at the London School of Economics.

"Don't ask questions until after the Consul has retired. He understands your need to cross-examine, but it should not be done until he leaves. That would violate their protocol.

"He will be accompanied by Vice Consul Chenh who is Kuthani warrior-class responsible for the consulate's operations and more used to Western ways. Now, this concept of warrior class is critical for you to know. The Kuthanis value tranquility, but they are also practical. They must have police officers, judges, and soldiers—bureaucrats if you will. Two of the clans have taken on this role historically, although there has been much intermarriage and the distinctions are softening. You are warrior class in their eyes, effectively middle class."

Horne looked round the room. "You can question Vice Consul Chenh as long as you are respectful. He has a degree in international policy from George Washington University. His English is excellent, and he is well versed in American law. However, I need to caution you that Kuthani laws are different from ours. Mr. Liu will be brought in after the Consul leaves. He will be accompanied by the head of security, Mallik, who comes from a refugee family and speaks excellent English. I'm not sure how much Liu or Mallik's deputy, Tien Han will understand. I speak Kuthani myself so can translate if asked."

"I'm curious," Jill said, "what the other virtues are. You mentioned spiritual connection and tranquility. What are the other three?"

"Justice, honesty, and gratitude. Keep these things in mind and you should be fine." Horne then stood up and started gathering his papers.

"Before you go," Kaj said, "could you expedite our request for information on a Cheterinda Gowda? He's a possible witness, and we can't locate him. The university tells us he's a foreign student but won't give us further details. We've asked for any information on his visa."

Horne looked thoughtful. "That name's familiar. Cheterinda is a Kuthani name. Gowda is not. I'll look into it for you when I get back to the office."

After Home left, Kaipo collapsed into laughter. "Goats that you can't tell back from front? Do I hear the Arabian Nights?"

Kaj did not look pleased, and Kaipo calmed down. "What did you think, Jill?" Kaj asked just to change the subject.

Jill frowned deeply and didn't answer.

Kaj sensed an awkwardness and redirected it. "Okay, that's it. Everyone, back to work."

"Is there something I should know?" Kaj settled uninvited into the chair next to Jill's desk.

She knew right away what he meant. "Was I being unprofessional?"

"Not at all." Kaj kept his voice low. "I'm just concerned that there's something wrong."

"I'm fine. You don't need to worry about me." Jill straightened out the pile of finished reports on her desk and did not look at him.

"I have to," Kaj said, "if it involves a case we are working on. You obviously know something about Kuthan."

"I'm fine. I don't allow my personal life to affect my professional responsibilities."

"Now I absolutely must insist that you tell me what is going on." Kaj looked directly at Jill and, when she finally looked up, held her gaze. He was prepared to wait.

"I was engaged to a climber who was building an expedition to climb in Mount Sawanotsuro in Kuthan when he was killed." Jill said this in a rush. She did not allow her face to register emotion.

Kaj settled back in his chair and chose his next question carefully.

"I'm sorry to hear of your loss. Can you tell me about him?"

"His name was Stephen Harkin. He was a photographer for *National Geographic*." She spoke matter of factly, but Kaj could sense the well of emotion behind the words.

"That name's familiar," he said. At first, he didn't place it, but then the context returned. "Didn't he do a photo spread on Kilimajaro a couple of years ago?"

"You knew his work?" Jill's face melted for a moment in surprise.

"My daughter, Annie, was writing a research paper about post-independence Tanzania. She brought the magazine home because she enjoyed the pictures of Kilimanjaro. They almost made me want to try climbing myself. I stress the word *almost*."

Jill smiled for the first time. "I was with him when he took those photographs. That's where he proposed. We decided to wait because he wanted us to be married in Kuthan. He'd been there before and loved the country. He said I'd wear a traditional bride's dress—red for joy and yellow for happiness—with a headdress of dragons and seeing eyes. I wish we hadn't waited."

"How did he die?"

"He was checking out a beginners' slope on Mount Rainier when a rock dislodged and hit him. I couldn't believe it. He'd climbed the most technically difficult mountains in the world but died on an easy climb"

"Is that why you decided to come to Hawaii?"

"It was part of it. I had no family left in California. I'd just joined the police force when my parents died. Then I met Stephen only to lose him as well. I needed a fresh start. I didn't feel I belonged anywhere."

"Jill, I don't know what it was like for you in San Diego. It can't have been easy."

"I don't let anything interfere with my work." Jill straightened her shoulders in a motion both of certainty and defiance.

"I don't doubt that," Kaj said gently. "I don't pretend to know how people deal with life, let alone death. But I do know something about loneliness and feeling disconnected. You know the old saying, *ichigo ichie*. Life happens only once. We must seize any joy in the moment. Perhaps the Kuthanis have something with their idea of the connection between people. I'm going to hope that Hawaii can give you what you're looking for. But even more, I hope that our team here at CID can one day earn your trust."

25

LINDA WAS WATCHING for his car as he drove up the road to the house and came out into the garage as he drove in. She hung by the car door as he opened it, almost jumping up and down with excitement.

"You're not going to believe what happened today."

"You wrapped a gift with no ants?"

"Silly. No. It's much more than that. Your professor, the one who was killed in Manoa—Harrison Whitworth—he bought some jewelry at Liberty House and had it sent to the Mainland. Did you know that?"

"Maybe someone had a birthday?"

"Yes, yes. But it's more interesting than that. The girls at work were all talking about it. Come on inside. I stopped at the Korean food place for kalbi beef on the way home. You know, the one where the gourmet fellow groaned with pleasure at each mouthful and kept saying the Koreans ought to travel to Hawaii and relearn how to cook. I'll tell you while you're eating."

"Okay," Kaj said as he sat the kitchen table, "tell me what happened."

"Today Annie and I went to our primary location at gift wrapping.

We had to learn all about prices and methods for wrapping and using the cash register. It's all very strict. You have to cut the paper off the rolls just so. Anyway, as we're learning all this, the other women working there started talking. They're regular staff, not temps like us. It seems that your Harrison Whitworth came into the store about two weeks ago. He picked out a diamond bracelet and arranged for it to be gift wrapped and sent, insured heavily, to an address on the Mainland. No note. Just his business card. They sent it out on the day he specified. The bracelet wasn't cheap. It was a nice one. I saw it."

"How could you have seen it?"

"I'm getting to that. The girls were intrigued and said they went all out on the wrapping, ribbon roses and stars—complimentary given the price he paid. There was envious talk about it. Boy, wish I were getting it and all that. It was that special. Not your everyday gift at all.

"Well, we got word today that it was returned. It was the talk of the lunch room. Returned? How could someone return something so beautiful? I even went to the jewelry counter and looked at it in the display case. It was gorgeous, little diamond rosettes in a tennis bracelet. It couldn't be the wrapping or the bracelet that was wrong. It had to be personal. It had to be a message. Somebody didn't like the sender."

"Who was it sent to?"

"It went to an address in California. I'm sure you can get it from the store. But that's not the most interesting part. You see, it was sent to the Mainland, but it was returned in person. That's why it was noticed. Whoever received it came to the Islands within days. That made me think. If they were upset enough to return such a beautiful gift, maybe they'd be angry enough to do something to the sender?"

"Did you say anything about this possible connection at the store?"

"Of course not. But the news coverage was so extensive that the ladies recognized Whitworth's name and remembered the bracelet."

"I hope you're not going to discuss the case with them," Kaj said.

"I know better than that. But do give me credit for spotting something unusual and figuring out it might be helpful," Linda winked at Kaj.

"Stay tuned. If the tip is useful, I'll see you're rewarded."

"By the way," she said happily, "after we get off from work tomorrow, Annie and I are having dinner with Malia. We thought we might see the Society of Seven show. But that's in Waikiki, so we'll have to see about the parking. She said she'd see if Alan can join us. I didn't want to blindside you again in case you get home before we do, but with your hours, I don't think that will happen. Hope that's okay?"

"Alan's a firefighter now, Moses told me. Strange how time flies."

"By the way, I want that reward whether the bracelet is useful or not. Dinner at M's Ranch House would have been nice, but it's not there anymore."

"Let me work on that, " Kaj said. Then he reached over and kissed her.

26

I**T MUST HAVE** been a slow news day. The *Advertiser* was out in full force regarding the Whitworth murder. The pundits and second-guessers were silent for the moment, replaced by a page full of letters to the editor as the public had their say.

Eight letters were reprinted under a header "Whitworth Murder" on the editorial page. One bewailed the end of the Aloha spirit and asked whether the murder meant the State was sinking into barbarism like the Mainland. Another accused the police department of sabotaging tourism by not arresting someone by now: "Who's going to feel safe coming here?" the letter writer asked. The third had a political motivation: "It's time," the writer said, "to consider supporting homegrown business rather than relying on fancy ideas from the university." The next three expressed condolences to Whitworth's family and asked them not to judge Hawaii by this one awful act. The seventh approved the concept of thinking about Hawaii's people first, and addressing local problems before trying to solve world problems. The eighth and final wanted to know whether the police were looking into the possibility of terrorism by someone wanting to destroy Hawaii's economy.

Kaj read them with varying interest. He had spent the days since the murder avoiding the local media, leaving the Department PR office to issue updates of what could be shared without compromising the on-going work. But he knew news releases would satisfy no one until an arrest was made.

And now there was Kuthan to make matters worse.

Greg was waiting for them in front of a white square building enclosed by an imposing carved lava rock wall. At first glance, it was impossible to tell what lay inside. The give-away was the Kuthani seal set into the lava wall. The seal was a gold circle with a central seeing eye and five dragons chasing round the rim, bearing the words, "Consulate of Kuthan." Greg rang the bell, and they were ushered in by a smiling man in a brown uniform. He led them through an arched entrance way with a recessed double door and then on into the center of the building.

The Consulate must have had a professional staff of horticulturists because before them was an oasis of bougainvillea, orchid, and fern growing under skylights. A cascade of water was directed through bamboo spouts, each tuned to a different pitch so the dripping water sounded like bird songs. The water's destination was a pond laced with lily pads and floating hyacinths. Meandering pathways went through the garden, and there were stone seats carved with dragons and eyes at various spots. All the consular offices opened onto this courtyard.

Their guide directed them to a room with open windows looking onto the pond then gave a small bow and left them. The room was furnished with deep leather couches and an armchair arranged around a coffee table whose glass top revealed a carved mountain scene underneath. Kaj and Jill settled into one couch while Horne sat opposite them on the other.

Kaj assumed that by sitting apart from them, Horne signaled that he was not part of the police business that had brought them there. Kaj understood. Law enforcement wasn't serene. To pass the time while they waited, Kaj studied the scrolls hung on the walls. They were weighted at the bottom by braided tassels threaded through jade balls and depicted a mountainous country with many waterfalls. A frieze along the ceiling depicted variations of the nation's all-seeing eye.

After a short while, the Consul entered the room with two other men. Kaj could tell the Consul's rank from the deference paid to him. He was impeccably groomed: his hair was cut close with a perfect part, his silk shirt was in muted beige and green, and his soft slacks so well-fitted that Kaj wondered if they were made from the famous goat fleece. Of the other two, one looked stylishly casual in a well-tailored jacket and pants, while the other wore form-fitting t-shirt and slacks, with a bunch of keys, sunglasses, and what looked like a walkie-talkie hooked at his waist.

Kaj stood, expecting to exchange the polite bow he had been coached to provide, but the Consul crossed to him and extended his hand. He shook hands with Jill also and then turned to Greg. Greg put his hands together and gave a deep bow. The Consul returned it and winked at Kaj before introducing Vice Consul Chenh, the man in the casual jacket, and sitting down in the armchair at the head of the table. The Vice Consul sat beside him. A smiling woman in trousers and tunic topic emblazoned with gold birds brought jasmine tea, poured it without being asked into small porcelain mugs, and left without saying a word. She did not serve the man with the sunglasses who was left to stand by himself against the wall. Each at the table sipped the tea to be polite, and then the meeting began.

"His Serene Majesty, King Soöng has expressed his most profound regret concerning Dr. Whitworth's death," the Consul began. "He considered him a dear friend, as I am sure you have heard. His Majesty wishes us to assist your investigation in any way possible." The Consul spoke with a perfect Etonian British university-educated voice, a combination of aristocracy and sophistication.

Kaj understood he was now expected to say something, but Greg hadn't warned him, so he had nothing prepared. He struggled to find something that would not undermine the five virtues. Protocol weighed him down.

"Mr. Horne and the State Department have told us a lot about Kuthan," he began. "but I do have a question." Horne's eye bored into him. Kaj didn't have to guess what he was thinking: Say something offensive and feel the US State Department come down on your head, and that's just the start.

Remembering that in Kuthani eyes he was warrior-class, respected but not high ranking, Kaj reached for the pleasantly irrelevant. "I understand, Sir," he began, "that his serene majesty enjoys surfing here in Hawaii. I was wondering how often he has the opportunity to do so and where he likes to go."

The Consul laughed. The question was perfect. It broke the formality and allowed things to proceed through small talk before the Consul left and more serious things could begin.

"He flies his aircraft here twice a year, unrecognized with the help of the State Department." The Consul nodded toward a now relaxed Horne.

"These are not official visits," he continued, "so there is no notice taken. It's busy at the Consulate when he is here, but a delight. We have persuaded him that the North Shore is too vigorous as he must be accompanied by security, and our security force members are not as accomplished surfers as he is."

The Consul chuckled. "In fact, several of our security staff had an experience—I believe you call it 'wiping out'—before His Majesty understood what we meant. When he comes now, His Majesty surfs on your southern shore and sometimes on Maui." Then he stood up and the visitors all did the same. "I will leave you to your business," he said. "I hope that this matter can be resolved well." Then he shook hands with them again and left.

The Vice Consul moved into the armchair the Consul had vacated and took over the meeting. In that small move, the meeting's tone changed. He gestured to the man on the side to come forward and told him to introduce himself. He looked like a schoolboy about to be disciplined.

The man introduced himself as Mallik, head of security for the embassy. He then spoke into the radio and a younger man came in to join them. Mallik introduced him as Teng Han, his deputy. The Vice Consul did not invite either man to sit.

"The Consul asked us to assist you in whatever way we can," the Vice Consul said smoothly. "We want to apologize for the unfortunate incident between Mr. Liu and your staff this morning. Professor Whitworth was a friend to Kuthan, and we are all saddened by his death. We want you to know we do not know anyone in the consulate who have wished any harm to him."

"We are glad to hear that," Kaj said. "However, we would most like to talk with Mr. Liu, who was at Professor Whitworth's house."

"He was not at Professor Whitworth's house. But that can be explained." The Vice Consul spoke some words in Kuthani and Mallik signaled for his assistant Han to do whatever had been requested. Han left the room at once. "Mallik and I will remain with you while you question Mr. Liu. I think you will understand why once he answers your questions. His English is not fluent."

After a few moments, the door opened to admit the unhappy Liu who looked even more dyspeptic than he had before, along with Wilfred Fong, who looked just as smug.

"Good afternoon, Detectives," said Fong. "Mr. Liu is my client, so I must be present during any interviews." Fong and Liu took their places at the table.

Kaj began the questions. "Mr. Liu, I appreciate your willingness to talk with us, but can we start with the obvious question of how long you had been watching Professor Whitworth's house."

Liu looked at Mallik for a translation and then responded in Kuthani.

"He was not watching Professor Whitworth's house," Mallik said.

"Then why was he apprehended in an area marked off by police tape?" Kaj asked.

Again, a short burst of language and an interpretation.

"He was nowhere near the house."

"But he was observed on the hill above the house on a ridge marked as an active crime scene," Jill pointed out.

"May we ask what was he doing up there?" Kaj asked.

"His assignment was to watch Professor Stone's house." This time Mallik answered the question. "I drove him to his post each evening so he could observe if any packages were delivered."

"An assignment? From whom?"

"From me," Mallik said. "I asked him and Han to take turns watching Mr. Stone's house for the past week."

"Might I ask why?"

Mallik smiled. "Because we believe that Mr. Stone is a thief."

The Vice Consul stepped in to explain. "We believe this man has been dealing in antiquities stolen from graves in the southern part of our country. Our consulate in Singapore learned that a new shipment was on its way to him. We wanted to know how the goods were shipped to the United States and how he was distributing them. Once the artifacts are here, it is hard to prove where they came from, and he has been clever in concealing them. He has even arranged for a donation to the art gallery at Hawaii State University; if they accept the art, the university will be accepting our stolen heritage."

"That's a point the university seems unable to understand," Fong said. "The administration can't see past the value of the proposed donation. As you can imagine, Kuthan is unhappy at their treasures being in a foreign museum."

"Why hasn't the consulate gone to the police about this?" Kaj asked the Vice Consul.

"They did," Fong interrupted. "But without specific information, there was little Interpol or local police could do beyond make inquiries. Because these deliveries were random, it was very difficult to set a trap to catch Stone. This time, the consulate wanted to see if they could find out for themselves. I warned them that there might be legal consequences, but the hemorrhage of their art was too serious for them to do nothing. I would represent them, of course, should any legal matters arise."

"Mr. Liu was in the trees above the road, then, watching the driveway to Stone's house on the night that Whitworth was killed?" Jill looked slightly sympathetic. It had been raining at night all week. The assignment must not have been comfortable.

"He was," Mallik agreed. "Han's assignment was morning. Liu was meant to watch later in the evening."

"Please ask Mr. Liu to tell us what happened and in what order the events took place," Kaj said to Mallik.

There were several minutes of conversation conducted in Kuthani before Mallik continued.

"Mr. Liu says he went to his usual place to observe at the usual time. He sat on a broken tile wall under a large tree. It was not pleasant, because it rained, and even after the rain stopped the tree dripped water on him. He observed several cars drive up to the houses along the road, but no one went down Mr. Stone's driveway or that of his neighbor Professor Whitworth."

"But eventually one did?"

"Yes, he says, somewhere before midnight he saw a car turn into Professor Whitworth's driveway. He thought it was the owner. Then he heard a noise like a door slam. It could have been the professor entering his house. Liu did not think anything of it."

"He didn't see the professor fall?"

"Mr. Liu was not at his post at the time of what happened."

Kaj sat back confused. "Where was he?"

"He was somewhere behind a tree." Mallik's face was contorted with scorn. Lui looked almost in tears.

Kaj watched as a heated discussion broke out between Mallik and Liu. It was interrupted by the Vice Consul who barked out a few words. Liu then hung his head and looked at the floor.

Now it was Kaj who felt sympathetic, remembering what Forensics had described as a chronic, painful, and embarrassing condition. He was unsure how to proceed.

"I must apologize," the Vice Consul said finally. "There was some disagreement over whether Mr. Liu was authorized to leave his post."

"Did Mr. Liu see the professor's body?" Kaj asked.

Mallik continued his translation with ill humor. "Liu says he could not see anything. There were no lights in the house or the driveway, only in the garage. He had no reason to believe that anyone had been hurt. He thought the man had forgotten to put down the door, but that did not seem alarming."

"Did he see or hear anything else?" Kaj addressed his question to Mallik.

"He heard birds chattering. He thinks he might have seen a shadow moving in the trees where the birds sleep, but if it was someone, it was someone small. He thinks it might be a large dog. He heard a car park. He remained where he was until the police car arrived next morning. He watched the policeman and saw the policeman was looking at something. That's when he realized something bad had happened. He walked down the trail and called the consulate.

"When we realized what happened that evening," the Vice Consul continued. "We did not want to interfere with your investigation, but we wanted to watch Mr. Stone. We decided to send Mr. Liu back to his post. But this time during the day. Later, we learned from sources in Singapore that Stone had received the delivery. We still do not know how that was possible."

"Mr. Han," Kaj said, "Did you see anything out of the ordinary when you were watching the house that day?"

Han took out a notebook. "Young people enter driveway at 4:30 p.m. One female hair tied up. One man, long hair, with shorts and t-shirt and slippers. They carry nothing. The postman come every day. He never go near house, He put mail in box. I look. Letters, no more."

"Did you notice anything unusual about Professor Whitworth's house?" Jill asked.

"I not make notes," Han said, "but I remember lady with buckets. She there over one hour. Then delivery lorry in afternoon. A package. When the lady was back of house, I went look. I was curious. I took chance. The package for Professor Whitworth. Medical instruments."

"Did you see who sent it?"

"No. Sorry, but it was not concerned Mr. Stone."

"Do you remember anything about the delivery truck?"

Han seemed to struggle with the words. He looked over at Mallik and spoke in Kuthani. Mallik translated. "He says it was yellow with writing on the side in red letters. There was a strange animal that he didn't recognize."

"How big was the box?"

Mallik translated. "About one-meter square. The box was plain with no list. Only a customs form. Of course, if addressed to Mr. Stone, he would have recorded the license number of the truck. But his instructions were clear. That is all he saw."

"I understand. You have been very helpful."

Is there anything more you need from us?" the Vice Consul asked. It was a clear hint that the meeting should start to close down.

"Please?" Liu broke in and spoke for himself. "I sorry no see. If I see, I call help."

"There was little you could do," Kaj replied. "Our medical examiner says death was immediate." Kaj took the Vice Consul's hint and stood up, as did Greg and Jill. "Please thank the Consul for his assistance in this matter. We appreciate the cooperation."

"It is our pleasure," the Vice Consul said. "Mallik will see you and Mr. Fong to the door."

Once they were outside, Fong looked slightly surprised when Kaj took him aside. "I assume your client-attorney privilege applies equally to foreign clients?"

"Of course," Fong replied. "But why is that a concern?"

"I have something to tell you in the interests of your client, and it needs to be kept confidential."

"Now you have my full attention," Fong sniggered.

"Tell your client that he has a serious illness and needs to see a doctor immediately."

Fong's smirk disappeared. "What's wrong with him?"

"Nothing that stress reduction and antibiotics can't cure, but he needs to get started. If he doesn't, I'm told it can be fatal."

"I suppose I don't want to know how you know this?"

"You don't."

As Fong left, Kaj had a question for Horne. "How accurate were Mallik's translations?"

"They were okay until he got to the truck. Then he got sketchy. What Han said was that there was a cartoon animal that looked like a mongoose with wings."

"AirIbex?" Kaj said.

"Sounds like," Greg said. "An interesting omission, don't you think? I'm not sure Mallik knows I understand Kuthani. The State Department works with the Consul and Vice Consul, not the staff."

As they got into their car, Kaj turned to Jill. "We need to finish up the interviews on campus, find that delivery truck, and locate this Mrs. Sam. She may be the cleaning lady Han saw. We also need to talk with Liu alone before they send him back to his country."

"How do you know they plan to do that?"

Kaj felt surprised that Jill had not seen the obvious. "Liu just told me," he replied.

27

IT SEEMED A long shot, but there wasn't anyone else who might know anything about Whitworth's life outside the university. As the dean had described it, Whitworth's relationship with Helen Malcolm sounded impersonal, but perhaps that was what the couple wished it to appear.

After they left the Consulate, Kaj and Jill drove to the campus and parked in the faculty lot where they displayed their pass on the dashboard. A pass like that would have been a life-changer for Kaj if he'd had one when he was harassed by students and even some anti-war faculty.

But he couldn't say everyone on campus was bad. He remembered the time when a long-haired hippie type with wire-rimmed glasses and leather sandals suddenly stood up on the first day of one of Kaj's classes. "Guess it's time to get this show on the road," he said. To Kaj's surprise, he was the instructor. He was to become a good friend. But there weren't many other examples.

Helen Malcolm's office was in Pendleton Hall, an older building that made no pretense at modernity. It flaunted its Grecian columns, defying the science buildings across the road whose chrome and glass screamed grants and money. Pendleton housed the history, philosophy, and English departments, the bastion of pure humanities as far as Pendleton was concerned, tasked with standing firm against anything with practical application to which could be applied the appalling label "vocational."

Included among the latter were the schools of business, engineering, agriculture, and education, not to mention the universally scorned and obscenely well-funded athletics department. It was a never-ending battle, but one the Pendleton denizens willingly fought to defend Western Civilization.

The History Department was on the top floor, occupying half the available office space. The Philosophy Department occupied the other half on the opposite side. There was no shared conference room in the middle, so it appeared the two departments had little to do with one another. Helen Malcolm's office was down a long-tiled hallway and behind a sharp bend that isolated three offices in a cul-de-sac.

Hers was the last one, the only one with an unobstructed view down the central campus promenade. She had decorated her space with intellectual and self-conscious daintiness. Two walls were covered by packed bookcases. Her desk was placed on an angle to them, no doubt following the best feng shui principles, leaving the wall behind her free for art work. A Georgia O'Keeffe painting of a longhorn skull hung behind her.

Ms. Malcolm radiated as much austerity as the painting under whose shadow she worked. Kaj thought he saw a resemblance to the skull. Her neck bones stood out under her red shirt, and her tailored linen jacket was not able to conceal a skeletal frame. Perhaps to counteract a masculine cast to her presence, she had a red plastic rose in a crystal vase on her desk.

Kaj and Jill introduced themselves and were invited to sit. Before their eyes, Ms. Malcolm became Professor Malcolm.

"How can I help you?"

"We understand that you are a friend of Harrison Whitworth's," Jill began.

"Were is more appropriate, isn't it?"

"Were a friend of Harrison Whitworth's," Jill corrected herself.

"Could you please tell us what your relationship was with him?" Jill continued.

"Why do you want to know that?"

"Because we are conducting a murder investigation," Kaj broke in, "and we need to know everything about him and about the people closest to him. If you have any information for us, we need to know it."

"What do you want to know?" Ms. Malcolm straightened in her seat. Her face lost the languid look and her tone had a new curiosity.

"How would you describe your relationship with him?"

She studied Kaj before she replied. "We were friends. We went to university functions and sometimes out to dinner. He needed a companion for social events, and since they were often in interesting places and involved meeting interesting people, I agreed to accompany him."

"There was nothing more between you?" Jill asked.

"We weren't lovers if that's what you're asking. Our evenings were formal, almost business-like. He wanted certain things, and so did I. Our needs overlapped."

"What things did he want?" Jill asked.

"Harrison came from a cultivated background. He was private about himself but still liked going to symphony receptions and dinners at Washington Place, the governor's mansion." Her explanation suggested that she did not expect Kaj and Jill to know where the Governor lived. "He enjoyed meeting visiting dignitaries, I suppose because it reminded him of his childhood. His family was American aristocracy if one is allowed to call it that these days. He even liked being invited to watch a football game from the president's private box at the stadium. These were semi-ceremonial occasions when it might be awkward to go without a companion."

"What did you want?"

"I wanted to meet people and be seen. I'm eligible for promotion to full professor, and I knew becoming known in the community might help my chances this time."

"Aren't promotions based on a publications record?" That much Kaj seemed to remember from his time on campus.

"I've published four books and twenty articles over the past ten years, and I've been passed over twice. I don't intend to see that happen again. I hoped that Harrison's friendship might influence the review committee. His death is very inconvenient."

Kaj looked into her face with its steely gray eyes and felt repulsed. They seemed as vacant as the empty eye sockets of the skull above her.

"Can you tell us about him as a person?" he asked.

She settled back in her chair, resting her hands on the desk and fingering a book cover with long bony fingers that seemed out of proportion to the rest of her hands. They reminded Kaj of spiders' legs, long appendages attached to unnaturally small bodies. Kaj noted the book on her desk; the title said it was about colonial emancipation.

"Harrison had an intuitive feel for balance and opportunity. He sought order and wanted acceptance. He did not oppose authority, but quietly subverted it to meet his needs. He would have become the lawyer his father wanted if not for a professor telling his father he would honor the family name better through being a scientific genius rather than a mediocre lawyer. He sometimes appeared self-centered and lacking empathy, not because he was malevolent, but because he didn't notice if others were offended. If it could be brought to his attention in a manner he could understand, he was often apologetic and tried to make amends—although that was partly his need to be admired. Is this what you wanted to know?"

"You seem to have made a particular study of him." Jill had to resist mirroring Malcolm's coldness. The woman made no pretense at charm.

"I have. He was a fascinating subject. You must understand that to a historian like me, someone like him is an irresistible research subject. It was difficult to know where he stood. He'd argue with the vice president about the need for pure science undefiled by outside pressure at the same time that he agreed with the president and Governor about the need for political support. He seemed to hold contradictory positions. This made him ambiguous and ironic, a quality that many people found alarming, particularly if they wanted to count on him. Yet it was this quality that attracted me most. Shall I continue?"

"Please do," Kaj said with a tinge of sarcasm. He wondered how he would feel if someone were to dissect him with this degree of almost malevolent objectivity.

"He was charming when he chose to be, but he was at heart a loner despite his desire to make everyone, including his critics, respect him.

His authoritarian family background sometimes made him mean spirited with his subordinates. I've never seen anyone carry a grudge so well. There was no way he would forgive and forget. Consider his squabble with Arthur Stone—not that Stone is any paragon. There's something shifty about Stone, but I never discovered what upset Harrison so much."

"Have you been keeping notes on Whitworth for a reason?" Jill asked.

"I thought he might make a good subject for my fifth book. I didn't think the book would be about the death of Hawaii's Nobel Laureate, but in some ways that's even better, isn't it? It might have popular appeal, although it will be academic."

She took out a plastic note file from a desk drawer and let her chalky fingers flick through the cards. She began reading from them:

"Harrison never saw the difference between personal advantage and new scientific knowledge. To him they were the same. If he could conceive of it, it was, by definition, perfect. Anyone who opposed him was standing in the way of progress. He believed himself sincere in this feeling. In his mind, he was the intellectual and scientific future. To oppose him was to be wrong. In his intellectual brilliance, when there was controversy, he simply waited to be proved right."

"That's quite an analysis," Jill said. "But beyond some advantage to your promotion, why would you want to spend time with someone like that?"

"Because Harrison was also a truly fascinating man. He knew everyone and could tell wonderful stories. His family had been invited to the White House during every presidency since Taft's.

"Let me explain it this way. Most people try to crawl their way up the social ladder; he was at the top already and had the pedigree to avoid the whole process. In the sciences, he rose to the top, although I suspect he was never comfortable with it. I think he came to Hawaii to escape something. He never explained why he was here. I assumed it was something he wanted to forget."

"It sounds as if you are well into that book," Jill observed .

"I might try starting to write it and see what happens." Malcolm delicately shrugged her bony shoulders and tapped her note cards into an orderly formation.

"When was the last time you saw him?" Kaj asked.

"At the institute party before he left to accept the Nobel Prize. I was a little surprised that he left without saying goodbye to me, but there were people clamoring around him, so I'm sure he was just distracted."

"Did he phone you during his time abroad?"

"No, but that was not his practice. I would hear a few days after he returned."

"Can I ask you," Kaj said, "where you were on Thursday night?"

"Am I a suspect? How lovely. I'll have to include that in the book. I was at the Christmas performance at the Blaisdell Center. I have the ticket stub somewhere if you want to see it."

"Were you alone?"

"I was with my friend, Cathy Eaton. She's a women's coach here on campus."

"When did you get home?"

"Around eleven thirty I should imagine, but we wanted to eat supper, so we picked up some food at Foodland on Beretania. She didn't leave my apartment until around 1:00am. I live in the Marco Polo on Kapiolani Boulevard if that's helpful."

"Do you know anyone who might want to harm him?"

"There were a few disgruntled students. Harrison's attitude to them was quite uncompromising. An exemplary student would merely be called competent, and it would go down from there. His highest praise was to say that the he would be willing to employ the student again as an assistant on his projects. I never heard him talk about them except the process by which they were useful to the project. On the other hand, his graduate students have won prestigious awards and prominent careers, so I assume Harrison's colleagues understood his rating system."

"Were his students as indifferent to him as he seems to have been to them?" Jill furrowed her head in bewilderment.

"Oh no. That's what's amazing. One was in love with him as far as I can tell. His secretary was also his graduate student. She even gave up her marriage for him. You must have spoken to her. Harriet Nogawa. Did she tell you? Some women want to give their lives to serve powerful men. I suppose it must have something to do with reflected glory and a sense of purpose. I don't know what she will do now without her illusions. I hear she's possessive and the only time she's away from him is when she goes home to a family reunion on Moloka'i. They have some ritual shooting goats with bows and arrows on the cliffs. Quite awful way to spend a vacation, but I suppose if you've been raised that way."

"He never said anything about his family?"

"Not that he mentioned, but I'm not sure he had time for a family. Poor Harrison. He was like a salmon swimming upstream to spawn, and when he arrived, the only thing left for him was to die."

Malcolm returned the cards to her filing cabinet and snapped the lid down. "Is there anything else?" she asked Kaj. Her tone was dismissive. She had better things to do. Kaj wondered if she wanted them gone so she could make notes about her interview with them.

He and Jill thanked her and left. In the hallway, out of Malcolm's hearing, Jill suddenly stopped.

"Professor Malcolm is very bitter," she said. "I wonder what she has had to deal with in her career."

Kaj was reluctant to speculate. "I think it's important what she told us. Mrs. Nogawa is possessive about Whitworth. And she's a bow hunter. I think we need to find what the lady uses to bring down those goats."

T HEY HAD JUST reached the car when Kaj's phone rang. It was Cliff telling him that Fred from the student newspaper had called, demanding to speak to him. It seemed the newspaper office had been broken into, and it all had something to do with Kahoʻolawe. Since Kaj had talked to the reporter yesterday, Cliff wondered if Kaj wanted to follow up since they were already on campus.

The other news was more welcome. Cliff was able to confirm that the delivery service at Whitworth's house was indeed AirIbex. Kaipo was getting the details. Also, they had reverse checked the phone number on Mrs. Sam, and it was an address in Waialae-Kahala not far from where Kaj was. Did he want to detour there on the way back from the campus? Kaj did.

Fred was highly indignant when they reached the student newspaper office.

"My files on Kahoʻolawe have gone. They broke into my desk. The bastards. They've torn everything apart. We can't publish the paper." Fred's face was red and he was waving his hands wildly. "This is harassment, and Sergeant Goof-off refuses to believe that we had anything worth stealing. He thinks we did it ourselves to get attention. Who does he think we are? Children?"

"Let's calm down here," Kaj said, feeling rather like Fred's father and trying to resist it. "I doubt you are going to gain much from venting about campus security, so let's take this step by step. When did this happen?"

Fred sat down at a desk, drumming his fingers in agitation. Kaj took a chair next to him while Jill wandered around the room talking with the students who were trying to restore order.

The editor was not to be consoled. "We'd beaten the deadline for once, and hallelujah it looked as if we might not need more late nights this week. We needed one more run-through through today, and that was it. We locked up and left last night. Everything was fine until we got here today after class and found this mess. The bastards. The absolute bastards."

"Who's the we you're talking about?"

"Me, the assistant editor, and the production editor."

"Just you three?"

Fred nodded.

"Did you notice anything when you left last night?"

"No. The light in the hallway was out, but that happens a lot. It takes facilities forever to replace burned-out bulbs when we report them, so it was no big deal to us."

"You didn't see anyone other than you?"

"No. But as I say, it was dark."

"What stories were you running?"

"A preliminary on the Kahoʻolawe plan, an interview with the president about replacing Whitworth, details about the upcoming memorial service, comments from various people on campus, plus a poll on Whitworth's name recognition—did the students know who he was? Did they care?"

"Did they?"

"Most hadn't heard of him. The ones who had any opinion were the students who'd taken his classes or worked for him, and those were mixed."

"Has anyone seemed more interested than normal in your Kahoʻolawe files?"

"Not in the office."

"Who then?"

"The other day, we had students from the Hawaiian Studies program asking where the newspaper stood on the Kahoʻolawe project. It seemed they learned about the project just like we did. They were sent an anonymous email originating from a campus computer lab. We told them the newspaper did not take stands on issues, but we were having difficulty understanding the justification for building anything on Kahoʻolawe except for bomb disposal sheds. Same thing I told you."

"Who are these students?"

"Maile, Kaui, and Chris from Hawaiian studies. They said they were opposed to desecrating yet another Hawaiian Island, and that the university should be ashamed for adding its name to a fraud on the Hawaiian people."

"Did they make any threats?"

"No. Why would they? We agreed with them. Why break in? What would that get them? I'd think they would want us to publish the story and get the word out. Oh, and I forgot, a week ago, Whitworth's secretary—whatever her name is—asked if she could see what we planned to print about her boss. Told her no, we never do that, so she left. No big deal. Otherwise, the Kahoʻolawe project is a non-starter. No one is willing to admit they know anything about it. I don't know what's going on. Did you learn anything from his majesty up in the president's house?'"

Kaj ignored the question. "We don't deal with vandalism," he said.

"I know. I just wanted you to know because it dealt with Kahoʻolawe. I hope you'll give us a scoop if you find something out."

Kaj doubted that was going to happen.

"Did you find anything?" Kaj asked Jill as they walked back to the car.

"The back door has glass inset panels. One is broken. The copy editor said it had not been like that last night. There was no alarm, so once inside the intruder had access to everything. Whoever it was knew what they were looking for. They went straight to the editor's drawer. It's too bad the campus police didn't secure the scene. Judging from the damage, my impression is that the front office vandalism was more staged than real. There's no damage except for the glass in the door."

"Any real evidence that the Kahoʻolawe files were the target?"

"I'd say so. Apparently, the campus police weren't any help."

"I imagine there's history there," Kaj replied. "He told me that Whitworth's secretary had been nosing around, so it sounds like we have even more reason to interview her again. I want to talk to Dawes again too, so let's roll them into one trip up here again tomorrow morning. For now, let's see if we can locate this Mrs. Sam."

29

MRS. SAM LIVED on Hunakai Street in Waialae Kahala at an address listed as belonging to an M. C. Crosswell. The name seemed familiar. Kaj assumed Mrs. Sam must live in the servant's quarters provided by her employer. He and Jill rang the doorbell and heard a Westminster chime sound deep in the house.

The door was answered by a willowy woman with almond eyes that could be described as golden. She was wearing slacks and a cream blouse that emphasized her narrow neck. Everything about her was perfect, from her sleek hairstyle and flawless complexion to her long, manicured nails and designer clothes. She moved like a ballerina, and the tilt of her head was a portrait in itself. Yet she was understated, which enhanced her polite reticence.

Kaj was impressed—not many women could carry this poise without appearing self-conscious. She was like Ming porcelain, delicate, every part a graceful curve. He felt they were intruding.

He introduced himself and Jill and watched her eyes widen. He knew that look, although it was gone in an instant. This was a cultivated woman well versed in concealing her feelings. He wondered why their presence had triggered this response.

"We're looking for Mrs. Sam."

"Can you tell me what this is about?" She stood in the doorway undecided, peering at their credentials and studying their faces, trying to read them. Kaj found himself studied and his character read. It was an unusual yet not unpleasant experience. He noticed that her attention was directed all to him with little attention paid to Jill.

"We're investigating the death of Harrison Whitworth," Kaj said, "and we need to talk with her."

"Is she here?" Jill cut in.

"Please come in." The woman stood back to admit them.

She led them through the entrance hall, past a turquoise swimming grotto dominated by a large Kwan Yin statue, and into a central atrium filled with orchids and ferns. The house glowed with indirect light coming from skylights. There were no real walls. Japanese chests, carved chairs and tables, and silk cushioned sofas defined the living spaces, each marked by shoji screens that could be pulled forward to create privacy or open the house for a large reception. It was a spare house created for luxurious entertaining. From where she invited them to sit in the atrium, they could see through the butler's pantry with its samovars, gold edged plates, tea sets, and crystal glasses, into the kitchen, a fantasy of silver, koa wood, and granite, with stained-glass fronts on the cabinets depicting bird of paradise, plumerias, and orchids.

They were invited to sit at a low table. Kaj heard his knees creak as he settled into place.

"May I offer you a coffee or a cool drink?"

"Thank you anyway, but is Mrs. Sam here?" Kaj asked.

"I believe you are looking for me. I'm Sam to my friends and sometimes Mrs. Sam to people who knew my late husband. I'm Samantha Crosswell. My husband was Morgan Crosswell."

"The developer?" Kaj remembered where he had heard the name.

"Developer, financier, investor—many things."

"He died not too long ago, didn't he?" Jill asked. "Under mysterious circumstances?"

Mrs. Sam bowed her head in acknowledgment. "For a long time, I believed he was murdered. Perhaps that's what I wanted to think, because I did not believe Morgan would go out on a boat and fall overboard. He hated the sea. He became seasick at the slightest wave. But it was ruled death by misadventure. I was told I had to believe he killed himself, even though I shall never understand why. After his death, his partners inherited his business share and found a way for me to stay in this house."

"Who were your husband's partners?" Kaj asked.

"There was a primary *hui* composed of my husband, Wilfred Fong the attorney, and Hitoshi Takai the builder, plus some blind investors. I don't know all their names as they came and went, but I know George Bayliss was one."

"The president of Hawaii National Trust Bank?" Jill remembered his smiling picture in the bank lobby where she opened an account..

"Yes," Sam said, "and I think Bruce Stillman also was involved."

"The HSU athletics coach?" Kaj was impressed. "Do you know what they were working on?"

"They wanted to build a technology park. Morgan was never forthcoming about his projects until they were well underway. He said he didn't want to bring business home with him. I heard later that the project was still moving forward."

"Was Harrison Whitworth involved with your husband's *hui*?"

"He had been offered the chance to be a blind investor, but he didn't accept."

"Do you know why?"

"He told me it would be a conflict of interest and might obligate him in other things."

"He used those words?" Jill asked.

"Yes. We had many conversations about how interwoven affairs are here in Hawaii."

"How did you meet him?' Kaj inquired.

"Harrison called me one day about a month after Morgan's death. He said he wanted to talk about Morgan. He wouldn't say why but asked me to meet him for lunch. I knew who he was, because Morgan had mentioned his name. I hoped he might have more information about Morgan's death, so I agreed."

"What did you talk about?"

"He talked about his misgivings about how people wanted to use his research. He was gracious enough not to discount my grief, and we became friends."

"What misgivings?"

"He felt that the university was being torn apart for profit. I knew very little about the university. I do remember him saying that it didn't seem ethical to him to obtain federal funds for a project and then make commercial profit from it. He used to talk about what he called pure science, knowledge for its own sake and for benefiting human life. He wanted to know if Morgan had expressed any similar concerns."

"And did he?"

"As I said, Morgan seldom discussed business affairs with me. I told him what little I had heard which was as much as I have told you."

"Yet," Jill pointed out, "you became friends?"

"Harrison was charming and I enjoyed his company. We talked about family, happiness, and disappointments. He enjoyed reading and could recall poems from memory. I sensed in him a great sadness he never talked about. My impression was he seemed not to have many friends."

"Were you more than friends?" Kaj asked.

"I don't think anyone can be more than friends. Friendship is an art in itself. But no, we were not lovers if that's what you're asking. That wasn't our connection. We were lonely for different reasons. I had lost my husband. He, for some reason, lived as a solitary man."

"As routine, I must ask you," Kaj said with a slight smile, "where you were on Thursday night."

Mrs. Sam gave a small smile. "I did not harm Harrison. I have no motive. I shall miss him as a dear friend."

"Still, we need to ask you."

"I hosted some people here for dinner. If it is necessary, I can say who it was. But I would prefer not to."

"I'm afraid it is necessary," Kaj said.

"I understand," she said and shrugged. "Wilfred Fong wanted to entertain his associates that evening. This may seem strange to you, but his house is not suitable for the evening he planned, and he preferred not to use a public restaurant or hotel. He asked me to prepare a small party for them. I was here with the catering staff and the guests."

"What time did the evening end?" Jill asked.

"It was a pleasant evening and the guests lingered. It was close to midnight when they left. Then I supervised as the staff restored the house to order."

"These are regular staff?"

"They are on call as needed, supplied by the Aloha Temp Agency. Most have been here before on similar occasions. If you add on the catering staff, there were many here who can tell you that I didn't leave my guests at any time during the evening."

Jill looked perplexed as she and Kaj wended their way out from the house, passing the tranquil Kwan Yin figure by the pool. She waited until they had reached the car before she asked her question.

"Why didn't you press her for the names of her guests.

"Because I have a good idea already, and it will be easy to find out if we need to." Kaj leaned across the front seat. "I think Mrs. Sam is a modern-day geisha, a lovely tradition. She provides a Hawaii version of gracious respite for wealthy business and political leaders who want elegant dinners where they can discuss private business. I'm not sure why she married Morgan Crosswell, but I suspect she is drawn to vulnerable men."

"That sounds very costly," Jill said. "Who's paying for all of this?"

"I imagine they have membership dues plus expenses. She's a professional hostess and caterer. Nothing wrong with that. When they conduct business, her clients want discretion, and she can become invisible when she needs to. She still owns her house, and they can still believe there is beauty in the world. The setting is created to form the mood where agreements can happen. I'm sure a hotel or good restaurant would be as expensive and far less satisfying. It's a wonderful illusion, like a private club. The world needs more of these fantasies."

"You're taken with that idea, aren't you?" Jill laughed with genuine amusement.

"Yes, I suppose I like teamwork, but I'd be crazy to imagine I could ever afford to be a member of that club."

Jill smiled slightly. "So, no one associated with the *hui* is on the suspect list?"

Kaj paused with his hand on the car door handle. "Did I say that? Not on your life. Wilfred Fong is showing up everywhere, and I think it's time we made a call on him and found out what his plans were for Whitworth."

30

KAIPO AND CLIFF were waiting with updates when arrived back to headquarters.

"We've confirmed times when Dawes dropped off the three students," Kaipo said. "The Kaimuki beat officers saw the rickshaw being unloaded; they were intrigued and pulled over to watch the struggle to get it off the truck. The dorms confirmed the time when Paul Nguyen and David Marks checked in. Lucky for us, Eddie Gao was unlucky. He got a speeding ticket on Kalanianaole Highway on his way home to Aina Haina. Curtis's alibi after he dropped them off is still dodgy, but so far things corroborate what he told us. We're still trying to locate Mark Gottschalk and Brendan Hope."

Cliff handed Kaj a clipped batch of copies of shipping bills of lading. "AirIbex confirmed the delivery to the Whitworth house. The shipper was Pacific International Center for Asian Art Auctions in Singapore. But that's just the start. They've been doing regular runs to Whitworth's house. I've got the dates. Their regular delivery time is between 2:00 and 4:00pm. I'm thinking that the cleaning service screwed things up when they came in the afternoon rather than their regular morning time."

"Did the cleaners see the package?" Kaj asked.

"That's the next thing on the agenda," Cliff said. "I'll check with them first thing in the morning."

"Did Horne get back to us on Cheterinda Gowda?" Kaj asked Kaipo.

"Not yet," Kaipo replied. "State's still being slow. But we did check all the sports shops and no one recognized Oliver Stone, so we can't confirm that he ever bought arrows. All the people down at the Blaisdell listening to "Winter Wonderland" are accounted for. Half the university seems to have been there."

"We need to know more about this Pacific Center in Singapore," Kaj said tersely.

"First thing tomorrow," Cliff said. "We found the recipient of the bracelet. It was sent to a Janice de Mello. The address Liberty House gave us was the Women's Studies Department at UC-Berkeley. When we phoned, they told us that she's away for the holidays. She had to be here in Hawaii, so we pressed hard for an emergency address. The department didn't have one but had us talk with an associate who thought she was staying at the Hawaiian Village. We checked it out. Sure enough, she checked in the day Whitworth arrived home."

Kaj and Jill stared at one another. "The author of the books that Whitworth had in his library?" Kaj shook his head. "The more we look at these people, the more complicated it gets. That's another thing we need to follow up with tomorrow."

"We also met Mrs. Sam today," Jill said. "She's a professional hostess for the local bigwig business people. She said she was hosting a dinner for Wilfred Fong the night that Whitworth died. Her guest list provides an alibi for Fong and President Halstead."

"The same Fong who represents the Kuthani Consulate?" Kaipo looked quizzical. "Is that just another coincidence?"

"No, it's not," Kaj said grimly. "They all seem to be involved with this Kahoʻolawe business. There are too many unanswered questions. It's looking more and more that Wilfred Fong is the center of all this, and it's time to get to the bottom of it."

31

"**I met one** of your history professors today," Kaj told Annie when he reached home that night. She was rolling dough to make almond sugar cookies. The fragrance of the almond essence made Kaj's nose twitch.

"Okay, I give up. Who was it?" Annie looked up at her father with her eyes dancing in fun. Kaj had enjoyed playing guessing games with her as she was growing up. It was something they both enjoyed.

"Helen Malcolm." Kaj pronounced the name with an ah-hah moment grin on his face.

The rolling pin stopped in midair, and Annie looked up at her father with a knowing, cheeky smile. He loved that smile. It made him remember Linda at the same age.

"So, you saw Lady Bi." Annie said with a mischievous and very knowing glint in her eye.

"Lady what?" he asked.

"Behind her back, we call her Lady Bi—after Lady Di."

"Sounds very clever and modern." Kaj looked at his daughter with his eyebrow raised.

Annie set down the rolling pin and wiped her hands on the towel wrapped around her waist. "That's one way of saying that she swings both ways."

Kaj tilted his head to one side. He felt that the world had moved on and left him behind.

Annie sighed. "You know, it means she dates men but also has a female partner, a women's coach. You really haven't heard that expression?"

Kaj shook his head. "We're not Vice. CID is innocent. We deal with straightforward murderers."

"Oh, Daddy," Annie said in mock anguish. "Word is that when Lady Bi came up for tenure, the committee didn't recommend her, so she claimed discrimination because they were denying tenure to the sole lesbian in the department. The chairman freaked. He said he hadn't known her sexual preferences and all evaluations had been on her work. She threatened an EEO investigation, Fed stuff, where they come in assuming you're guilty and go from there. The university caved. The administration had to give an extra position to the department for her, so the faculty senate wouldn't vote no confidence.

"Well," Kaj said. "She's one tough lady."

"Dad, she's had to be. She's the only woman in a department of contentious men. Historians have that reputation. She's used to being talked over, talked down to, and her opinions and research topics dismissed. She's been passed over for promotion even though her publishing record is better than most of the full professors'. She'd see someone like Harrison Whitworth as having it easy. He'd fit into the old boy network where she can't. Rumor has it that there's no way they'll give her the promotion she's been angling for, so she'll probably have to sue them again and deal with their retaliation."

"If things are that bad, whatever made you want to major in history?"

"History's like English. It's a doorway to a lot of careers. I never said I was going to teach history, particularly not at a university. But, Dad, if you don't know history, all you've got is opinion and no way to evaluate it. I learned more about human nature from the Greek historians than I do from our modern writers."

Kaj shook his head in amazement. "When did you become so sophisticated?" he asked her. He still remembered the tiny human laid in his arms a few minutes after birth, her face so much looking like Linda's.

"Oh, Dad, all you have to do is listen. Universities are hotbeds of gossip. But they're not the only ones. I bet there's an active rumor mill in your office."

"I've never heard of such a thing."

"You wouldn't, Dad. You're such a straight arrow. But trust me, it happens. The university has more leaks than a water mattress on a bed of nails, if that's not too cliched. But why were you talking to her?"

"It has to do with a case," he replied.

"Oh, I know. You don't want to discuss it. It has to be the Whitworth case. That's all anyone's talking about."

Kaj said nothing. He watched as she used a glass to cut the dough into circles and arrange them on a baking tray. Even uncooked, the batter smelled good. She opened the oven door and slid the tray in.

"Are those the almond cookies I like?" he asked hopefully. A bite of almond cookie could go a long way toward making up for the confusing overlapped relationships he'd had to deal with during the day.

"Sorry, Dad, these are for Mom's school bake sale. We can't do the Jingle Bell run this year with her school group, so she said we'd make cookies instead."

"There won't be any extras?" he asked, smelling how the oven's warmth had already made the kitchen smell good enough to eat.

"Better check with Mom about that." Annie laughed and flicked a piece of dough at him. He caught it and popped it into his mouth. It tasted as good as he remembered.

"So how was your dinner with Malia?"

"It was all right," Annie said. She concentrated on cleaning up the spilled flour on the counter .

"You're home!" Linda came bounding into the kitchen. "I didn't hear you come in."

"I was asking Annie how the dinner went with Malia."

"We went to the China House and had dim sum. It was good to catch up. I hadn't seen Alan since he went off to college. That's one good looking fellow. He's quite the man. Malia's bursting with pride."

"What did you think, Annie," Kaj asked.

"He was all right. Just a guy. Mom, Dad says he wants cookies."

"Not on your life," Linda said. "These are for the school. But I tell you what, if you're good this weekend, I'll make a whole batch for you. Deal?"

"Deal," Kaj grinned. Now there was something else to look forward to besides ending the Whitworth case.

31

JANICE DE MELLO was staying on the 23rd floor of the Rainbow Tower. When Kaj knocked on the door, a male voice answered and the door opened a crack.

"Police," Kaj called out. "We'd like to talk to Janice de Mello."

The door opened an inch or two wider. It took Kaj a few moments to recognize Brendan Hope. There had been a transformation. In the rickshaw video he had worn a Save the Seals t-shirt and looked scruffy. Now he wore a blue shirt and khaki pants that looked new, his beard was gone, leaving pale patches on his face, and his hair had been trimmed. He also looked somewhat self-conscious. Kaj could feel Jill stiffen in surprise as she also recognized him.

"We'd like to speak to Janice DeMello," Kaj repeated.

"She's in the shower." Brendan stared at them and did not open the door any wider.

"That's all right." Kaj held up his badge, "We'll wait. May we come in?"

Brendan hesitated but Kaj had sensed the kid was used to doing what he was told. The door slowly opened. Once inside, they could hear the shower running in the bathroom. Jill canvassed the room while Kaj engaged Brendan. The room was a half suite with two queen beds, a sofa and chairs, a kitchenette with dishes in the sink smelling of fried eggs and toast, and a balcony view of Diamond Head and Waikiki Beach.

"You haven't been to work. They're worried about you." Kaj offered this as an explanation for his and Jill's presence.

"Are they angry with me?" Brendan looked worried. "I haven't been at the lab. Something happened." He glanced toward the bathroom door where the shower had ended. His eyes were sleepy, and he looked stressed.

"How long have you been here in the hotel?" Kaj knew a room like this would be pricey. Someone had money, and Kaj doubted it was Brendan. Both beds had been slept on but the covers had not been drawn back. Kaj assumed the woman was paying.

"A couple of days," Brendan said distractedly as if he had lost track of time.

"Do you stay here often?" Kaj's tone was placid but laced with insinuation.

Brendan's eyes opened wide. He glanced again at the bathroom door and then back at Kaj. "I never come down to Waikiki. It's too expensive."

Just then the bathroom door opened, and the woman came into the room. She was about fifty, wearing blouse and slacks and drying her dark hair with a towel. She stopped when she saw Kaj and Jill.

"The police are here, Mom," Brendan said. "I had to let them in."

Kaj's eyebrows shot up. "Janice de Mello?" he asked.

The woman nodded and peered at the badges Kaj and Jill showed her. She frowned for a moment, rubbed her hair some more and hung the towel over a chair back. She was tall like her son. Her hair was tangled but showed no gray. She didn't look much older than the picture she used on the back cover of all her books.

"We understand you know Harrison Whitworth," Kaj began.

"I wondered when you'd get to me. How did you find me?" She sat in an armchair and gestured for Kaj and Jill to occupy the sofa.

Her son sat on the nearest bed.

"Would you like coffee?" she asked. "Brendan can make us some. No? Well, I could use some. This is going to be a long story."

Brendan got off the bed and started the coffee maker. He seemed as interested in hearing what she had to say as Kaj and Jill were. He doesn't know the whole story either, Kaj thought.

"We read about Harrison's death in the paper yesterday. Someone was going to see a huge coincidence in my being here just as it happened. But I assure you that I didn't have anything to do with it."

"How did you know him?" Jill took the lead and started the questions out with the obvious ones.

"Many years ago, it seems like a lifetime, Harrison and I were graduate students at Harvard. We lived together for three years and went our separate ways after graduation." She spoke without emotion.

Jill picked up the implication that the parting had not been pleasant. "How did the relationship end?" Jill let implied sympathy creep into her voice as if to say, men can be such bastards, can't they?

Janice gave a slight, grim smile and ran her fingers through her wet hair. Brendan leaned forward with interest.

"Call it the prince and the pauper syndrome. I wasn't on the same social level as Harrison, and he couldn't or wouldn't lift me to his. Harrison was old money. I visited his ancestral home once, and there was his family, hung in oil paintings around the dining room. Their paintings were done by famous artists, not like my family's caricatures done at the state fair."

Janice gave a laugh that sounded more like a bark. "Harrison's father wanted his son to run for president, except Harrison didn't like politics. He wanted to be a scientist. Once they agreed to his chosen career, he was expected to become a major scientist—being important was what the family did. I was his first and only real rebellion. But even as he rebelled, he always looked over his shoulder for his mother's approval. Whitworth men are allowed a few wild oats along the way but always go back to mother. Perhaps because the mothers have the money. I was Harrison's wild oats."

"When was the last time you saw Whitworth?" Jill asked.

Janice watched Brendan place a coffee mug on the table for her. She took a sip before she answered.

"On the night I told him I was pregnant." Her matter of fact tone did not match the obvious anguish in her eyes.

"Did you discuss marriage?" Kaj knew it must have been a difficult conversation. Even twenty years ago, attitudes were very different about unwed mothers.

"I did. He didn't. He told me his delicate mother could never accept his marrying a scholarship student from a second-generation Italian family living in Dorchester, Mass. That's where they made shoes for

God's sake. I was intelligent, he said, but my education could never make up for my background. I was furious. I'd believed education was the way up. Pretty naïve. But you know what—all the pomposity seems sad now and an unworthy stereotype of who he was. He wasn't even very original about it."

"You say you hadn't seen him in years, and yet he sends you expensive jewelry?" Kaj frowned slightly at the seeming inconsistency.

"That's how you found me, isn't it? I didn't want it. It frightened me." Janice glanced at Brendan as if she were protectively hugging him.

Kaj noticed the glance. "What made you frightened?"

"I was afraid that Brendan had identified himself as my son. My late husband, Bill, and I raised Brendan. I didn't tell Brendan until after Bill's death that Harrison was his biological father. I didn't want Brendan to come to Hawaii. He could have attended any university on the Mainland. When I saw that I had to allow it, I made one condition. He was not to tell Harrison who he was. If anyone was going to do it, I would. I didn't trust Harrison, and I didn't want Brendan to be devastated by his rejection. After the package arrived from Hawaii, and I saw what it was, I booked the next plane to make sure Brendan was all right. I returned the thing to the place where Harrison bought it and hoped that he would get the message I intended, which was to leave me alone."

"Do you have any idea why he sent it to you?"

Janice looked at Kaj and threw up her hands. "Who knows? After all these years, I'd be the last one to know."

"There was no explanation or a note?"

"Nothing except his business card. But Harrison often did things you were supposed to figure out. He was offended if you couldn't read his mind. Because there were always servants around him whose job it was to cater to him, he just made assumptions."

"And he never made any other effort to contact you?" Jill could see a series of possible motives. "Could he had been feeling guilty about the past? Could he have wanted to resume your relationship?"

'Who knows what he was feeling." Janice's voice had a bitter edge. "He could have found me if he'd wanted to. I kept my maiden name for my professional work. But why do we have to go through this? It's yesterday's news. We didn't kill him."

"Brendan," Kaj said, "why don't you and Detective Nakamura go out on the lanai for a few minutes. Maybe you could tell her some more about that greeting at the airport."

"I know this is uncomfortable for you," Kaj said after Jill and Brendan left, "but we need to know all we can about what he was thinking before he was killed. You lived with him, even if it was a long time ago, so you might have some idea."

Janice ran her fingers through her hair again. She seemed more relaxed with her son out of hearing. "Harrison always had a reason. All I knew was that I wasn't going to share Brendan with him or his mother. Let them get their own son and grandson and leave my boy alone."

Janice looked at her son and Jill through the glass sliding doors. She didn't resume until she was sure they couldn't hear her. Even then she dropped her voice and leaned into Kaj.

"There are certain things I don't choose to tell Brendan. He was raised by a wonderful man whom I married when Brendan was a toddler. Bill didn't just adopt him and give him his name; he became Brendan's father in all senses of the word. I wouldn't have said anything if we hadn't lost Bill to cancer a few years ago. Death makes life seem too short for lies, doesn't it? One day I'm looking at Brendan, and I can see Harrison. Same eyes and profile, same body build. It hit me that I was being selfish by keeping the truth from him. On an impulse I told him."

"How did Brendan take it?" Kaj wondered how he would have reacted if Ai had suddenly told him that Goro was not his father. He wouldn't have liked it.

"Well, he was an adult and had some sense that things don't always go right in the world, but he was still shocked. He and my husband were close, and it took him time to realize that being a good father didn't require a shared blood line. It also took him time to get past feeling betrayed by me. He refused to talk to me for weeks.

"Many times, I wondered if I'd done the right thing, or if I'd destroyed my relationship with him forever. In the end, I was glad I hadn't told him before, because he would never have to see my bitterness toward Harrison. I loved Harrison and, by the time I told Brendan about him, I'd replaced the bitterness with compassion. I recognized how trapped Harrison was. He was like Midas—everything he touched turned to gold, but he could never be happy. He died a Midas death. When his duty to his family conflicted with his duty to me, he prioritized his commitments, and I didn't come out on top. But that doesn't mean he wasn't a decent man, even if warped by the expectations drummed into him from childhood."

"Where did Brendan come out with it?"

"In the end? Mainly curious. He'd been happy with things as they were—so was I for that matter—but with Bill not there to be hurt, Brendan could take a scientific approach. He wondered what he'd inherited. Give Harrison his due, he passed on good genes. His son is bright except for the Whitworth wild oats phase."

"Save the Seals?" Kaj smiled.

"Yes. He was arrested with Green Peace for trying to block the seal killings a few months ago. The Canadians put them in jail. He's rethinking his causes right now, but I imagine he will go right back into the fray. I'm proud that he's standing up for his beliefs."

"Did finding his father become another cause? Is that why he wanted to come to Hawaii?"

"In a way, but he understands, as I do, that things carved in granite seldom change. He hasn't told me what he learned about Harrison. But someone who wins a Nobel Prize is probably overwhelming—and Harrison was like that even before the prize."

"Whitworth never tried to contact you? Never wondered about his child?"

"No. He knew it wouldn't have been any use. You see, when I told him I was pregnant, he made an awful blunder. He questioned whether he was the father and seemed surprised when I was angry. He did admit in the end that it couldn't be anyone else's. I told him I was going to have the baby, and he could go to hell. I went home— to Dorchester—and had Brendan. My mother had died of cancer when I was in high school, so Dad was excited to have us; the only thing he asked was that I avoid people in the future who could hurt me. Then, when I got on my feet, I applied to a new program on women's studies at Berkeley, moved to California, met and married Bill, who was an assistant professor in Economics. I moved on with my life."

"You said you were bitter?" Kaj leaned forward.

"I was. But not anywhere near wanting to harm him. If anything, I would have been satisfied just to yell at him and call him a fool for losing me and Brendan. Harrison was a victim himself in a way, constrained by family duty. I wasn't sure if he could ever be happy. He was the perennial puppy, eager to please and looking for the approving pat on the head."

Janice rubbed her hair with the wet towel and threw it toward the bathroom door where it fell on the floor.

"I met his mother once. She was gracious enough, but I could see her take in every detail of my clothing and manners. I thought her burdened herself by the same expectations as he was. I couldn't imagine her doing anything impulsive or making messy mistakes. I bet her maid ironed her underwear. Harrison couldn't deal with conflict when it involved competing forces in his life. He just wanted peace."

She stopped for a moment to look at Kaj. "Eleanor Whitworth was everything I found impossible to emulate and difficult to admire. Perhaps Harrison was right. I was Dorchester through and through. My first book was about women in so-called democratic societies with de facto colonial class structures. Right now, I feel sad that he missed so much. If I'd known what was going to happen, I wouldn't have asked Brendan not to talk to Harrison. I regret that he didn't know his beautiful boy. I could have been at least that generous. Now I have to live with that."

"You've had no contact with his department or the university?"

"Just with Brendan, although I did talk several times with someone named Dawes. I can't remember his first name. When Brendan was jailed in Canada, he asked me to call this Dawes about keeping his research assistantship open for when he was released."

"Was he able to?"

"As it worked out, yes. The Canadians could have given him a year in prison. In the end, Canada deported him and told him not to come back. Brendan was a week late returning to school, but he made it in time. Dawes told me that he had prepared letters from the anemone project to send to the Canadian judge; he'd also arranged for the university president to express support. He said he'd try to get a Hawaii US Senator to write as well, but in the end, it wasn't needed."

"Do you know of anyone who might have wanted to harm Whitworth?"

Janice shook her head. "All I know about his work is the Nobel Prize announcement. The Harrison I knew played everything straight, except for me." She laughed with genuine amusement and Kaj glimpsed the vivacity and spontaneity that must have attracted a man controlled by family and destiny.

"I have to ask you this," Kaj said apologetically. His gut was telling him that this woman wasn't the killer, but was that just sympathy? "Where were you on Thursday night?"

Janice nodded as if to assure Kaj that she understood the need for formalities. "I flew United from San Francisco, landed at six Thursday night, rented a car, and checked into the hotel. I hadn't had time to tell Brendan I was coming. I left messages for him once I got here, but he didn't call back until after one in the morning. I suppose that means I don't have an alibi. I picked Brendan up early the next morning from his apartment. We had breakfast and then went down to Ala Moana to get him the services of a barber and buy him some clothes. I still have the receipts if you want to see them."

Janice squared her shoulders and looked suddenly proud. "But let me tell you something. I see Harrison every day in his son. Brendan has his sense of duty, his passion for history, his charm, and his vulnerability. I could never harm Harrison, because it would be the same as harming my son. No parent has the right to impose issues on their child. I wanted Brendan to like him; I wanted Harrison to like his son. I just didn't want to be involved. If I were to meet Harrison's mother now, I'm not sure what I could say to her. She was the primary reason there was no future for Harrison and me."

"You said before that he could have found you if he wanted to?" Kaj remembered Whitworth's computer and the collection he'd made of anything to do with Janice and their son.

"Yes. Someone with a computer could Google me, and there I would be."

"We think he did," Kaj said. "He had your books in his home, and when we searched his computer, we found pictures of you and your family."

Kaj watched as Janice struggled with her emotions, surprise yielding to confusion, and then annoyance that she had been placed in a vulnerable position without warning. "Oh my God," she said. "That means he knew who Brendan was? And he didn't say anything?"

"It looks that way. But weren't you expecting this might happen? If it was easy to find you, would it be so hard for him to find your son?"

Janice shook her head. "I don't know what I was thinking. But if Harrison knew Brendan a little, maybe that's what I was hoping for and didn't know it. This changes everything. I don't know what to think now. Why didn't I figure that out?"

"There's a memorial service for him on the university campus on Monday," Kaj said. "I hear the Governor will be there and many of his university colleagues. If you come, you and your son might learn more about his life here in Hawaii."

"Let me think about it. There's nothing I have to rush home for. Bill's not waiting anymore." Janice looked at her son through the glass lanai door, and when she looked back at Kaj, her eyes shone with a glaze of tears.

32

KAJ AND JILL drove straight from the Hawaiian Village to Fong's office. It was located on the top floor of a Bishop Street high-rise building and was furnished to impress. A large piece of tapa bark hung on the entry wall. Beneath it was a highly polished dark wood credenza displaying museum-quality Hawaiian wood bowls and calabashes. Pictures of old Hawaii sleekly mounted in Koa frames hung on the other walls. Most impressive of all, though, was the view of Iolani Palace, the State Capitol, and the Koʻolau range.

Kaj and Jill had deliberately not given Fong warning that they were coming. They planned instead to take up position in his waiting room and sit there until he talked with them. Fong did not appreciate their strategy and kept them waiting.

"When people make appointments to see me, they pay for it," he sniffed when they were shown in.

"Which is why we didn't make an appointment. I am sure you can make an exception," Kaj said crisply. "Your name crops up wherever we go. The Crosswell death. The Kahoʻolawe project. Hawaii State University. The Kuthan Consulate. We're practically tripping over you. Were you and your partners planning to invest in Whitworth's institute?"

"You're here because you think I killed Whitworth?" Fong snorted. "Is that what you think? That's absurd. You're wrong, and I can tell you why. But what I say is off the record. I mean that."

"You know I can't promise that."

"Then I won't tell you."

The two men faced each other across Wilfred Fong's capacious Koa wood desk. For a moment, the sole sound was tick of the pendulum swinging in a large, grandly-carved grandfather clock bearing the crest of the Hawaiian royal family.

"I'll promise this," Kaj said finally. "If what you tell me has no bearing on the case, I'll forget you ever said anything."

"It has no bearing, so you can file this away in un-useful knowledge. Morgan Crosswell was not murdered, despite what Mrs. Sam thinks. He killed himself, because he wanted to protect her. He made unwise investments outside the *hui* and faced bankruptcy. He knew that Hitoshi and I were fond of Mrs. Sam. Not in a carnal way. Stifle your policeman's brain of yours. If he had gone through with his bankruptcy, the house in Waialae Kahala would have gone and she would have had nowhere to go. He asked me what he could do. I laid out the facts."

Kaj and Jill looked at one another. Jill was wide-eyed. "You encouraged him to commit suicide?"

"Absolutely not," Fong replied instantly. "No such thing. I was pragmatic and tried to help him by laying out possible scenarios. He came to his own decision and never discussed it with me. After his death, the *hui* took over his debts, called in some favors to make sure his life insurance was paid, and advised Mrs. Sam not to look a gift horse in the mouth."

"The *hui* assumed his debts?" Kai furrowed his brow. "Why would they do that? They must have added up to a considerable amount if he was facing bankruptcy."

"They did. But in a small community like this State, reputation is everything. You should know that, Inspector. You were born here. Businessmen who hate one another will sit together on a platform with no visible animosity between them. This is the Island Way. Had Morgan gone through bankruptcy, it would have cast a shadow over the *hui* and its members. Morgan had not lived here all his life, but he understood what was at stake. Not that he did it for us. He loved his wife and did it for her."

"And where does Whitworth fit in?" Kaj was starting to see the lay of the land. Big money investors had no time for sentiment.

"He didn't. He was invited into the *hui* business as a peripheral player. Sometimes, when someone represents a strong business interest to a *hui* member, he'll be invited to invest a small amount, perhaps a few thousands, with the expectation of a payoff somewhere down the line. It's a useful way to slip money in specific directions. Completely legal."

"That's how Coach Stillman was included?" Kaj began to connect the dots.

Fong crinkled his eyes in amusement. "I see Mrs. Sam has been talking. Still off the record. Hitoshi happens to be a big fan of HSU football. He was devastated when he heard Nebraska was courting Coach Stillman. Hitoshi hates Nebraska from his days as a business major at the University of Colorado. Since Stillman had taken HSU to national ranking and could be expected to repeat it, Hitoshi figured if we included Stillman on a limited investment, we could induce him to stay. Again, completely legal. And the coach did stay at HSU."

"But Whitworth didn't bite on your offer?"

"Well, for starters, George Bayliss, as a banker, knew the financials and dropped the hint that Whitworth was so wealthy that whatever the *hui* could offer would be small change. In my experience, money can either improve or ruin you. You can have so much it means nothing, or you can be consumed by it for its own sake. In Whitworth's case, it was the former.

"He professed to be horrified when business interests believed they could invest in his ideas and even expect a profit. I say professed, because I'm skeptical myself. I don't know. Perhaps the man was sincere. But he did everything possible to maximize the science and minimize the profit. It was idiotic, because science is nowhere without money, and unless the scientists up in Kamaboko Institute have developed a new system for printing US currency, science and money intersect. New buildings are expensive and someone needs to build them."

"Why not your *hui*, is that it?" Kaj kept his face stolidly calm in the face of what sounded like financial gymnastics. He had a sudden image of Fong picking his way along a seawall dodging huge waves on one side and sharks on the other. If making money took that kind of dexterity and risk, Kaj was content to be poor.

"Of course. We help wherever we can." Fong gave a smug smile as if he had read Kaj's thoughts and wanted to assure him that the seawall was quite safe as long as one had connections and lifelines.

"And what about Kahoʻolawe?" Kaj wondered what tale of financial derring-do he was about to be told.

Fong leaned back in his leather chair and cradled his fingers. "You have to distinguish between Kahoʻolawe the concept and Kahoʻolawe the project. The concept was useful. The project was not."

"You'll need to explain that." Kaj had the idea he was being toyed with and didn't like it.

"Senator Kamaboko was impressed with Harrison Whitworth. I'm sure Whitworth thought the senator was attracted by his scientific work, and a Nobel Prize would seal the deal with international reputation and endorsement—notice the endorsement part. Hawaii responds primarily when there is outside recognition. It's a frail insecurity, but you have to work with what you have.

"The Senator is a senior politician whose popularity ensures his reelection, so he focuses on bringing jobs and investment to the Islands. Whitworth represented an enormous opportunity for economic development. The HSU president thought along the same lines as the senator, although his primary focus was increasing prestige for the campus. The Governor quickly came on board and, with him, the *hui*.

"What we wanted was for Whitworth to provide scientific impetus and credibility to help the senator direct federal dollars to the State. Whitworth's part was to do the science, write the grants, and provide the image while we built the infrastructure around him."

Fong looked at Kaj with a slight sneer. "But—and I don't mean this unkindly because we had plans to deal with it—Whitworth's big problem was that he was an academic, the opposite of a realist. He thought his scientific work alone would attract grants and funding without behind-the-scenes work and lobbying here and in Washington. We were in the process of educating him when he was killed.

"This means, if you're understanding me—his death is the worst possible thing that could have happened to the *hui* or to this State.

There is no one on the horizon to replace him, and we all stand to lose millions and the jobs those dollars represent. That, Inspector, is the real disaster."

"I'm still confused about Kahoʻolawe," Kaj said.

Fong chuckled at Kaj's slowness to grasp the obvious. "I'm surprised you don't get it. Nobody ever intended to build a scientific facility on Kahoʻolawe. We had a basic problem within the *hui*. Two members had associates who owned land suitable for the institute as the senator envisioned it. One was on Oahu, the other on the Big Island. The Governor favored one. The university favored the other. Both islands wanted the investment and the jobs. There was no way we could divide the institute equitably between the islands, so George Bayliss and I cooked up this diversionary plan for Kahoʻolawe. We persuaded the HSU president to go along, knowing full well that the Hawaiian community would rise up in arms about the possible misappropriation of Kahoʻolawe, and the heat would be so intense that we could persuade the two competing islands to negotiate in the interests of community."

Fong chuckled. He was clearly enjoying himself. "That's another Island Way. Obvious controversy needs to be dealt with behind the scenes. That's what happened. It has not been announced yet, but the institute will be sited on one island, while the other will receive other projects to soften the disappointment. The university will be persuaded to accept that the decision was made downtown rather than on campus, but, come budget time next year, the university will be rewarded. Everyone's face is saved, and life can continue."

"Did Whitworth know that building on Kahoʻolawe was a myth?"

"We hadn't concluded our negotiations, so not at that point. We were planning to discuss it with him. Unfortunately, Hitoshi let slip something about it, not understanding that Whitworth hadn't been brought on board."

"What if Whitworth hadn't agreed?"

"He would have received a phone call from the Senator's DC office. If necessary, we would have called in favors at the White House. The Governor would have held a reception in his honor at Washington Place with invited State legislators from both houses and parties as well as the university administration. There would have been a persuasive dinner at Mrs. Sam's with the *hui* and President Halstead, followed by a front-page newspaper article and an editorial praising the plan. I assure you he would have come along."

Fong smiled benevolently. "You may see violence every day in your job. But that's not how things work in Hawaii's business world."

Kaj withheld judgment. "Mr. Fong, what your role is in all this?"

"As part of the *hui*, I manage legal matters as my contribution, but outside the *hui* I also work with corporate investors. One way or another, I am nearly always involved in major projects."

"Does anything get done without you?" Kaj's eyebrow rose in its quizzical arch.

"I try not to let it." Fong made a cathedral again out of his laced fingers.

"And the Kuthani Consulate?"

"Embassies are a new practice. I can't discuss my clients with you, but I can tell you that my international practice is recent. I received a phone call from one local embassy asking for assistance with the State Department. I dropped everything to deal with it. From there it has been word of mouth."

"What can you tell us about the Kuthani Consulate?"

Fong leaned forward with interest. "Not a lot because of attorney-client privilege. But I can tell you that the Kuthani Consulate is a closed shop. The staff do not often interact with other embassies and are seldom seen at public gatherings. Some of my consular clients were even surprised to hear Kuthan has a presence here. Most serious business, if they have any, is negotiated between the US Government and Kuthan in DC or through a third party. The local staff seem to process tourist visas. It's a big question mark what the embassy is doing here at all."

"But if that's all they do, are there that many tourist visa applications to keep them in Hawaii?" Jill looked confused and intrigued at the same moment.

"That's the point," Fong said as he scratched his chin. "They want tourism, but on their own terms. From what I hear, they have a quota on visitors and go so far as to interview the applicant before they grant an entry permit. They don't say what they are looking for, and they don't give a reason if they turn someone down. It took my nephew two years to get a visa, and then he had to provide references on his good character. Amazing. On the one hand, this makes visiting the country a status symbol, because it's hard to get in and it's not an overcrowded Nepal. On the other, the growth of their tourism is glacial. Nepal needs the money from climbing licenses. Kuthan does not. It's all that hydroelectric money."

"You have no idea then why the consulate is here in Hawaii?" Kaj was secretly amused. Here was one piece of information that they had and Fong didn't. He wasn't about to enlighten him.

"None at all, and I'd be interested in learning. The State Department may know, but I certainly don't. Still, there are advantages. Now and then they throw a very nice reception—not like the local political fundraiser crap I get stuck with. Pure extortion: fifty dollars or more for homemade sushi and over-fried egg rolls. If you ever get invited to a Kuthani reception, accept immediately."

"I'll keep that in mind," Kaj said dryly. "Now, where were you on Thursday night?"

"As you very well know, since you talked with Mrs. Sam, I hosted a dinner at her house to sort out this Kahoʻolawe mess. The *hui* was there, so were President Halstead and State leadership from the two islands involved. It was heated at times, everyone stayed to the end, and we left after midnight with an agreement. The food was superb. Trust me, that's another invitation you want to accept."

33

"**Y**ou were very quiet," Kaj told Jill as they went down in the elevator after leaving Fong's office.

"I watch, and I learn." She crinkled her eyes in amusement. "It's not often I get the chance to see Hawaii politics on display. I would have been direct with him and cut to the chase."

"And he would have backed off," Kaj laughed, feeling a little of Fong's glow himself. "The trick was to start him talking. I knew he wanted me to know how cleverly he and the *hui* work. All I had to do was give him permission."

"And you know that how?" Jill tilted her head to look at Kaj almost playfully.

"When he complained that we hadn't made an appointment, he meant he would have liked more time to prepare. That meant he either planned to lie to us or to share something that made him look good. I guessed the latter. It was confirmed when he started to negotiate how the information could be shared. He also wanted to know if we had any information that he didn't. I wouldn't play his game. But he did get some satisfaction. He strung out the drama and created suspense.

I imagine he's feeling pretty good right now. Scratch a lawyer and you get an actor. I'm told he puts on a good performance in court."

"If you look at it that way," Jill said as she got into the car, "using Kaho'olawe as a red herring was quite inspired. But did anyone really take it seriously?"

"The Hawaiian students did." Kaj started the car, pulled out of parking lot, and began the maneuvers Honolulu's one-way streets required on the way back to headquarters. "Fong was counting on them to protest loudly. Whitworth was priming a rich vein of resistance when he talked to the Hawaiian students. Only problem was that he was wrong and didn't know it."

Kaj's phone rang as they approached headquarters. It was Cliff. "You wanted information on any movements from the Kuthani Consulate. We've just heard that Liu is booked on a flight to Bangkok this afternoon. If you want to talk to him," he said, "you'd better get a move on."

Kaj put the blue light on the car roof and turned on the siren.

"Let's see if we can do better this time with Mr. Liu," he said.

38

THEY REACHED THE airport shortly before Liu checked in and were waiting for him on the other side of security. They watched as he was guided to the security line by the man they recognized as Han, Mallik's second in command at the consulate security office. Once Liu was in line, Han left him to it.

Liu looked dazed when an officer picked up his hand baggage and escorted him to the room where Kaj and Jill were waiting.

"Mr. Liu," Kaj said slowly as he gestured for the man to take one of the three chairs around the table. "We know you speak a little English."

Liu bowed at them several times, then sat down and nodded his head.

"You wanted to talk to me?" Kaj sat down and waited.

"Sometimes, things not right." Liu frowned. He struggled with the words, pausing as he spoke each one. He seemed to understand more than he was able to speak.

"Was I wrong?"

Mr. Liu shook his head vigorously. "Darkness bad."

"I agree," said Kaj. "I look for people who hurt others."

"Difficult. You understand? Harmony?"

"I understand. What did you want to tell us?"

Liu looked relieved. "In Consulate, trust only tranquil people."

"I understand." Right there, Kaj remembered with gratitude the lessons Ai had taught him about nuance. He sat back in his chair and looked significantly at Liu. "Do you feel better?"

"Yes." Liu stood up and bowed several times again. "I see doctor. I have pills. I go home now, be well. Thank you. Thank Mr. Fong."

Liu gathered his belongings eagerly and Kaj did not try to stop him. From the doorway, he bowed again to Kaj and then to Jill, his expression suggesting that a large load had been lifted from him. Kaj watched him scuttle away.

Jill looked perplexed. "What just happened? Did he tell you what you wanted to know?"

"Yes, he did." Kaj looked down the hallway where he could just make out Liu disappearing into a waiting lounge. "He was actually quite courageous."

"You're going to have to explain all this code and understatement to me again."

"He told me that there is something wrong in the consulate. I'm not sure if there is a connection to the Whitworth case yet, but I suspect there may be. He says there are people in the consulate who don't belong or are not pure Kuthani."

"How did you even know what he was talking about?" Jill looked completely confused.

"It's a knack. It comes with practice," Kaj's eyes were twinkling. He wished Jill could have met Ai. His mother would have liked Jill's earnest sense of duty.

"It's really just putting two and two together," he said. "You know Kuthanis can't expose one of their own. He had to find a way to tell me what he knew without violating their code, and he had to justify it to himself. Thanks to Greg, I knew their code."

"Practice, huh?" Jill looked at him doubtfully. She suspected it had more to do with being born in Hawaii. She knew she had a long learning curve ahead of her.

"Now we have to figure out how to identify them," Kaj said. "But it means we need to get back into the consulate, and I have no idea how we're going to pull that off."

34

WHEN KAJ REACHED home that night, he was done in. Campuses, consulates, and *huis* were almost too much for one mind to grasp. At that point, he wanted to solve the case and get some sleep.

Linda, though, was waiting up for him as always. This time she had a wry smile as she put out the leftovers from the past few days. Early in their marriage, they had agreed never to waste food. On the nights when they ate whatever was left in the fridge, Linda said they were eating filet of leftover.

He never minded. It was like reading a food diary of the past week. This evening, she put kalbi and chicken down on the table along with fresh rice and potato salad. At that point he would have eaten macaroni cheese and spam and pronounced it gourmet.

She sat down beside him. "Hard day?" she asked.

"Busy, frustrating, the usual."

"Well, we've got an invitation that I don't see any way we can avoid."

"What's that?" He looked at her with tired, anguished eyes. What now, he thought.

"We've been invited to Moses and Malia's for dinner."

Kaj's shoulders fell in discouragement. "I thought we agreed that I could get through this case before we talked about that. Is this what you and Malia planned when you met up the other day?"

"No. It wasn't me or Malia. It's Annie and Alan. They hadn't seen each other since high school. They couldn't take their eyes off one another. They met for lunch today and decided that it was time that the families got together. Kaj, I'm not kidding. Even though they've just met again, I have a feeling this could become serious."

"Annie didn't think he was so special the other night when I asked."

"Annie's your daughter. Do you think she's going to admit anything personal to her parents? You didn't tell your parents that I was your girlfriend until you were ready to propose. Why would she be any different? The kids are curious about when you and Moses served together in the army."

"Don't you realize that I've been avoiding Moses for that very reason?" Kaj was too tired to think about what he was admitting.

"Now you have to explain yourself," Linda said. "What are you talking about?"

"Moses tells everyone about what happened when we were in Vietnam. I have repeatedly asked him not to."

"That doesn't make sense, Kaj. You were upset, because he told everyone that you're a decorated war hero?"

"I don't need that attention. It's over. I don't want to hear about it. There were other men did much more than I did."

"There probably were," Linda agreed, "but there were enough people who thought what you did meant something, and they gave you the medal to honor it. But is that the real reason? Or is it the nightmares?"

Kaj put down his fork and looked at her in dismay.

"You know about them?"

"Of course, I do. I keep notes on them, and I can tell you that they started getting worse once you decided to stay away from Moses. Did you make that connection? I did."

"It was the other way round. I tried to stay away because they had come back, and I didn't want to burden anyone with my problems. I'm an adult. I can deal with them myself."

"Really?" Linda replied. "And who convinced you that you would be shamed if you asked for help?"

"I try to keep things private. I remember wanting to keep our engagement secret for a little while. I wanted to enjoy it alone with you. Our lives don't have to be on someone's front page."

"So that's why you proposed during a Cazimero concert at the Waikiki Shell," Linda laughed. "You knew I couldn't tell anyone right away."

"It was ours to know for a moment," Kaj admitted. "Once you told everyone, then there were parties and planning and photographers and food. The world took over our lives. I'd have been just as happy eloping to Las Vegas and being married by an Elvis impersonator."

"You realize you've just changed the subject," Linda said.

"And I need you to allow me to do it," Kaj replied.

"Well, honey, here it is in a nutshell. I fell in love with you, because you are steady and calm. In my house, everyone yelled at once. I like how you watch people and learn from them. I love your sensitivity and thoughtfulness. My family kept on going until they hit a wall. You don't move until you've decided how thick the wall is and have made plans for how to get over it. Do you have any idea how comforting that is? I can't speak to the baggage you and Moses brought back with you from the war, but this business with Annie and Alan is different. You're our hero and we need you."

"Not everyone. When I came home, a medal and a dollar would have bought me a cup of coffee. The HSU campus was no place to talk about the war. The faculty were even worse than the students."

"It was the times, Hon. The war polarized people. Campuses were where guys went to get deferments. What do you suppose they felt when you came home? They had to argue that you were a fool, because every time they looked at you, they were reminded that you went and they didn't. But there were many others who opposed the war and still respected your service. I was one of them. I told Moses about the nightmares. We just want you to be happy and find peace."

"Dad came home from Europe and handled his experiences okay. He had much worse fighting with the 442nd in Italy."

"You thought it was weakness that you couldn't just set the memories aside? But, Kaj sweetie, what makes you think your dad handled them so well?"

"He never said anything about it to my sister or me. I thought he was superman."

"And that's how he dealt with it. He refused to talk. But your mother told me of many nights when she sat up holding him while he cried. They just didn't want to bother you children."

"I didn't know." Kaj looked stunned. "They never said anything."

"Samurais, both of them," Linda smiled. "But your dad's generation were much clearer about why they were fighting. They came home to a heroes' welcome. The Viet Nam vets were alone in an unpopular war. Their war was violent and brutal, yes, but they were much clearer about why they were fighting."

"Moses seems to have handled it okay. I didn't feel I'd done anything to deserve a medal. I wish people would stop talking about it." Kaj looked moodily out of the kitchen window. It was dark outside so all he saw was his own reflection thrown back at him. He wanted the conversation over.

Linda was unwilling to let him slip away. "Moses says he came through because he had you. You've never let him tell you how much you meant to him and the rest of the platoon. He says you shut him down if he tried."

"I wish he wouldn't talk about it like that." Kaj folded into himself, seeking that place where he could escape and shut down his emotions.

Linda reached out and dragged him back.

"He wants to tell you that the world needs you to give us hope. That's what I'm telling you, and that's what we're asking of you. Please let's go to the Mahi's for all of our sakes. Let's get beyond the past. There's no knowing what lies ahead for Annie and Alan. I don't want to face it without you."

Kaj looked into Linda's eyes and remembered all the late nights when he worked difficult cases, the times that she had covered for him when he couldn't be at Annie's school events, and the disappointments when he had been forced to go back on his promises of vacations. That was the common life of a CID detective. It was no one's fault. If anything, it was the ebb and flow of human life.

CID headquarters was where life's frustrations came to work themselves out. It wasn't pretty and it wasn't predictable. Kaipo's wife had left him because of it. But it was also one of the few places where it was possible to make a difference, if you could only envision what that difference was and how to make it happen.

Linda had stayed with him through all the difficult years and put up with everything. It wasn't often that she asked for anything, and he knew he owed her far more than an awkward dinner. Facing Moses might even be something he needed to do for himself. He knew that when he saw Moses again, there would be no turning back. For a moment, he hung on the precipice of his emotions, but then he resigned himself to what he already knew. It was time to face the past.

"All right," he said slowly, "if it's that important to you, we'll go."

35

KAJ WENT TO work the next day, feeling out of sorts with the world. He would not back away from his promise to go the Mahis. He owed that to Linda and Annie, but, even as he said that he would go, he had not promised to enjoy it. That was his secret reservation, and it powered his new, gritty determination to shake truths out of the HSU campus.

As he and Jill approached the Kamaboko Institute, his mouth set in a grim line. This time he was going to deal with the campus on his own terms.

Mrs. Nogawa was not at her desk, so he and Jill went to the lab in search of her. They found Curtis Dawes in his office and settled on him.

"We're tying up loose ends," Kaj told him in his best no-nonsense voice. "Tell us what happened to Douglas Williams."

"You know that privacy laws don't allow me to discuss him," Curtis heard the command in Kaj's voice and didn't like it. "I told you that before."

Kaj ignored him. "We know he had some sort of a breakdown. We know that he threatened Whitworth and tried to set fire to the institute. You can insist on not talking with us, but that won't protect him. We'll get a warrant for his contact information and waste everyone's time. I'm told you stay in contact with the graduate students, so you must know where he is. All we need to know is whether it was possible for him to come back to the Islands and finish what he started. It's that easy."

Dawes looked down at his desk resentfully. He didn't like being thrust into a corner. He didn't doubt Kaj could do what he said, but he also didn't want to see harm come to the student or the project. "I don't know who's been talking to you. You don't know how serious this could be if there's a complaint."

"No one's going to complain," Kaj growled.

"We just need to exclude him as a suspect." Jill's tone was more soothing. "If you can clear this up, it won't have to go any further."

Dawes sighed again. "All right. But I want it known that I'm doing this only because I feel coerced. I can tell you categorically that it's not possible for Doug to be involved. He started hearing voices telling him to set fire to a trash barrel in the lab. We extinguished the fire quickly before there was much damage, but it could have been disastrous if the flammable chemicals had caught fire. There was no way we could continue to employ him.

"When I contacted his sister, she told me he had a history of instability. Rather than see him charged with arson, she offered to fly here overnight from Oklahoma and take him home. The anemone project rented a hotel room for him until she arrived and paid for security to stay with him to make sure he didn't run away. Harrison met with the sister and then convinced campus security not to report the incident officially.

"That's what happened. The registrar's office withdrew him from school, and Harrison paid him for the duration of his contract, which was decent. So, no, Inspector, there is no way he could have returned to harm Harrison. He is still receiving treatment at an in-patient facility in Tulsa. I spoke with his sister the other day."

"Thank you," Kaj said. "That's all we needed. You've helped him and this investigation as well. Now, do you have any idea where Mrs. Nogawa is?"

Dawes looked at his watch. "The support staff meets once a month in the auditorium downstairs. She should be back by now. I haven't seen her so far today."

Mrs. Nogawa was still not in her office, but this time, they decided to sit down and wait. As he looked around, Kaj noticed a large framed picture of goats on the Molokai cliffs. He gave Jill a nudge, but she'd seen it too. About fifteen minutes later, the lady came through the door and stopped dead when she saw them.

"We have a few questions," Kaj said.

Mrs. Nogawa did not look happy, but Kaj's frown convinced her not to resist. She walked to her desk and gestured for them to pull up chairs. She kept the desk between them.

Kaj gave no opening pleasantries. He got to the point. "Why were you asking about the Kahoʻolawe project at the student newspaper office?"

Mrs. Nogawa's eyes opened wide in fright. "I wanted to know what the newspaper was planning to write."

"Why?" Jill asked.

"Meddle you mean? Harrison was due home, and I was sure he was going to ask me about it. Also, I wanted to protect Harrison. I heard him shouting at Vice President Napa on the phone. It was something about Kahoʻolawe. I could hear what he was saying out here. He threatened to close the project down and move it to California. He said the university and the State would steal his research over his dead body. Later that day, I know he contacted the Hawaiian studies department and the student newspaper and encouraged them to protest. I only wanted to know what they were doing with the information."

"Then let me ask you," Kaj said bluntly, "were you the one who vandalized the newspaper office?"

Mrs. Nogawa reared her head indignantly. "I most certainly did not. I did nothing of the kind."

"Then what were you doing at Harrison Whitworth's house the night he was killed?"

Mrs. Nogawa started and jerked back in her chair. Her lip trembled and her eyes grew moist. "Why would I be there?" Her voice was weak and her denial unconvincing.

"That's what we're asking you. We know someone took lab boots and left footprints on the slope above his house. The boots were too large for the person who wore them, so we knew it could have been a woman. We could account for everyone else who had access to the lab after hours, except you. You told us you were home, so you had no real alibi. So, let me repeat the question: what were you doing up there?"

"I didn't kill him," she choked out. "I could never hurt him."

"That doesn't answer the question," Jill said sternly. "Why were you there?"

Tears trickled down Mrs. Nogawa's face. It was several minutes before she could bring herself to answer. "I had to know," she whispered. "I had to know if he had taken that odious Helen Malcolm with him to Stockholm. I pictured them coming back to his house from the airport and having champagne. All those years I gave up to support him and his work. It should have been me who went with him."

"Because you loved him?" Jill gave a small apologetic smile. The scenario of jealous secretary and unaware employer was as cliched as murders committed by generations of guilty butlers. But still, it had to be asked.

"No. Out of justice and fairness. I was the one who made his work possible. I deserved better than her taking what should have been mine. I hadn't thought through what I would do if I saw them together, but I had to know."

"So you stood under a tree in cold rain to see if a rival had won the prize you thought you'd earned?" It sounded like something out of a gothic novel.

"Not if you put it that way," she sobbed. "I never saw him. I knew when he was due home, because I booked his ticket. I allowed an hour for him to clear customs and half an hour to drive back from the airport. I got to his house around ten thirty. I didn't park on his street because I thought he'd recognize my car. I parked one-road down and walked up the ravine beside his house. There was a party in the house below his. It was dark in the trees, and I thought no one would notice my little flashlight. When I woke the mynahs, I was afraid someone would hear. After half an hour I realized that he must have stopped somewhere on his way home. Perhaps he'd even gone to her place. It was wet and muddy, and I started to feel ridiculous as well as cold."

Mrs. Nogawa took out a tissue from her desk and blew her nose.

"When it turned eleven, I gave up and said she could have him. I was starting on my way back towards the ravine when I heard a car drive up and stop on the road. It wasn't Harrison, or he would have opened the garage. Footsteps came towards me. I was too afraid to use my flashlight, so I hunched over and used my hands to pick my way down the ravine. It was difficult until someone in the lower house opened the door and came out on the lanai. The light made it easier for me to get down. I heard a sliding door open and, then the boards creaked. I heard someone talk on a phone."

"Could you hear what was said? Was it a man or a woman?" Kaj was suddenly very interested.

"A man. He was talking in a foreign language. The only sound I could make out was an occasional yes. He said it several times and then went back in."

"Did you hear the door close?" Kaj asked.

"Yes," Mrs. Nogawa said, "but all I wanted to do at that point was get to the road below and get away. But when I got to my car, I was curious about who had been in the trees with me. I decided to drive up Harrison's street. All I saw was a silver or white car parked down by the street light. I couldn't see inside because the windows were tinted, but I noticed that the license plate wasn't green and white. It was pale blue. I couldn't see anything else, so I left and drove home."

"Mrs. Nogawa, we understand that you do bowhunting on Moloka'i," Kaj said, abruptly changing the subject.

"My family has a cabin over there, and we meet each year to go goat hunting. But why's that important?" Mrs. Nogawa looked non-plussed by the question.

"We need to ask you about it. What type of bow do you have and how is it equipped?"

"I have a compound bow with 60- and 70-pound draw weights. It's a light bow that I can carry easily. But why are you asking?"

"Where is the bow right now?" Kaj's voice was stern and no-nonsense.

"At my house." Mrs. Nogawa suddenly put her hand to her mouth. "Oh my God, Harrison wasn't . . ." Her voice trailed off. "You don't think that I . . . ?"

"We'd like your cooperation. We need to inspect it."

She nodded dumbly, the horror of realizing how he died making her loss both more real and more appalling. They left her preparing to meet Cliff at her house to transfer the bow into custody.

"Could the car she saw be the one registered to the Kuthani Consulate?" Jill asked. "The patrol officers noticed it when they picked up Liu. They said it was silver. We've been assuming that Liu parked it on Whitworth's road. But what if it had been driven by someone else?"

Kaj had made the same connection. "Whoever was driving it was also watching the house. The Consulate may have a sign-out system on their cars, but we would still need a reason to ask them for access."

Kaj sighed. "Horne isn't going to like this one bit," he said.

36

Kaj rose from his desk with dread that afternoon when he saw Vice Consul Sengh standing at the reception desk. Had he come to complain about their questioning Liu at the airport? But Sengh looked more awkward than angry. With him was a young member of the consulate staff Kaj hadn't seen before. He resembled a serious graduate student, with dark-rimmed eyeglasses, dark hair sprung over his forehead, and a fleeting smile that conveyed self-conscious apology and polite awareness.

"I hope you will forgive this unannounced visit." Sengh offered his hand for a handshake. "Mr. Chendh and I hoped you might have a few moments." Chendh nodded in embarrassment at being singled out. Kaj imagined that Sengh had chosen the young man because, as an underling, he would be too scared to talk. Score one for the Vice Consul.

"Let's go into the conference room," Kaj said, hoping that morning's paper coffee cups and donut flakes had been cleared. The room was depressing enough with its caramel walls and lifting brown floor tiles without spilled coffee and sticky crumbs. Once he opened the door, he was glad to see the table top was clean. He looked up in time to catch Jill's little smile as she settled into a chair beside him. How had she known the room would be needed? She must have seen the Kuthanis arrive.

"This is a pleasant surprise," Kaj managed as Sengh settled into the chair at the head and said something in Kuthani to his assistant. The young man tried to object. Kaj could guess what was happening: Sengh was telling the young man to wait outside. Chendh replied and made nervous movements with his hands. The Vice Consul listened then issued a decisive command, upon which the unhappy man backed away, gave a bow, and pulled the door shut behind him. Through the glass, Kaj could see him take up position outside. Chendh was going to see that no one harmed his superior, not while he was on duty.

"Our security is sometimes a little overbearing," Sengh said. "I doubt I am in any danger here in your police station. Chendh took your CIA workshop for chauffeurs on how to avoid terrorist abductions. He has been looking for kidnappers ever since."

"May we offer you tea or coffee?" Jill asked.

Kaj cringed as he pictured Sengh sipping tea from a paper cup with a tea-bag string hanging over the edge, or, worse, sipping coffee that even the department described as lethal. But the consul wished neither.

"How may we help you?" Kaj felt as if he was taking a first solo flight. He remembered Horne's instructions not to provide offense and to evaluate all possible meanings in whatever the man said. That was easier said than done. Until the Whitworth murder, he hadn't known that Kuthan even existed. Now he was representing Hawaii's law enforcement, anticipating what the State Department would say if he bungled it.

"I have something to give you," Sengh said. "I think it is going to be unfortunate."

Kaj wondered at the word *unfortunate*. Unfortunate for whom? Kaj knew Sengh was using his words with great delicacy. The man took a white legal-sized envelope from his inside jacket pocket and laid it down on the table.

"Before I give this to you," he said, "I know you must look into it, but the Consul has asked that you proceed with good intentions."

Kaj wasn't sure what good intentions might look like in this case. "The Consul is aware that you have come here?"

Sengh nodded. "Yes, he is aware, and I am here with his permission."

Kaj took a deep breath and said what he believed would pass for sincere and credible. "I assure you that we do not wish to disturb the consulate or cause harm to Kuthan."

The Vice Consul seemed satisfied. He pushed the envelope across the table. Kaj opened the unsealed flap at the back and took out a torn piece of brown paper. He slid it over to where Jill could see it as well. It was from a package sent to an address in Manoa. Although the street address was partial, there was enough left to show that the addressee was Harrison Whitworth and the shipper was AirIbex. There was no date stamp left nor any indication where it had originated. But how had it turned up at the Kuthan consulate? Kaj raised his eyebrows and looked at the man across the table.

"A groundskeeper found it inside our rear gate, perhaps dropped from the refuse lorry this morning. After your visit, I asked to be informed when anything unusual was found no matter how small. Anyone finding such a thing was to bring it to me directly. When the man saw the name, he recognized it and brought it to me. I am offering it to you for justice, because I know no reason why any correspondence addressed to Professor Whitworth should have been at the consulate."

"A very interesting question," Kaj agreed. "We have no information about a connection between Professor Whitworth and the consulate except for the warm relations between the professor and His Majesty. We would like to consider this further."

Kaj carefully avoided using the words *investigate* or *suspicious*. He felt stilted and constrained by protocol but also wondered if he was over-thinking the situation. Still, there was diplomatic immunity. As Horne had made clear, the consulate grounds were part of Kuthan, where the police lacked authority. Kaj had never dealt with international protocols before; most criminals having business with CID were homegrown.

"I hope you will do so, because I am curious about how this paper came to be on our grounds. However, since I am sure no one on our staff is involved, I must ask you not to talk with any consulate staff without my approval."

"Might we ask more specifically how this came into your hands?"

"As I said, a groundskeeper found it. The man brought it to me."

Kaj mentally noted how many people had handled it.

"And this was this morning?"

"Yes." The Vice Consul paused for a moment and furrowed his forehead. "I sometimes envy the West. You talk about winning and losing and debate and argue. You make decisions, but you create people who lose with bad feelings. In the East, we believe individuals belong to one another and want to maintain harmony between them. It's possible for us not to reach a decision, and if we do, we can be slow, because we seek consensus. It's what is important to us. We are a very traditional people."

Sengh paused and looked troubled. Kaj did not wish to interrupt until he was sure that Sengh was finished speaking. He looked at Jill and gave her an imperceptible caution not to speak. She folded her hands in her lap and looked down. He appreciated her quick learning.

"I have spent many years in the West, and I have come to understand the differences. I am sure Mr. Horne has described our five virtues. I am trusting you to understand it is delicate that I am here today."

"I understand that you have sacrificed tranquility to protect it for others," Kaj said. "But, Sir, may I ask you something. I know that archery can be an important avenue to meditation. Have you been able to practice this form here in Hawaii?"

Sengh frowned for a moment as if trying to digest what lay behind Kaj's question. "Does this have to do with Mr. Whitworth?"

Kaj nodded. He knew he was taking a chance, because they had still not revealed how Whitworth died, but he had a hunch he wanted to go with.

"Yes," Sengh replied. "There is a place to practice that meditation within the consulate."

"Would you be willing to allow us to talk once more your staff? And would you permit Detective Kahana and Detective Lee to see where you meditate?" Kaj held his breath. Without this permission, he could not see a clear way to prove or disprove his growing suspicions.

Sengh seemed lost in thought for a moment. "It will be arranged tomorrow," he said briskly. Then he stood up, shook hands again with Kaj and Jill, and pulled the door open the door before Kaj or Jill could do it for him. Chendh quickly fell in behind him, glaring at the CID office as if he believed he'd been among Western devils bent on tearing apart his employer.

Kaj watched them almost jog toward the elevators. Most people were happy to flee CID, especially if they weren't in handcuffs, but he was surprised that the Vice Consul was actually in a hurry. Kaj wondered if something had also clicked in Sengh's mind.

Kaj barked at Kaipo once the elevator doors were shut behind the Kuthanis. "Tell Horne we need to know about everyone in the Kuthani embassy. State has to have it, since they give out the visas. Tell him we expect to be invited to the consulate tomorrow, and he needs to be there. We need to know where the consular staff come from and who they are. Tell him it's urgent. The Vice Consul came here today to ask us to help them. I don't even know if that's legal, but we're in too far to quit now. You know, I'm starting to understand these people, and it's scaring the hell out of me."

"What else did he tell you that so critical?" Jill asked.

"He told me that there is an archery range somewhere in the consulate. Get everyone together. We need to get to Stone's house. He may be in danger."

37

MOSES' BLUE AND white patrol car was parked across the top of Stone's driveway when they arrived. 'No movement," Moses reported. "We've been standing by as requested."

When a sharp rap on the door and several loud attempts to raise Stone produced no answer, Kaj felt the old, sick feeling in his stomach. Something was wrong. He waved Kaipo and Cliff around the back and pushed against the door. It wasn't locked and swung open to reveal total chaos. Everything in the room, from the shabby rattan furniture to the paintings on the wall, had been systematically slashed and thrown on the floor.

Kaj and Jill went in slowly, weapons drawn. They checked each room expecting to find a body. All the rooms were damaged. Drawers had been turned out, artwork broken, and mattress springs cut from their protective casing, but Stone wasn't there and no sign of blood. If Stone had been killed, this wasn't the crime scene.

"The owner is at the top of the driveway," Jason Rogers came down to tell them. "We've detained him. What do you want done with him?"

"Bring him down," Kaj said. "Maybe he can throw some light on this."

"What have you done to my house?" Stone almost screamed as he stood in his doorway surveying the damage. Jill prevented him from entering, or he might have thrown himself on Kaj right there.

"It wasn't us," Kaj said. "You tell us what happened here."

"You broke in. You've destroyed my house. I'm going to sue the police department for millions. I'll see you all lose your jobs."

"Before you do that, Mr. Stone. We have some questions."

"I'm not answering anything without my lawyer."

"That's fine. We'll do the talking."

Kaj directed him out onto his lanai and had him sit in one of the few chairs still left intact in the house. Jill stood in the doorway to watch. "We entered, because we had reason to believe you were in danger."

"What crap is that? Who's going to believe that?"

"We believe you have been receiving packages from Singapore addressed to your neighbor Harrison Whitworth. They arrive when he is away, and you arrange for them to be picked up."

"I don't know what you're talking about." Stone's bluster could not hide a desperation in his eyes. He looked as if he had been caught in an earthquake without a desk to duck beneath.

"Right now, we are concerned that whoever killed your neighbor intends to kill you. If so, the question is whether he gets to finish the job or whether you are going to tell us who it is."

"No one has any reason to kill me."

"Then why was your house ransacked?"

"How do I know it wasn't you who did it?"

"We also know you have been receiving artwork that the Kuthani embassy believes was plundered from their country."

"The Kuthani embassy?" Stone broke into caustic laughter. "You want to watch out for them. Is that what they told you? That I'm an art smuggler? They'd sell their souls if you offered enough. They're no high-minded saviors of their artistic heritage. They're the biggest crooks in the Pacific region."

"You're saying you did not collect parcels addressed to Whitworth?" Jill asked.

"No, I did not. I would not set foot on his property even if I knew he wasn't there. For all I know he's set up a video camera to catch dogs peeing on his grass. That's the kind of thing he'd do."

"But you know who did," Kaj said. "It couldn't have been done without your knowledge. That was the set-up. You threw a party when you knew Whitworth wouldn't be in town. A delivery was made, the package collected, and no one was the wiser. How did they pay you? With art for your collection?"

"There was something here when we came to interview you last time. Where is it?" Jill asked.

"You can visit it anytime at my office on campus."

"Was that your payment?"

"It was sent from the Pacific International Center for Asian Art Auctions in Bangkok. They are licensed by the Thai government. I have dealt with them several times before and found them reputable. All official paperwork and permissions were signed, and I have them in my office with the piece."

"The Thai government informs us that Pacific-International is being investigated for trading in smuggled antiquities. Did you know that?"

"Of course not," Stone bristled.

"Mr. Stone," Kaj said, "unless you help us, we are going to look into every art piece in the donation you are making to the university. We will bring in our experts and look for matches to every stolen or missing antiquity."

"This is harassment. It's blackmail."

"If all your art pieces were obtained legitimately, you don't have to worry, do you?"

"You can't hold back my donation," Stone said plaintively, "I need to release the collection to cover my back taxes."

"We're not interested in your art collection," Kaj said, "We want to know who killed Harrison Whitworth."

"I don't know who killed him."

"Tell us what happened that night," Jill said. She had adopted Kaj's mixture of demand and appeal. She was learning from the master.

"We were drinking and hanging out, that's all. Some of the kids had a little too much to drink."

"Except Gowda," Jill reminded him. "You told us yourself he was not drinking. What you didn't tell us is that his uncle is the head of security at the Kuthani Embassy."

"Why would that be relevant? If I knew it, that is."

"He had to be your contact. You told him the dates Whitworth would be gone. He knew the AirIbex schedule of delivery days. He picked up the parcel, stayed in your house, gave you your cut, and drove off with his fellow party goers with no one the wiser."

"Why would I go through such an elaborate charade? If there were parcels as you suggest, why not have them sent to my house?"

"I imagine you wanted a drop site so you wouldn't be charged with receiving stolen art work. The Kuthani smugglers also needed a drop site because they couldn't use the consulate address. The packages supposedly came from a legitimate art dealer in Singapore, so you thought you were covered. It worked for a while, but it went wrong this time, didn't it? The cleaners found the package and took it inside. Once they left the house, they set the house alarm. The only thing any of you could do was wait for Whitworth to come home. But that was a problem too, wasn't it? The package was addressed to him. He'd expect it was his. Why would he give it to anyone else? The only solution was to kill him."

"But I didn't do it. I didn't kill Whitworth. I swear." Stone looked cornered and frightened.

"Then you tell us what happened."

"Some of what you're saying is right," Stone seemed to shrink before Kaj's eyes. "Chet told me that his uncle had a valuable art collection stored in Singapore that he wanted to bring into this country. He said his uncle would be willing to give me valuable pieces for my own collection if I helped him avoid taxes and duty. It sounded easy. All I had to do was figure out how to get the package delivered safely. I swear it was only supposed to be one time.

"Whitworth was constantly traveling, so we worked it out that the package could be delivered when he was out of town. Chet was to pick it up from Whitworth's house and bring it down to mine. It's difficult to see into his yard and the neighbors are away during the day, so it was easy enough. But that's all I did, except they kept coming back and demanded I accept more deliveries. I never saw what was in the shipment or dealt with anyone other than Chet. He unpacked, gave me whatever they wanted me to have along with a certification of authenticity, and packed the things he was taking into a backpack."

"What happened this time?"

"The timing of the shipments was always a problem because the package could be held up on arrival at the airport. AirIbex couldn't tell me when they could deliver until the day before. Whitworth's cleaning service always came in the morning. This time, they came in the afternoon. It was all so stupid. They'd never made changes before."

"Then what?"

"I'd already planned the gathering at my house as usual, and I told Chet about the cleaning service mess-up when he arrived with the others. He went outside and made a call. I don't know who he called. He came back and said it would be taken care of. That's all I know."

"When did Chet leave the house that night?"

"During the party he received a call and took it out on the lanai. I don't know what he did after that. All he told me was that he'd take the students back to the campus and then come back to unpack as usual. I didn't even see the package."

"Where did he take the art pieces after he left here?"

"He never told me. I told you that I didn't speak to anyone but Chet. I wanted to stop, but Chet told me that if I tried to, they'd expose me. I was trapped. You have to believe me, I had nothing to do with Whitworth's death. I had no idea what they were going to do."

Kaj shook his head as he looked at the cowering Stone. It was hard to imagine that someone educated would fall for such an obvious trap. What had the man being thinking of? But then the answer was obvious. Stone saw it as a way to get out of his financial difficulties with the IRS. He shook his head again. Life was about to become even more difficult for Stone, and the IRS might be only a small part of the trouble.

"Well," Kaj told Stone, "you'd better arrange to sleep somewhere else tonight. You can't stay here."

38

Tʜɪs ᴛɪᴍᴇ, ᴛʜᴇʀᴇ was no ceremony when Kaj, Jill, Kaipo, and Cliff arrived at the Kuthani consulate. It was a business call and all those who valued tranquility were in other parts of the building. Greg Horne was waiting for them outside looking sober. This was not a call he liked making on the sovereign grounds of a nation that the State Department did not want to offend. Kaj had kept his word to the Vice Consul, and he had told no one beyond CID about his visit. Horne might not have been comforted even if he'd known.

They walked in together, but Cliff and Kaipo were quickly escorted away down a hallway. Kaj and Jill and Horne were directed once more to the conference room. The people Kaj had requested were waiting for them: Vice Consul Singh, Mallik, Han, and a younger, sullen dark-haired man that Kaj took to be the missing Cheterinda, along with consular security staff. The room was crowded when the principals sat down at the table. Kaj was surprised that Fong hadn't been invited, but he seemed not to be needed since his client Mr. Liu had left the country.

The Vice Consul gave a small, tight smile and nodded to Kaj as if to give him permission to start. Kaj saw that it was up to him to conduct the meeting. Kuthani protocols were being suspended.

Kaj looked at each man across the table from him. Mallik was scowling. Gowda looked uncomfortable. Han looked confused. The Vice Consul had a small little smile that suggested he was intrigued by what was coming next.

"As I am sure you know, we are investigating the death of Harrison Whitworth. We have received permission from Vice Consul Singh to ask you questions. We are grateful for this cooperation. But first, in order to save time, I am going to share with you what we already know. We interviewed Arthur Stone this morning."

Mallik gave a snorting guffaw. "And you believe him?"

"Why should I disbelieve him?" Kaj let his eyebrows rise.

"Because he's a thief and an art smuggler. We told you that we were watching his house for the shipments we know he received."

"Well," Kaj said, "we're focusing here on the murder. I suppose Stone could have left the party and gone up his driveway to kill his neighbor. But let's get to that later. I want to look at what we know happened.

A package arrived at the Whitworth house on the day of Stone's party. It was on a day that you, Mr. Mallik, had arranged for Stone's house to be watched. The package was addressed to Harrison Whitworth, and the label said it was surgical instruments. The package originated in Singapore, shipped by the Pacific International Center for Asian Art Auctions via AirIbex. According to AirIbex their regular delivery schedule for Manoa is between 2pm and 4pm. Coincidentally, the Suite Leilani cleaning service changed their schedule from morning to afternoon since they knew that Whitworth was away."

"How does any of this concern us?" Mallik sneered.

"That difference in schedule is important. Because the cleaning woman was there later than usual, she took the package into the house, as any thoughtful person might. When she left, she reset the house's high-tech alarm system. This meant that whatever was in that package was trapped inside.

"Now from talking with Mr. Stone, we understand that someone was to pick up that package in the dark and transport it down to his house where it could be unpacked and the contents distributed.

"So now you know how he did it," Mallik said derisively. "Why are we here?"

"There's a little more to it. Only Whitworth knew the code. Imagine the shock when the person meant to pick up the package arrives at the house to find it is not on the porch where it should be. He can see it through the window beside the front door, but there's no way to get in."

Mallik leaned back in his chair. Gowda still stared down at the table.

"We know from AirIbex that packages had been delivered previously on days when the home owner was away. Those were also the days that Mr. Stone arranged social activity at his house. Now we can see a pattern, a routine. It tells us that we need to identify someone who was present at all Mr. Stone's parties. As it turns out, there was only one. The other art students identified you, Mr. Gowda, as that person."

"Being at the house means nothing," Mallik spat out. "Who are you trying to fool?"

"We have more. We also have a witness who heard you, Mr. Gowda, on Stone's lanai talking on your cell phone in other than English. Since no one else at the party speaks a second language—trust me, we checked—it had to be you. You were heard to say yes several times. I assume that you identified the problem to whoever you were working with and agreed with the solution. I assume further than it was an agreement to kill Mr. Whitworth when he returned home that night. The question I am left with is whether it was you who killed him or the person you are working for."

Gowda looked terrified. He glanced at Kaj then at Mallik, who glared at him, and then looked back down at the table. At that point Cliff and Kaipo entered the room and stood back by the door. Cliff caught Kaj's eye and nodded.

"Now you are probably thinking that there is no way to prove this theory, but actually there is." Kaj held onto the moment to create suspense.

"The place where the killer stood to shoot from has a unique , rare grass that goes to seed in December, and the tree above is home to nesting mynah birds. Our killer will have seeds, mud, and guano on the soles of his shoes. It is also likely that the murder weapon will have mud and rain traces. Manoa Valley soil is unique, so we will tell a lot from it."

"What murder weapon?" Mallik sneered again. "I don't see you have anything."

Cliff at that point stepped forward holding a bow in his gloved hands, along with an arrow fledged in red and black. "We found these downstairs in the archery range." he said, "It looks like there is mud on the bow."

"We'll have Forensics check that out," Kaj said, "But with Vice Consul Singh's permission, I want to ask everyone to remove his shoes."

The first reaction around the table was stunned silence. The Vice Consul stared for several moments Kaj with a look that suggested that being asked to remove his shoes was the rudest request he'd ever received. Horne looked as if he were choking but said nothing. The body language from Mallik, Gowda, and Han implied that all five virtues were being violated at once. But then the Vice Consul chuckled and reached down. He handed his shoes to Kaipo. With such an example, the others were forced to comply.

When Mallik's turn came, he stood up suddenly. "This is nonsense. I won't submit to this."

A barked order from the Vice Consul made him sit down. Gowda was trembling as he took his off, while Han shook his head in bemusement. Five pairs of shoes eventually lined up on the floor. Kaipo and Cliff then made a big demonstration of scraping the soles, putting what they found into plastic envelopes, labeling them by name, and returning the shoes to their owners. Cliff placed the envelopes on the table. The suspense in the room was starting to mount.

Slowly, ceremoniously, Kaj arranged the envelopes on the table and flattened the plastic on each to study the contents. The moments ticked by. Kaj then put on his discouraged face and stared at the men in the room. He picked up one envelope and pointed at it. He motioned for Cliff to come over and look. By then the suspense was unbearable. Apparently, it was too much for Gowda who suddenly jumped up. "I didn't kill anyone. I didn't kill anyone. I wanted to stay here and study art."

Mallik also sprung to his feet, yelling for Gowda to shut up. For a few moments the conference room was anything but tranquil until the consulate security staff were able to restore order.

When things calmed down, Mallik sat glaring at Kaj while Gowda had tears pouring down his face. It was a scene unprecedented in the consulate's history, and Kaj sat there in silence, not knowing what to say. He didn't dare look at Horne. He looked instead at Han who was white faced with shock.

The Vice Consul broke the silence. "What does this mean?" he asked.

"It means that Cheterinda has admitted to being an accomplice," Kaj said. "Perhaps he can explain."

Gowda looked in fear at Mallik but then trained his eyes on Kaj. "I picked up the packages and took them to the building behind Professor Stone's house. I opened them and put what I found in my backpack. That was all that I did. I never hurt anyone."

"You were not there alone," Kaj said. "Who else was there that night?'

Gowda looked down at the table and hunched his shoulders. Kaj expected him to break into tears again. "My uncle," he whispered.

Mallik started to yell again, pounding the table and cursing.

"Enough!" said the Vice Consul in very Western outburst of authority.

Kaj waited for the furor to die down and then turned again to Gowda. "So where were you if you did not shoot the arrow that killed Harrison Whitworth?"

"I told my uncle about the package. He said I was to wait until I heard from him. Then he called and said he had the package for me. I walked up Professor Stone's driveway. My uncle met me and handed the package to me. I went back down to the shed and opened it. I left one piece on the table and put the rest into my backpack. People were asleep when I went back to the house."

"No one saw you return?" Jill asked.

"Everyone was asleep. I pretended I was too. Then when they woke up, I drove them home. Then I came back to get the backpack."

"What did you do with the backpack?"

"I gave it to my uncle."

"Liar," Mallik shouted. "You wouldn't be here without me. I made all the arrangements for you. Your mother begged me to help you. He's an artist, she said. All he wants to do is study in Hawaii. Family needs to take care of itself."

"You never said you were going to make me do bad things for you," Gowda yelled back. He seemed to be finding his voice against his uncle at last.

"We have our answers now about who has been doing the smuggling," the Vice Consul said. "But where are these pieces?" He looked at Mallik. "What did you do with them?"

Mallik sat mute, so the Vice Consul looked sternly at Gowda, who shrank down in his seat.

"Where did they go," the Vice Consul demanded to know.

Gowda looked terrified again. "There are people who sell art to private buyers. My uncle knows who they are. He sold the pieces one at a time. He posted them to these people."

"Do you know who he worked with in Singapore and Kuthan?" Kaj knew he was going far afield from the Whitworth murder, but he could also see that the Vice Consul was absorbed. This must be the consular equivalent of a university dean kicking a political problem upstairs.

Kaj was doing the job for the consulate who wanted to know but didn't want to ask.

"There are some cousins in Kuthan, but no one I knew. The shipper in Singapore arranged everything."

Interpol's going to love this, Kaj thought. Then he asked the question he had been holding back. "Is your uncle good with his bow?"

The Vice Consul broke in at this point. "Mallik is a master archer. If you had said that was how Professor Whitworth died, I would have told you this before. If you are indeed saying that Professor Whitworth was killed by an arrow, and if the bow came from this consulate, I am ashamed for my country."

"We will know once our forensics lab has tested the shoe scrapings and the bow. Kaj looked at Horne desperately. He wanted guidance for what one says to a diplomat who has learned that his country's values have been violated by his own people and under the auspices of his own consulate. The silence was deafening.

"Please, Sir, let us know how you wish us to proceed," Kaj said.

The Vice consul's mouth formed a straight, tight line. "I shall consult with the Consul, and we will advise you."

He stood up then and nodded to the security staff who removed Mallik and Gowda.

"I must say though," the Vice Consul said as he looked at the four detectives, "that I have never encountered such an unusual police interview. There has been nothing on television like it."

He allowed himself a slight smile before he left the room.

Kaj didn't know if that was good or bad.

39

ONCE ON THE street outside the consulate, the detectives huddled with Horne. "Now what?" Kaj asked.

"No idea," Horne said. "He's right. This is unprecedented. They may waive diplomatic immunity, or they may not. If the consulate sends Mallik and Gowda home, they may meet a sticky end. If they decide to let them be tried in US courts, the younger one might do better if he testifies. Do you have enough evidence to charge Mallik with murder? It could still have been Gowda."

"Now that we know what we're looking for, let's follow the evidence," Kaj said. "But we're going to need those shoes back."

"I don't think there'll be a problem with that," Greg said. "But you're not getting mine, so don't bother asking. If Kuthan decides to turn Mallik and Gowda over to us, both of them will have reason to cooperate once they think about it. Being in an American prison is not a bad option, considering the alternative. But one way or another Kuthan will get them back. Once they're released from our jails, they'll be deported. We'll have to wait and see what Kuthan wants to do. Any idea why Mallik had Liu and Han watch Stone's house?"

"He had to. The consulate suspected Stone, and Mallik wanted to appear to be checking on him. He was probably watching Liu and Han himself, which might explain how Wilfred Fong got involved. Mallik saw Liu get picked up."

"By the way," Greg said as they parted, "could you really see the grass seeds and is Manoa soil unique?"

"I'm glad no one in the consulate reads detective stories," Kaj said.

"Really?" Greg looked momentarily confused.

"There's nothing particularly unique about Manoa mud," Kaj said, and he left it at that.

40

Two days later, Horne bounded into Kaj's office uninvited and grinning like the Cheshire cat. "It's been a big morning. It's just been confirmed by Mongathuā that the consulate will remain in Hawaii. And it's thanks to you."

Kaj sank back into his chair and closed the case folder he had been working on. He left eyebrow rose. "Me?"

Horne sat down uninvited next to Kaj's desk. "It was the fifth virtue. When Mr. Liu was debriefed in Kuthan, he said you and he were so connected, he did not need to use words. You understood him. Incidentally, pulling him aside at the airport was very risky. You should have told me before you did it. Someone not spiritually connected might have used the wrong techniques and brutalized him. He said you read his mind."

"Did he?" Kaj was finding Horne's excitement tiring.

"In so many words. Vice Consul Singh is also singing your praises. He says that you are better than the detectives he sees on television. The king is delighted to have found another American he can trust, and so are we. The Kuthani Consulate will remain open. The consulate, in fact, checked with us and then phoned the Governor's office to request you be assigned to consult on their security."

Kaj looked hard at Horne. "For becoming warrior class and letting them be tranquil? Or for doing the State Department's dirty work and letting Kuthan become indebted to US justice?"

Greg lifted his hands up and grinned. "We never intended for you to feel used, but when we get a win, we take it. Besides, you're becoming a Kuthani national hero. Not many of us get to be called a hero."

"Just routine work," Kaj growled. This was the nonsense he hated.

"Really. Well, his majesty was also deeply impressed with your war record. He paid you the highest tribute possible. He said he wished you had been born Kuthani."

"My war record," Kaj said with an irritable start. "How did that get involved?"

"You didn't think we'd let you enter the Kuthani Consulate without doing an intensive security check on you, did you? We put together a dossier overnight. Plus, we spoke to people who worked with you over the years."

"Moses! I see. That's who told you."

"He gave us details on your service and how you earned the Silver Star, but the general facts were all there in your military record. Don't look so shocked. We can access any government records we need."

"I don't talk about my time in the service," Kaj's lip curled as he tried to contain his annoyance. "I keep it private."

"Not possible anymore in a high-tech world. We all have to live with it. But cheer up. Food's important in Hawaii, and the consulate knows how to throw the occasional good reception when they feel like it. I believe they are planning one to honor you. It'll take a while, though. Also, I wouldn't be surprised if the king sends the royal jet for you at some point. Please do take me along as your translator and protocol officer. In the meantime, try not to get yourself killed. It's too difficult to find Kuthani soul mates."

"Aren't you enough for them? You speak the language and you understand them."

"Not enough, I'm afraid. They tell me my knowledge of their form of Buddhism is intellectual. When I talk about it, I analyze it. That makes me too Western. They tell me I do not understand their concept of tranquility. I can't get past seeing it as being stoic and detached."

"Instead of meaning balance and the middle way?"

"See, you get it. I understand the words but lack the feeling for them. Maybe one day I will grow into it. Who knows? In the meantime, I'm serious. You're the closest thing we have to a Kuthani soulmate."

"If it helps, I can assure you I'll try not to get killed," Kaj said drily.

"By the way, I'm to tell you that Kuthan is waiving diplomatic immunity for Mallik and Gowda. This was after we worked out provisos and assurances with them. Mallik will confess to killing Whitworth and Gowda will testify against his uncle. My bet is that Mallik's counting on not getting a life sentence and will try to collect money he must have stashed away in Singapore once he's deported. Time will tell. Gowda will do time for smuggling and then get sent home. He's seriously going to regret that he did not have a better class of relative."

"Above my pay grade," Kaj said. "Still, I'm curious to know how the Governor is going to explain who killed Harrison Whitworth. We briefed Bob Wilson and the police commissioner last night, and they had the same question. Who's going to believe that a Nobel Prize winning scientist died because his cleaning service came late one day?"

"Is it any more unbelievable than saying that Whitworth was victimized by an international art smuggling ring? Yet, it's true. The consulate security staff, or what's left of it, searched Mallik's room and found looted artifacts. They immediately called in the art academy to authenticate them and alerted the university that they want their stolen pieces back. Tien Han has been promoted by the way. He was also under suspicion but seems to have convinced them that he had no part in the smuggling or murder."

"Customs has been grilling Stone," Horne said. "He's cooperating as much as he can, but he doesn't know much about the art smuggling. They're getting more from Gowda. The district attorney's office has been working with the university, and I understand that the campus has refused to hold Stone's job for him if he goes to prison. The IRS is next in line. It turns out that his so-called collection is mostly fake. The one real piece was a teak dragon that he had in his office. Kuthan immediately claimed it. Not surprisingly, the university has declined to accept the collection."

"Again, above my pay grade." Kaj indulged his mischievous side. "Maybe the art department can mount an exhibition on how to spot fake Asian art."

Horne seemed unimpressed. "You must be relieved now that the Whitworth case is over."

"Well," Kaj replied with a wicked grin, "you know how you feel when the garbage truck picks up your *opala*, your trash? Relief and sense of completion?"

"It was that bad?"

"No," Kaj replied, "it's actually good now that it's over."

Horne looked unconvinced by Kaj's humor. "What did your forensics lab conclude about the shoes?"

"The FD said the mud was consistent with soil from Manoa. But then that soil could have come from anywhere. It was the mynahs that cinched it. Mallik's shoes were the only ones with mynah droppings on the soles, so we got the right man."

"How did you know they'd still be wearing the same shoes?"

"I didn't. It was fifty-fifty, so I took a chance."

Horne shook his head in disbelief, and to Kaj's relief started to leave. On his way out, though, he stopped at Jill's desk. Kaj watched as Jill's cheeks turned a slight pink, and then she smiled. Horne went off with a jaunty wave to the office.

"What was that about?" Kaj asked her a little later.

"Greg has invited me to have dinner with him on Christmas Eve. He says there's a little Thai restaurant that is almost as good as having dinner in Kuthan. I said yes."

"Good for you," Kaj said. "Have a wonderful Christmas."

41

MALIA AND MOSES Mahi lived in a one-level, bungalow style, wooden-slat house in Kapahulu. It had an overhanging roof to protect against downpours, louvered windows to let in the breezes, and a front yard full of wooden benches loaded with orchids in wooden boxes, bark shells, and cement pots.

Kaj could see the mango tree in the front yard had nearly doubled in size since he'd seen it last, and the papaya trees down the side yard all were heavy with green fruit. The house was similar to the one Kaj grew up in Palolo: the front door opened directly into the living room, the kitchen was directly behind, and off to the right were a corridor, a bathroom, and three bedrooms.

It was a modest house, but Kaj remembered how Moses and Malia agonized over the payments. In hindsight, the mortgage was a pittance, but back then it was a lot. Once they settled in, though, it seemed the house had been waiting for them. It was a welcome haven for two tired beat officers after a long shift.

Kaj noticed that the house had been repainted pale green and a new tile roof put in place. Somehow, he'd pictured it never changing.

The front door was open and Kaj could hear voices from the backyard, so he went in unannounced as he had so many times before. He put the case of beer he'd brought in the fridge, and walked through the kitchen to the backdoor. "Hey," he said through the screen, "is this party open to everyone?"

"Well, hello, stranger," Malia called back at him. "Welcome."

Kaj stepped down the stairs and into the past. Linda was sitting with Goro and Malia at a round iron mesh table lacking its glass top.

He hadn't realized his dad would be there. Goro was a few drinks ahead and feeling quite at ease. Kaj was glad he was finding some happiness in a season likely to remind him of Ai's death.

Linda waved him over. Annie was nowhere to be seen. Moses was standing over a large hibachi under an avocado tree, spraying the flaming coals with a water bottle. He put it down and gave Kaj a slap on the shoulder. Malia got to her feet with some effort and gave him as warm a hug as her advanced pregnancy and voluminous flowered muumuu allowed. She looked as if she was about to deliver on the spot.

"You look beautiful, Malia," Kaj said.

"I look pregnant. Very *hapai*. Now you're here, we can start. Mo, why don't you bring out the poke. We can last only so long on spinach dip and crispy won-tons."

"Help yourself to a Bud Light in the cooler," Moses told Kaj as he went into the house. They could hear the refrigerator open and close.

When he came out, he put a large bowl on the table and tore off its silver foil cover. Then he went to the grill and put on the burgers and teriyaki chicken. A satisfying sizzle greeted the meat along with good-smelling smoke.

"Mo's cousin John went fishing this morning off Koko Head and shared his catch," Malia explained. "We got the limu from the fish market on Hotel Street. Mo chopped the onion and ginger and marinated it in shoyu this afternoon, and those are our own peppers."

Kaj helped himself to poke and offered some to Linda. "Where's Annie?" he asked.

"Gone to Leonard's Bakery with Alan," Linda told him. "Malia needed bread, so Alan said he'd drive her."

"Alan's a good boy," Malia said. "He finished his firefighting course in the top ten. He wants to go to graduate school when he gets a chance. You know how kids are. They think they've got their whole lifetimes. But then they do, don't they?"

"These are cooking too fast," Moses said as he flipped the burgers and turned over the chicken pieces. "I'm going to set them aside for a bit until Annie and Alan get back." He sat down on the vacant lawn chair and took a large mouthful of poke that he washed down with beer. "It always surprises me when Mainland folk don't like poke or poi," he said. "Must mean you have to be born here."

"There's plenty that's strange even to people raised here," Malia said. "My auntie on the Big Island liked to chew on chicken feet. Her skin was beautiful, so maybe it was the collagen."

"Big Portuguese holiday thing was pickled pigs' feet," Linda chuckled. "We knew it was Christmas when Dad brought home a box and marinated them in a barrel out back in the garage. He was upset with us, because we kids wouldn't eat them. Sometimes, I think it's better not to watch when food's being prepared."

"Goro, what did your folks do on the holidays?" Malia asked.

"Smoked meat," Goro said. "Char Siu was good. A friend on Moloka'i sent over dry-ice goat and wild pig during hunting season. We made jerky. Remember that, Kenji?"

"I remember the jerky," Kaj said. "I wouldn't eat it, because you told me it was bear meat."

"And you believed me?" Goro burst into laughter. "My boy thought I shot a bear."

"How are you doing, Goro?" Moses asked. "You need another beer?"

"I'm fine," Goro said. "I made a big decision today. I'm celebrating."

"What's that, Dad?" Kaj asked quizzically.

"Kenji, I'm seventy-eight, and it's time you do your own yard. I'm selling the Palolo house and getting a place in a senior building. I know that's why hard, but you need to take responsibility for your yard and give your old man some freedom. I know you need me, but now I want to kick back, talk story with my friends."

"Why didn't you tell us that's what you wanted?" Kaj nearly fell out of his chair. He couldn't bring himself to look at Linda. He knew if he did, he would burst into laughter. When he did glance over at her, she was studying the writing on her beer can label.

"You never ask," Goro said. "I figure you disapprove because maybe I don't do your yard."

"I'm glad you made the decision, Dad," he managed to get out.

"Yes, sir," his father said and waved his beer can in the air. "Three meals a day on time. Cleaning service every week. Movies and bingo. Maybe some ladies to look at. Old friends from the army. Good stuff."

Kaj wasn't sure if his father was referring to the retirement home or to the beer. In the old days, right about now, if it was a good day, Goro would be on the garage floor, hugging the dog, and maybe singing folk songs he'd learned in his childhood. It would have been followed by Fluffy going around to lift his leg and pee on everyone's car tires.

"How did Dad get here?" Kaj whispered to Linda.

"Annie picked him up. She wanted him to be here tonight. I think we should to take him home with us to make sure he's okay."

"What about work? You've got another few days at Ala Moana, right?" Kaj asked. "Don't you have to be in early?"

Linda shook her head. "I told them I had to quit. My feet hurt, and my back is going out. I can't do all the standing around anymore. Also, I couldn't take any more listening to 'Mele Kalikimaka' on the store speakers. Annie's okay. She'll finish up, but I'm done."

Kaj chose his words carefully. "I know it must be a disappointment to you."

"Actually, I'm more than okay with it. I got my Christmas shopping done. I think I'll look into selling Mary Kay."

Kaj's hair shot up, and she burst into laughter. "Just kidding."

Kaj heard Annie's voice before he saw her. "Hi, Dad, Grandpa," she said as she ran down the stairs into the garden. "We just got back. There was a busload at Leonard's buying malasadas. Kids coming back from a basketball game somewhere." She sounded amused and animated.

To Kaj's surprise, Goro stood up and held out his arms to her. "You look just like your grandmother at your age," Goro said. "I remember first time I saw her. So tiny. I could almost circle her waist with my hands. Just like a little bird. But she was strong. Beautiful. Just like you." Goro's eyes were moist.

So were Kaj's, although he wished it was his sister in Goro's arms. Maybe tomorrow, he'd call her. He could always say it was to wish her a Merry Christmas. Maybe he could say none of them was getting any younger, and maybe there was something she should know. He'd talk about that tonight with Linda.

"I'm proud to be like her." Annie accepted his hug and kissed him on the cheek. Then she called out into the house. "We're all out here, Alan. Come on out."

"Hey you," Malia said to her son when he appeared, "You see who's here?" She nodded toward Kaj.

Alan walked over to Kaj and shook his hand. Kaj was surprised at this formality. Upon meeting, most men in Hawaii nodded at one another, gave an awkward pat on the back, or just handed one another a beer. But manners are a good thing, he thought.

"Been a while," Alan said. "How are you doing?"

"You were heading to the Mainland last time I saw you."

"Eugene, Oregon Ducks," Alan said. "The Mainland was too different for me. I'm an Island boy."

"Then you joined the Fire Department?"

"Right after graduation from HSU."

"How are you liking it?"

"Love it. Great guys to work with."

"Hey Alan, your dad could use help with the food," Malia chimed in. "And Annie, maybe you and your mother could bring out the salad and stuff from the kitchen."

Malia grinned at Kaj. "Being pregnant has some benefits. Better enjoy them while I can. Sit down, Kaj. The food will come to you." She busied herself setting out the plates and knives and forks.

"Hey you guys," she yelled toward the kitchen door, "we need two more chairs here. Get something comfortable for Goro. And somebody bring out the rice pot."

After the dishes were cleared away, Kaj and Moses sat by themselves under the avocado tree out back and looked up at the stars. The night was warm and only slightly humid, much better than usual for December in Hawaii. The mynahs had settled down for the night and the only sounds were the neighbors down the way having their own cookout.

"What's ahead on the case?" Moses asked him.

"We've got a memorial thing on the university campus for Whitworth. The Governor is going to be there, so the brass is going. Jill wants to go, because she's been working with Whitworth's family, and I said I'd go along. You never know what's going to happen at these things. There could be trouble, but I expect it will just be speeches."

"Better you than me," Moses chuckled. "Being a detective on a major case is the most political job in the world. I'm glad I'm just a beat officer."

Kaj knew that it was time.

"I'm sorry there's been such a gap," Kaj replied. "Things happened."

"You don't have to explain."

"Yes, I do. I often thought about you both."

Moses looked concerned but also knowing. "The nightmares?"

Kaj nodded wearily. "I know Linda told you about them. When they started up again, I thought I could handle them if I didn't have reminders."

"Like if you didn't keep running into me?"

Kaj nodded. "But it didn't help. I think they got worse."

"What's happening now?"

"Usual thing. The jungle. The explosions. The uselessness."

"Useless, not. Without you there, I wouldn't be here. Without that sixth sense of yours, none of us would have got out. That's why they gave you the medal."

"But we lost so many men."

"That wasn't your fault. You did everything you could. You put yourself out there, bringing us ammo, acting like a medic, taking over when Sarge got hit. You were what held us held us together. You were the one who got us back to camp even though you'd been hit yourself."

"I don't like talking about it," Kaj said. "If you hadn't said anything, people might have forgotten."

"Anyone want coffee?" Malia called from the door. "We've got Kona-Mac brewing."

"Give us a bit. We'll be in," Moses called back.

"Okay." Malia disappeared. Laughter and conversation swelled from the living room. Goro was singing a folk song about bears and monkeys in Japan's snow country.

Moses furrowed his brow and looked intently at Kaj.

"None of us has forgotten. That's not the sort of thing you can just forget. I get it though. You didn't like me talking about what happened? Is that it?"

"Yeah. That's part of it. It made me uncomfortable, as if people thought I was cashing in on it."

"Kaj, trust me. No one sets out to be a hero. It's tough because once you are, people depend on you to define life for them. But all any of us can do is to keep on living. You're my hero, you know."

"Well, I don't feel it. Everyone there was a hero." Kaj made a sweeping gesture as if he were brushing away the past.

Moses leaned over to make the moment more serious. "Kaj, the only time I feel even a little bit heroic is when I tell people about you. I want them to know what you did. We knew you'd been hit, but not how bad until we got back. That's guts. You pushed through it to keep us going. As far as I'm concerned, they should have given you the Medal of Honor. When I talk about you, it's like a bit of stardust rubs off on me. I can feel that somebody cared enough to keep us alive because none of the REMFs did. I never meant to make you uncomfortable."

"I know." Kaj shook his head in sadness at the hurt and confusion he had caused Moses.

"Kaj, there are ways to deal with these nightmares now. They do things with lights. There are also groups that can help. I attend one. They're all good guys who were over there. We talk things out. Come with me sometime."

Kaj took a deep breath. He didn't feel ready yet. He needed time to work out the contradictions.

"Let me think about it," he said. "I know you're not going to give up. You never did. But give me a few days."

Moses let him sit in silence for a few moments. Then he gave a sudden roar of laughter. "I think you've been telling me that in future I should my big mouth shut."

"Sounds like a good place to start." Kaj gave a small smile that quickly gave over to his own laughter.

He knew he would talk with the others about what happened. He also knew that Moses would not resist every future temptation to talk. Still, he could hope.

42

THE SMALL WHITE-HAIRED woman, now wearing a dark burgundy suit, black silk blouse, and a single strand of pearls, stood outside the theater where her son was to be remembered. Jill and Kaj had driven her to the university from the Halekulani Hotel, but she said little on the short journey to the university campus. It was hard to know what she thought.

Accessing the campus was very different from when Kaj was issued a parking caution. This time campus security waved them through the guard stand. It was a relief not to have to argue with anyone. Jill drove straight to the theater and parked under the portico.

Kaj held the door while Eleanor Whitworth got out of the car and was greeted by the president's waiting assistant. The university president, it seemed, was on his way but running late.

Kaj wondered if the old woman was feeling warm in the sun and humidity, but she did not seem uncomfortable. So far, she had shown only a gracious appreciation for the police chief's allowing Kaj and Jill to escort her.

"If you'll wait here for a few moments," the president's embarrassed assistant told them, "I'll make sure everyone is seated. The president will escort you down to the seats at the front. The first row has been reserved for you and the university administration." She disappeared to look for the president's limousine.

Most people were already inside, but some were still walking through the doors, and Eleanor seemed startled when one or two seemed to know who she was and came up to give their condolences. She let her eyes run over the unfamiliar people dressed in unfamiliar clothing, colorful and more informal than she was used to. Then she stiffened and make a choked sound.

Kaj looked to where she was staring and saw Janice de Mello walking amidst the graduate students from the anemone lab. Kaj recognized Janice's son, Brendan among them.

Janice was close enough to hear the gasp and turn towards it. When she saw Eleanor, she stopped and took a step back, bumping into the student behind her. For a few moments, she was immobile. Then her mouth set, she said something brief to the students and moved toward Eleanor. The confused students moved closer to the theater entrance where they remained, watching her.

The old woman shrank back as Janice approached. Kaj moved to be beside her, although he didn't expect that either woman wanted a confrontation. From what Janice had told him, they had not seen each other since the difficult days when Harrison and Janice ended their relationship, both knowing a child was on the way and the forces that would keep them apart.

"Don't hit me," Eleanor said to Janice in a wavering voice, "I'm an old woman." She held her arm bent across her chest to protect herself, revealing a lace hankie clenched tightly in her fist.

Janice stopped dead and her eyebrows rose. "Why would I hit you?"

"Because I told Harrison not to marry you."

"I know," Janice replied. "You made a terrible mistake. So did he. But I know why you did."

"You do?" Eleanor let her arm come slowly down to her side.

"Of course, I do. I knew Harrison. He was obedient," Janice said. "I knew he loved me, but I also understood he wouldn't go against your wishes. I knew you were ambitious for him and thought I would hold him back. It's all so pointless now."

"You're still angry." It was more statement than question.

"Not now. I was. But I was angry with him too. But life does go on. My life would have been different with him, but I'm not sure it would have been better. Harrison's life was always his work, and his duty was always his birth family. If we'd married, he would have looked to you for approval, and I would have found that difficult."

"I'm so sorry." The old woman's shoulders sagged, and her eyes welled with the tears she had not permitted herself to shed before. "If only I'd known how things were going to turn out."

"We all have regrets. I have my share. We just do the best we can."

Janice glanced at the students still standing by the theater entrance. Her body language indicated she wanted this meeting over and her life returned to her. The students waved at her and pointed inside. She raised her arm and signaled they should go in.

"Have you been happy?" Eleanor asked, calling Janice's attention back to her and seeming reluctant to let her go.

Janice looked surprised and was slow to reply. "I had a good husband and a rewarding career. I have a great deal to be thankful for."

"I'm glad for you. Poor Harrison. That it should come to this. Killed in the way he was" Tears now trickled down her cheeks, and she made no effort to stem them.

Kaj stepped back, knowing he was an intruder. It was clear that Janice would do nothing more than talk. He looked at Jill who also looked uncomfortable. Eleanor was oblivious.

"The president is arriving now, Mrs. Whitworth," the president's assistant said as she returned. They could hear the rubber on the smooth cement under the theater portico.

Only Brendan remained now by the theater door, still waiting for his mother. Kaj watched him start out towards them; he seemed to pick up purpose as he approached.

"Mom," he said, "we should be going in now."

Eleanor's head snapped up when she heard him. "This is your son?" she asked Janice.

Janice nodded. She was reluctant to share him with this woman. She spoke carefully. "Brendan, this is Eleanor Whitworth."

The old woman's lips trembled again. She stared at Brendan, her eyes flicking up and down, taking in the details. "Brendan," she said at last in a whisper. "That's a good, strong name."

"He's named for my uncle, Brendan de Mello. He died in the war." Janice spoke the words defiantly, reminding Eleanor this was not a Whitworth but a de Mello from Dorchester, where they used to make shoes.

"Brendan is a good name," Eleanor repeated, accepting the family and its origins.

Kaj took advantage of the moment to head off the president and explain that they needed a few minutes.

Eleanor stood looking at Brendan, waiting for an invitation. Her eyes were moist, frozen between hope and regret.

Janice stared at Eleanor and felt the stirrings of pity. She remembered her father's loving acceptance of her and her baby and the years of love that had created the young man who was about to hear eulogies for a father he had never known. All the resentment seemed pointless now. She looked deeply into Eleanor's eyes, and gave a world-weary shrug. "Eleanor," she said, "this is your grandson."

"How do you do?" Brendan said awkwardly. He took Eleanor's hand and shook it. When he tried to remove it, she did not let go.

"You're so like Harrison was at your age," Eleanor whispered. "You have his eyes and his shoulders. Are you mad about science too?"

"He's part of Harrison's research project," Janice said. "He competed and won a spot on his own."

"Did Harrison know who he was?" Eleanor asked.

"I don't know. I thought not, but it seems he may have. We tried to keep it from him. I wish now we hadn't."

"He would have been so proud to know you," Eleanor told Brendan.

"We need to get started," the president tried to break in. "The Governor has just arrived. May I escort you to your seat?" He offered his arm, which Eleanor ignored.

"We're sitting in the back, Mom. I asked them to hold places for us."

"No," said Eleanor, turning her back to the president. She looked frightened. "I want you both with me in the front. I want the Whitworth family to be where they belong." Her voice was tremulous with emotion.

Janice hesitated and the world seemed to halt.

"Please," Eleanor said. Her voice was a request for forgiveness.

Still Janice hesitated.

"Please," said Eleanor again. Her voice wavered. All she had left was the hope that in this moment there could be forgiveness.

Janice looked down at the ground, still considering her options. Then she looked at Eleanor and gave a slight but perceptible nod.

"Thank you," Eleanor whispered. She slipped her arm into her grandson's and reached out for Janice's hand. "I want you to sit with me. That's where family belongs."

43

ON STAGE, FOLDING chairs had been placed before the drawn curtains; and someone had draped woody-smelling maile leis over the lectern. The mood was somber and the audience quiet.

Kaj looked around. For a man who was difficult to know, Harrison Whitworth had filled the place. He saw Helen Malcolm half way up on the right. He imagined she was taking notes for her book. Vice President Napa and Dean Goodyear were seated next to each other in the second row. Curtis Dawes and the graduate students sat behind them. Wilfred Fong was there with Mrs. Sam in an upper seat. And all around were seats were filled with legislators, university faculty, students, and the media.

Eleanor Whitworth was standing beneath the stage with Janice on one side and Brendan on the other. They were speaking with the Governor and President Halstead. Even from the back, Kaj could see Eleanor still held her grandson's hand tightly.

Kaj knew that he and Jill would not be needed any more. Eleanor Whitworth had her family. They could slip away quietly when they were ready.

The president opened the memorial by welcoming them and pointing out Eleanor Whitworth. He had the honor, he said, to welcome her to the campus and to announce that she had asked that her son's Nobel Prize award be used to endow an annual Harrison Whitworth Memorial Prize. It was to be awarded to a doctoral student at this university who shows exceptional promise in the field of pharmaceutical research. Large applause followed.

The Governor was then introduced and spoke eloquently about what Whitworth had meant to the State. He described him in personal terms as a good friend and great man. He was here today to pay tribute, he said, to a visionary scientist who left behind a promised legacy that the state would strive to live up to.

Finally, President Halstead returned to the podium. On behalf of the Whitworth family and Hawaii State University, he thanked everyone for attending and said that he was privileged to make a special announcement.

"We have been able to obtain the services of a colleague of Professor Whitworth's, a distinguished scientist who has agreed to spend a year here. He will ensure that Professor Whitworth's vital work is carried out according to his wishes and that it will continue in future to serve this state, the world, and those who will benefit from the pharmaceuticals this project will develop. He is coming to Hawaii as a tribute to his friend and colleague. We will be joined in one month by Dr. Trenton Wind-Sutter, rector of Cambridge University."

Kaj's hairline took a massive leap, and his left eyebrow flew into its quizzical arch. Who could have persuaded Wind-Trenton away from his comfortable bastion of unchallenged superiority? Like politics, academe made for strange bedfellows. All he knew was that he was going to do his very best to avoid him.

If Kaj had thought he and Jill could quietly leave after the ceremony, however, he was mistaken. Fred Lee from the student newspaper was lying in wait for them.

"About those break-ins," Fred said.

"What is it this time?" Kaj asked. "Please, not another conspiracy theory."

"We found out who wrecked the newspaper office." Fred was almost breathless. 'Can you believe it? It was that little weasel, Ronnie. He practically wet his pants over those threats we received over the Kahoʻolawe story, so he busted up the place to stop us printing it. Can you believe? He's not on the paper anymore. We fired his ass. But now it's too late to run the story, because I hear the university has selected a site on Oahu."

"Don't," Kaj said as he held up both hands to stop him. "No more university stories. We need time to recover."

Epilogue

EELING SUFFOCATED IN the humid night air, Professor Harrison Whitworth jerks his tie from around his shirt collar and tosses it impatiently onto his car's passenger seat. The offending silk slithers down between the console and seat before disappearing amidst the dark floor mats. Good riddance, he thinks.

He has reason to feel indignant. That nonsense at the airport just made a hard trip worse. Whatever possessed Curtis Dawes to think he'd want to ride in a rickshaw drawn by graduate students? Anyone in their right mind would have seen the absurdity of it: him sitting with his luggage at his feet, his briefcase on his lap, while the students, like Pharaoh's slaves, strained to pull the thing through the airport garage. He doesn't want even to think about the caption someone could write beneath a picture.

He's exhausted and knows now that he should have taken Harriet's advice about taking an overnight stop in Vancouver. She warned him he would be exhausted by the time he arrived in Canada, but he'd insisted that he needed to get back to Hawaii quickly. He didn't tell her why. Anyway, what's a few more hours in the air? He could always stretch out on the plane, he said, and catch a nap. Except, as it turned out, he couldn't. He was far too excited.

It wasn't the Nobel Prize ceremony that had generated this anticipation. The award evening was certainly impressive and profound, and the small, proud smiles of the other recipients underlined the honor of the recognition. He, on the other hand, had spent much of his time there wondering how someone could be hailed a conquering hero when he had screwed up his personal life so badly.

The champagne and congratulations, in fact, made him feel like an imposter. The reality was that there hadn't been a moment in the Swedish, wind-driven sleet when he didn't think of Janice and wish her with him. The thought of her was his companion across the Atlantic and the possibility of seeing her was the reason he couldn't sleep on the flights home.

He knew their breakup was his cowardice. It had been drummed into him that he was a Whitworth, and that it was his responsibility to be important. Any personal happiness was to be merely incidental. He'd bought into it then. But now, with the hindsight of experience and age, he can't believe that, for the sake of his family, most of whom were dead anyway, he'd given up the one woman he was never able to forget.

Yet he can't totally blame the generational Whitworths on the dining room walls, frozen into fashionable portraits by fashionable artists. It was his mother's disapproval that carried the day, and she was only a transplant into the Whitworth culture, being born a Boston Bradshaw. She turned out to be more Whitworth than the gaggle of painted senators and generals.

When his grandfather died, the old senator patriarch, his mother dealt with the pervasive smell of stale cigar smoke by closing off her father-in-law's study and saying it was not to be used.

How completely Whitworth that was: throwing white sheets over unpleasantness, and leaving his grandfather to collect dust. He had to rush to retrieve his grandfather's watch and the painting of the yacht the old man had named "The Traveler," so he would have something to remember him by.

He drives now past the black outline of Punchbowl National Cemetery and the wall of apartments and condominiums on its slopes. Their lights march up the mountain sides like lava laying claim to colonize the sky and stars.

Unstoppable lava—that ought to have been the Whitworth family crest. He wonders if even a Nobel Prize would have been enough for his grandfather. Probably not. He doubts that the old man would have been impressed.

He can imagine Grandpapa saying that the Nobel Prize was America begging foreigners for acknowledgment again. Hell, the old man would have thundered, if we don't have the guts to do without their approval, we don't deserve to be who we are. He would have drunk his (Scottish) whiskey, smoked a (Cuban) cigar, gone driving in his (European) car, and told his son to earn a Pulitzer next time.

He hopes Janice liked his gift. He wanted her to hold something of him in her hands. A necklace would have been too personal. A ring would have been an insult. He imagines her smiling as she saw the bracelet. He knows she will understand what the gift meant.

She had to have sent the boy to him, knowing that he'd recognize the name. Because of her, he'd made sure that the boy was accepted in the project, even though Curtis resented his interfering in the selection process. They exchanged heated words and Dawes had told him to go to hell. But it didn't matter. The boy was accepted, and Dawes apologized. In the months that followed, he made sure that the boy was mentored and ensured that he was safe. He wanted the boy, their boy, to tell his mother how well he was being cared for.

He was very patient, though. He knew she'd recently lost her husband, and he wanted to respect that. He never doubted, though, that she was sending him the message that she forgave him. He'd waited all those years for her. He could be patient until the time was right.

He stops at the Safeway in Manoa valley and picks up the few things he needs. He threw most of the perishable food out before he left. He hates roaches but they are the price he pays for living in a wooded lot with a view of the ocean. The supermarket is busy for that time of night, but it takes only a few minutes to pay and leave.

Black clouds cover the stars at the back of the valley when he drives up his road. The only lights are Christmas bulbs strung along the eaves and on front porches, along with muted lights from bedroom windows. The dim light and drizzle obscure the road, so he slows until his car lights pick out the mailbox at the top of his driveway.

He'll be glad to get inside and turn on his computer. He had the store include his business card with the gift. His email address is on it. He'll turn on the computer the moment he gets home, before he even unpacks. He is anxious to know if she has responded. That's why he's rushed home. He doesn't want to keep her waiting.

As he turns down his driveway, he is distracted briefly by the mynahs arguing in the trees by the gully next to his property. Something must have disturbed them. It might be a mongoose, although he's never seen one. He's used to the noise and pays no real attention.

He uses his opener to lift the garage door and drives in. Once inside, he switches on the main overhead light and uses the remote switch for the light outside his front door. Then he carries his briefcase to the house. He punches in the command numbers of the alarm system. He uses the first four numbers of her birthday: 0403. The alarm digitally confirms his selection. Alarm off, it says.

He puts his keys on the table beside the door and glances up towards the road. Everything up there is quiet now. The birds have settled and the neighborhood is still. He enjoys the solitude for a moment.

He walks back to the garage, lifts his suitcase from the back seat and snaps the handle upright. He notices how the rain has released the woody smell of vines. The drizzle hits the side of the house with a soft spitting sound.

He wants her to love this house as much as he does. He hopes she will help him furnish it. He wants her to be the hostess when King Soöng visits them. Them. Them. The sound intoxicates him. He wants her to love him again as he always has loved her. He promises himself that he will spend the rest of his life making up to her, and to their son, his absences and failures. This time will be different. He will make sure of that.

His feet slip a little on the rain-slicked mud of his sidewalk as he pulls the suitcase along the pathway to the house. His mind is ablaze with how he wants his future to be. There's nothing now to stop him. He can be the man he was meant to be.

He reaches the place where he knows the sidewalk is raised and he must lift his foot slightly to avoid tripping. He plans to have a company come in to repour the cement once the rains stop. He hears a noise somewhere up towards the road and glances up that way, unaware of anything but his own thoughts and gladness to be home.

It only takes a moment for him to realize that something isn't right before he feels a jolt and then a weightlessness that lifts him off his feet. He tries to reach out his arm to break his fall, but that arm is frozen. He stumbles backwards, landing heavily on his back, his suitcase left to stand sentinel above him. Final muscle contractions make the blood course through his body, filling in the ventricles of his heart, and forcing the cardiac muscle to cease its beating.

He gulps with incomprehension, and, in the last, few seconds of his life, his confused eyes rake the skies. It wasn't meant to end like this. Then there is only darkness.

Harrison Whitworth, scion of wealth and pedigree, heartbeat of a multi-million-dollar research project, fellow traveler with kings, politicians, and academics, and the engine upon which the State hoped to build a bright economic future, lies sprawled on his sidewalk, his death so sudden that he did not even have the chance to call out her name one last time.